Wicked Never Sleeps

Mysteries from the Sixth Borough, Volume 1

Gina LaManna

Published by LaManna Books, 2018.

WICKED NEVER SLEEPS

First edition. June 29, 2018.

Written by Gina LaManna.

To my husband - I love you!

To my family and friends, and above all, to my readers. :)

Acknowledgments

SPECIAL THANKS:

To Alex—Home is where the heart is. я тебя люблю!

To my family—and especially my mom who pokes me for her 'complimentary copy' of every book I publish, and to my extremely supportive dad.

To Stacia—My most favorite editor and friend. Thanks for everything you do.

To those LaManna's Ladies posting unicorns memes and sparkling cars and fancy cakes, thanks for making me smile every day!

Synopsis

W elcome to Wicked.

Wicked—the paranormal sixth borough of New York—is home to witches and goblins, werewolves and necromancers, elves and vampires...and former Detective Dani DeMarco. Dani's busy with the grand opening of her family's pizza parlor, when a knock on the door leaves her face to face with the stunning, yet lethal vampire in charge of the NYPD's supernatural branch—Captain Matthew King.

There's been a high profile double homicide in the Sixth Borough, and Dani's peculiar talent is the only hope to untangle the web of lies and magic connecting the dead victims. As the case spirals into a pulse-pounding chase, Dani's not sure what's worse: the fact that a ruthless killer has his sights set on her, or that her feelings for New York's most infamous vampire have returned...

All is fair in love and war, but passion is downright Wicked...

Chapter 1

"Are you *sure* it was a good idea to invite the trolls?" My mother wrinkled her nose as she scanned the vibrant party. "And really, Dani, the gnomes? They could have at least showered before coming to a cross-species event."

"*Mother*, give it a rest. DeMarco's Pizza doesn't discriminate." I pointed to a sign that clearly stated so behind the counter. "Everyone's just here for the food."

I topped off my mother's wine glass. She worriedly glanced over my shoulder but was wise enough to keep her comments quiet. Instead, she moved swiftly across the room to join my father and one of my brothers in conversation with Marv, an elf with a heavy lisp and a penchant for pickpocketing. I'd arrested him twice before, but after he'd learned his lesson and turned mostly legal, we'd become allies, if not quite friends.

Let me back up for a minute to explain. I'm Dani DeMarco, and I've been in the pizza business for all of five minutes. I hadn't always been passionate about pepperoni and parmesan, nor had I grown up debating the financial pros and cons of serving deep dish versus thin crust, but times changed.

I used to be the paranormal version of a cop. More specifically, I was a Reserve for the Sixth Precinct—a special branch of the NYPD—and I'd been great at my job. The chief had recruited me the day I turned eighteen due to my '*special talents*'. Reserves could see things other officers couldn't. Magical things.

My *special talents* helped me to become the youngest detective on the force, male or female, by my twenty-first birthday. Because I was the only Reserve for the NYPD, I worked across all units of the Investigative Division. Usually, I focused on the big cases, splashy, public homicides and tricky kidnappings, but every now and again there'd be a narcotics bust or the odd theft.

The force had gotten seven good years out of me. I had always loved my job—thrived on it, my mother might say—and I might still be thriving if I hadn't stumbled onto a case that very nearly killed me. More on that later.

That's why I'm semi-retired from law enforcement at the ripe old age of twenty-eight. With time on my hands and skills useless outside the realm of police work, I decided on a complete career revamp. I dug deep into Carl's cushions (my enchanted couch is named Carl) and took out a big fat loan from a goblin with questionable morals to cover the rest. *Voila*—eight months into retirement, I had a pizza business ready to open.

Tonight's the grand opening, and I have to say I'm impressed with the turnout. All I wanted was a quiet gathering, a slew of good food, and a burst of publicity to kick off the hottest new pizza parlor in Wicked. We'd achieved that in a big way.

"Dani..." My mother sidled over again. "A word?"

"Yes, mother."

My mom (though I love her dearly) is one of those helicopter mothers—the type that hovers just a little too close for my liking. It doesn't matter that I'm a decorated cop, an independent witch, or a small business owner. I am still her only daughter in a sea of sons.

"I know we discussed this when you signed your lease, but don't you think this building is a little close to the Dead Lands? I was just talking with Marv, and he said the feud between the elves and the necromancers is really heating up. I don't know that this is the safest space for you, and—"

"Mom! This is my grand opening. Can you please just enjoy it like the rest of us?" I gestured to my little space, feeling proud of the happy group of customers swaying to light music in the background.

"Jack's going to be here all the time. He was the first to sign up for the DeMarco Diet coupons—buy six pizzas get the seventh free."

My mother pursed her lips. The youngest of my four brothers ate food like it was going out of style, and without a doubt, he'd be hanging around the shop as much as his wallet allowed. Plus, I'd hired him on as part-time help. That small reminder was a win in my mother's book.

"And when Jack's not here, I can take care of myself." I leaned in conspiratorially and grinned, making my mother jump with surprise. "I might have retired, but who says I'm not still armed? I have a permit to carry."

"*Danielle Marie DeMarco!*" My mother rested a hand over her heart. "I wish you'd stop carrying around weapons. You are already... *different* enough. Stop making it hard for men to approach you."

"Right. Like it's my *gun* keeping people away." I snorted, and a random spellslinger to my left took a step back, looking alarmed. He really wasn't helping my case, and I felt snarly as I glanced at him. "What are *you* looking at?"

"That's exactly the attitude I'm talking about, Danielle," my mother said. "I know you grew up in a house full of boys and had to fend for yourself, but really, did they wash *all* the femininity out of you?"

"They didn't wash anything." I wrinkled my nose, remembering some of the smells that had turned up in the house during our teenage years. "They punched, kicked, tricked, and otherwise tortured the femininity out of me. Plus, all of that is overrated. The right man will like me exactly the way I am."

A knock on the front door pulled me away from the titillating discussion with Mrs. Rose DeMarco, my mother. I frowned as I crossed the room to greet the new arrival, wondering who bothered to knock at a party.

Then again, this wasn't your average pizza place. It was located on the first floor of a two-story building. The second floor held my private living quarters, while the first floor had been converted from a business space into a diner's delight with lofty windows, old tables, and worn wooden benches littering the roomy eating area. A state of the art kitchen had been added behind the counter.

We'd hadn't touched the wooden front door, nor had we added a ton of flair to the outside. The signage was dubious at best except for a DeMarco's Pizza above the door in flickering neon. I was counting on word of mouth and quality of pizza to bring in customers.

"Nash," I said, pulling open the door and quickly stepping outside. I shut the door as I offered a calculated smile at my second oldest brother. "What are you doing here? I thought you couldn't make it to the party."

Nash stood rigidly straight, the stick that was normally up his ass firmly planted in place. "Detective."

"Drop it, Nash. I'm your sister."

He cleared his throat, clearly uncomfortable, and that's when I discovered he wasn't alone. A shadow approached from the darkness behind my brother. It was a male figure no doubt, his build too tall and too broad to be mistaken for anything else. As he stepped closer, his face easing into the glow from the party, the wry greeting I'd prepared died on my lips.

Captain Matthew King. I hadn't even realized I'd said his name aloud, but it must have slipped out because his dark eyes landed on mine, hard, calculating, and all too familiar.

I inhaled the peculiar scent of him—something woodsy and fresh, a spice to it that warmed me despite the distance between us. Then again, it was hard to say if it was his cologne that sent shivers down my spine, or the mere proximity of him.

"Detective," he said, his voice a chocolatey river of alluring sweet undercut with a deadly danger. "Congratulations on your successful launch."

"Sorry I didn't send you an invitation, but I figured you wouldn't be interested in attending."

Matthew gave a hint of a smile. He rarely pulled his lips back enough for anyone to recognize the just-too-sharp edge of his canine teeth. His fangs remained retracted—except to feed, of course, and when he was aroused or sensed danger. I'd been a witness to all a long, long time ago.

The smile turned out to be hollow and disappeared with a snap as he gave a curious tilt of his head. "Detective—"

"Drop the formality. I'm retired." I wiped my hands against the apron tied to my waist. "I'm Dani DeMarco, owner of the Sixth Borough's greatest pizza shop now."

I said this with a falsetto that didn't have anyone smiling. Nash had been firmly against my leaving the force; Matthew even more so, although he hadn't said as much. It was merely understood. Things between Matthew and I often felt that way.

Nash cleared his throat. "We're here on official business, Dani. We need your help."

"Apparently it's a big deal if they sent my brother and the big guns." I nodded toward Matthew, captain of the Sixth Precinct Homicide Unit. "What do you need from me? I have an alibi for the entire evening," I joked. "Ask anyone here."

The Sixth Precinct is a well-buried program that started as an offshoot to the human NYPD meant to serve and protect the Sixth Borough of New York. See, everyone knows about the main five boroughs of New York: Staten Island, Manhattan, The Bronx, Brooklyn, and Queens, but only those with supernatural tendencies can enter the Sixth Borough—also named *Wicked*.

Wicked was slotted into New York like the rest of the boroughs—smack in between Staten Island, Manhattan, and Brooklyn. On maps, it looked like a sea of water. To humans, it looked like a sea of water. To us, it was a city ripe with culture, paranormal species, and now, the hottest new pizza parlor to enter the paranormal world: DeMarco's Pizza.

Needless to say, we had our own problems with crime, and we needed our own way to police the paranormal issues. Slapping a pair of regular old handcuffs on a sorceress was like sending a giant into a china shop—a useless and dangerous practice that was costly when things went south. Hence the reason we policed our own in Wicked and let the human NYPD take care of everyone else.

"We're not looking for an alibi." Matthew glided closer, his size an impressive wall before me. "I'm asking a favor."

"I'm a little busy right now, but sure. What can I do you for, Captain?"

Matthew's close proximity made the breath hitch in my throat. He was tall and broad and muscular—his physique enviable to male creatures everywhere.

His hair, a dark brown bordering on black, cut across a glint of pale skin—though a rare tinge of color in his cheeks told me he was either turned on, angry, or frightened. Since I doubted Matthew could feel fear, and he happened to not like me very much at the moment, I doubted it was the former or the latter, and I settled on anger. He was angry. But at what? The thought had me worried even before he spoke.

"We found Mayor Lapel dead." Matthew's voice took on a deep, rolling gait. He could be a silver-tongued devil when he wanted to be. Persuasiveness was a skill vampires used more than almost any other, without even thinking about it, but Matthew had learned to tone it down when talking to me because he knew it pissed me off.

"The mayor's body was discovered in a hotel room along with a young woman's—one who was not his wife."

"And?" I hesitated. "I'm sorry for the city's loss, but I don't know what you want me to do about it."

"Dani," Nash growled, finally dropping the formality. "Don't be dense. We need a Reserve to help analyze the scene."

"I trained Lucia to be my replacement. She's probably better than I am by this point," I said, thinking of the blond-haired pixie with a hint of envy.

Lucia had been born with the same rare talent that I, too, possessed: The ability to see Residuals—traces of spells left behind after they've been cast.

"Again," I reiterated, "I don't know how I can help you. I've been out of the business for eight—almost nine—months."

Nash's eyes flicked toward Matthew, asking an unspoken question.

My eyes narrowed at the men. "What aren't you telling me?"

"Lucia doesn't appear to be working for us anymore," Matthew said. "She stopped showing up to work two weeks ago."

My heart pumped a little faster. "Why?"

"We're not sure." Matthew tried to remain calm. "We've been investigating her disappearance in case of foul play, but we haven't found any evidence of... well, anything at all. By all accounts, it looks like one morning she just took off of her own free will."

I'd spent six months beside Lucia—training, teaching, introducing her to every technique and most of the contacts I'd met on the job. She was a bit flighty about personal matters, but when it came to her job, she'd been fierce and determined.

"No." I found myself shaking my head. "No, she wouldn't have run away. She's been gone for two weeks? Why didn't you come to me sooner?"

"Because you *retired*," Nash snapped. "We tried to get by without her, but in a case this big, we need help. Between the publicity it'll receive and its impact on Wicked, we need to act fast."

"We were hoping Lucia would return on her own when she was ready," Matthew admitted, "but it appears she has left for good."

"I'm telling you, she didn't just up and leave. There are two options, one more likely than the other. The first is that she saw something that scared her. I'm not talking about a sick murder scene—she's seen plenty of those by now." I paused for emphasis. "I'm talking about something that rattled her freaking cage. Yes, you both know what I mean."

Nash shifted uneasily from one foot to the other while I leveled my eyes at both men. The shared, bruised look that only those who've seen humanity at its worst can recognize passed between us.

"The second option," I said, "is that she was taken unwillingly."

"Which is more likely?" Matthew asked, though he could read the answer in my eyes.

"If I had to guess," I ventured. "My vote would be on a kidnapping."

"But we've been investigating—" Nash started.

"Well, you missed something," I snapped. I didn't mean to react emotionally—my brother and I had to delicately balance family life versus professional careers, and sometimes the lines blurred. "You should have come to me sooner. But you didn't, so I suppose we'll have to pick up the pieces from here. You know all of the Residuals will be gone by now, right?"

"You'll help?" Matthew asked.

I glanced at my brother, who appeared to be sulking. "On which case? Lucia's disappearance or the mayor's murder?"

Matthew's voice slid into a smooth drawl. "As much as you're willing to give us, DeMarco."

"I'm working on my own time, I get a badge, and the force is required to buy enough pizzas to feed the department lunch once a week," I said, crossing my arms. "That's my offer."

Matthew nodded. "But that's not all you're asking for—obviously. What else do you request from us?"

I was impressed with his ability to read me. The last thing I wanted to do was return to work in the job that'd broken me, but I didn't have a choice. When the head of Homicide showed up at my door with his fangs retracted asking for help, the situation was dire. Once a cop, always a cop, I thought, and my personal sense of justice wouldn't allow me to back away from the challenge.

But Matthew was right. There was one more thing that I wanted in exchange for my help. Something more valuable than my salary, more precious than gold, more desperate than the tangled strings of passion that hovered between the vampire and me. I stepped outside, away from the background noise of the party, and closed the door firmly behind me.

"The Hex Files," I said into the quiet of the night. "I want them. All of them."

"Those are sealed," he said with a growl, as if he'd already known my demand. Captain King's dark eyes bore holes into mine. "You know I can't give you those."

"Then you don't need my help." I stepped back into the warmth of the pizzeria, held their gazes for a long moment, and then slammed the heavy door shut.

I'd barely turned around before a loud *crack* ripped through the party, and the sound of splintering wood sent those with a little wine in their systems thinking a bar fight had broken out.

I knew better. Looking back, I found my sturdy front door splintered right down the middle and completely lopsided on its frame. As I'd slammed the door, Matthew had stuck his hand out to block it, and the entire door had shuddered and forfeited. A solid mahogany panel was no match for Matthew King's strength.

The man could be equal parts intimidating and sexy, and sometimes both at once. This was one of those times, and I hated my visceral reaction to him when I wanted to feel nothing but anger.

"The Hex Files," he said in an almost inaudible hiss. "You'll have twenty-four hours with them—off the record. No copies, no notes...*nothing*. Nobody aside from the three of us will ever know you saw them."

"Fine," I said, my voice a whisper. "Let me get my coat."

I reached for my jacket, avoided my mom's open-mouthed stare, and muttered to Jack to keep the party going until I returned. My youngest brother stared with bemused wonder at Matthew and Nash before giving a firm nod.

"King," I said, as I stepped over the smashed wood on the ground. "I've got one more demand."

"What's that?"

"A new door."

Chapter 2

M urder never smells pleasant.
    Especially when the source of death is a complex set of runes that only the most advanced sorcerer can perform. *Especially* when the victims' blood is frozen solid in their veins, freezing the victims' faces into a permanent contortion of pain.

That's how we found the mayor and his female friend—a possible companion, though we couldn't be sure until we ID'd her. As cars weren't allowed in the Sixth Borough, Matthew, Nash, and I had hopped onto one of the spell-powered trolleys that crisscrossed the length of the city and made it to the outer edge of the Goblin Grid in under five minutes.

The scene of the crime was a seedy motel in close proximity to the casino. It acted as a crash pit for those who'd lost their money or needed to buy an under-the-table supply of SpellHash—a relatively harmless recreational drug favored by the young paranormal crowd. It made people relaxed, hungry, and sometimes paranoid, but in the scheme of magically-laced drugs, it was pretty innocent stuff.

The only other reason to visit the Motel 6th was in the company of a Goblin Girl—an attractive female goblin outfitted in a little skirt and littler bra. These women roamed the casinos looking for customers, and while the practice was legal, it was a distinctly gray area of the law. In short, the Motel 6th was hardly the place Mayor Lapel would ever want to be seen, let alone found dead.

"He went out with a bang," Nash said, having perfected the dark humor so predominant in cop circles. "Or, seems to look that way. This one's clearly a Goblin Girl."

"We don't know that yet," Captain King said smoothly. "We're running down her identity now. We all know the records of Goblin Girls are a pile of smoke and lies. I'll be impressed if anyone admits to even knowing her real name."

"How old do you think she is?" Nash asked the question to the general public, but I could tell it was directed at me. "Do you think she's underage?"

I barely processed the question. Since I'd stepped into the room minutes before, my brain had been working on overdrive. It'd been cranking through an analysis so familiar it was like I'd never left my job.

The sounds of the techs toiling away, their hands covered with Fingerprint Eraser charms, faded to nothing as I sank into my role as Reserve. Nash's commentary filtered in one ear and found a storage space deep in the recesses of my mind to be processed later. Even Matthew—his form one I was always innately attuned to—couldn't crack my concentration.

Matthew knew better than to interrupt. He left me alone, urging Nash to do the same. I was vaguely aware of King clearing the crime scene completely of techs and other Sixth Precinct officers before retreating himself. I was left alone with the two bodies—the way I preferred to work.

I closed my eyes, took a deep breath, and returned to the doorway to begin my process. A process I'd perfected over seven years on the job, and a process that had led the Sixth Precinct to the highest rate of closed cases ever. When my eyes flashed open, I was back in business.

The room was full of old, desperately wilting Residuals that were mostly gone. In a hotel room with a constantly revolving door and customers fashioning all types of spells and hexes and charms after a drunken night at the casino, the Residuals never quite left. My breathing felt heavy, constricted—as if the room were incredibly dusty and filled with pollen.

My peculiar *gift* was that I could physically see Residuals, unlike almost everyone else. I was one of five registered Reserves in all paranormal realms. My talent happened to be stronger than most. Even Lucia, a worthy pixie to take over my role at the force, would never see the same detail in Residuals as me. It wasn't her fault; it was the nature of the beast.

It's difficult to explain how my talent works, but I have spent so many years attempting to help others understand that my spiel is well rehearsed and automatic. It goes something like this: All spells leave behind traces. It's part of Newton's Third Law that for every action, there's an equal and opposite reaction. All magic takes energy, and when a spell is performed, it doesn't just vanish. It leaves behind trace amounts of the energy used and sprinkles them into the atmosphere on a level that's invisible to everyone.

Everyone except me.

To me, these leftover bits of energy are like the breadcrumbs that Hansel and Gretel followed into the woods, leading them to the wicked witch. Except it's much more than breadcrumbs. I can actually see the remnants spells leave behind: I can tell if the breadcrumbs are from whole wheat or white bread, from a croissant or a cinnamon roll. Hell, I can tell if it's not even bread in the first place but rather a trail of crumbled cookies.

Residuals are valuable to me within twenty-four hours of the spell being performed in most cases. Longer than that, and the details fade. When the Residuals are fresh, I can pick apart pieces that point to the user of the spell, the type of enchantment cast, the results of it—did the spell misfire? Was it strong? Did it kill?

As soon as a spell is cast, that energy begins to be reabsorbed into the universe. From ashes to ashes, and all of that jazz. By the time a full day has passed, it's hard for me to confirm anything more than the existence of an invoked spell. The rest of the details are often muddied beyond recognition, like a footprint that's been out in the rain all day.

So, I set to work on the motel room, dusting back the minutia of magic—the incantations and magical traces that meant nothing to the case. Someone had performed a zap to warm up old takeout food in the non-functioning microwave yesterday morning. A Shaver invoked by a woman late last night had been spelled in the shower, and earlier this morning, a lazy maid had hawked an illegal form of a Cleaning Curse to get the room in shape for its next guest.

Once I'd sorted through the trace spells and catalogued them in my brain, I focused on the bigger ones. A streak of glittering red particles invisible to the human and paranormal eyes, save for my own, told me that a magical contract had been signed in this room. The red shimmered like dust particles visible beneath stunning sunlight, and I let my mind haze over as I teased apart the details and filed them into place.

The contract had been performed by a woman—someone older than the body at my feet. The spell was at least twelve hours old, while the bodies had been here for no more than four. I processed that and moved on to the next.

A cluster of green signaled an illegal drug trade had happened here with SpellHash—again, it had been about twelve hours before. It probably had something to do with the contract. I shook away the green and focused on a splash of pink that had seemed innocuous at first glance, but upon review, deserved a second look.

The spell had been performed by... I hesitated. I couldn't get a read on the gender, which often happened if the person had been trying to remain concealed. He or she might have used a charm to mask their fingerprints and footprints, which would have clouded the Residuals, but the spell itself seemed out of place.

It was simple Moving Magic—a quick spell a student might use to shift heavy equipment in their dorm room, for example—but the amount of energy it had taken was enormous. There was more concentrated pink near the door than anywhere else in the room.

My gasp drew Matthew to my side. His movements were liquid like mercury—a hint of supernatural to his very presence. Shimmery with speed and silent as a grave. Nash followed at a distinctly more human pace as I knelt over the bodies.

I quickly encased my hands with a Fingerprint Eraser charm to not disrupt the tech's work on the bodies and rested a hand on the young woman's arm. She had the look of a Goblin Girl, but a new one—her complexion tinged just slightly green, and not the deep, leathery green of the older ones.

"She wasn't killed here," I murmured. "This is obviously complicated rune magic, but there's just not enough energy in the Residuals here for the murders to have been committed in this room. They were killed elsewhere and moved here."

"You catch a whiff of the spell?" Nash asked. "What does it look like to you?"

My older brother seemed more curious than most about *exactly* how my talent worked. Though he'd never shown a hint of jealousy, I often wondered if he begrudged me the career advantage of being a Reserve. The truth was, he was an excellent cop—the best in the business. Probably better than me if we tallied up work ethic and drive, but there were simply things he couldn't do—like see Residuals. Fair or not, that was life.

"Pink Residuals. A normal spell—nothing that even set off my alarms at first glance." My knees creaked as I stood. I was instantly aware that even at my full height, I barely came up to Matthew's shoulder. "Speaking of—there was a SpellHash deal in here last night. Might want to get the drug team to look up the last residents of this room and trail them. Usually there's no legal contract if some-one's just buying some Hash for recreational purposes."

Nash snorted. He'd worked on the drug unit for his first five years on the force. "Like they gave their real names at check-in. And anyway, I know Donny," he said, speaking of the front desk recep-tionist who'd let us into the room. "He calls me when a wanted per-son pops up around these parts."

"Well, he didn't call you last night, and there was enough Spell-Hash in here for me to feel the high off the Residuals," I said. "I think Donny isn't as honest as you're hoping, bro."

Nash scowled. "We've got to choose our battles, Dani. Some-thing you don't understand, not having to—"

"The mayor," King interrupted. "Any Residuals around him?"

I studied the man sprawled on the floor. He had a bit of a belly in the way of most comfortable politicians, but he wasn't an un-hand-some man. His salt and pepper hair could be considered dignified, and he stood somewhere taller than me and shorter than King. In life, he had a friendly smile that had likely won him the position of Mayor of Wicked.

"From what I can tell, the mayor hasn't performed any spells in the last few hours." I focused more intently on his fingers. "Not a sin-gle Residual there. I'm guessing whoever killed him started the runes a while ago. If you want more information, you'll need to find the ac-tual crime scene. This is just the staging zone."

"Why stage here?" Matthew wondered aloud. "If the killer want-ed to make a scene, wouldn't he make a bigger splash? A seedy motel is hardly high profile."

"The mayor is high profile enough," I corrected. "The scene is just the backdrop. Maybe it's a message of some sort. Maybe the murder-er is trying to tell us, or the general public, something."

"Some sort of renegade killer?" Nash looked skeptical. "Deter-mined to expose the mayor for his tryst with a Goblin Girl?"

I shook my head. "It's gotta be more than that."

King's nod wasn't of agreement, it was of acknowledgement. "Why go through all the trouble of killing with runes when the murderer could've ended things quicker?"

I tsked under my breath. "I just don't know. There's not enough here to go on."

"You forget," Nash said with a bite to his words, "that the rest of us never have Residuals; this is all we ever get."

My eyes cut to him. "That's why you have me and Lucia."

My retort hung in the air. They didn't really *have* me, nor did they have Lucia anymore. It wasn't modest of me to admit, but a lack of Reserve on staff would most certainly hurt the force's close rates. Sometimes the answer to the case was written in the Residuals, and closing it was a simple matter. Unfortunately, that wasn't the case with the mayor.

"It doesn't make sense to me. Not yet," I quickly corrected, resuming my stroll around the edge of the crime scene. I paused at the doorway. "No sign of forced entry. There'd be gold Residual for a Lock Lifter, but there's nothing."

"We're holding Donny for questioning," King said, and it was an invitation. "Would you like to join?"

I sighed. "I'm not getting back to the pizza party tonight, am I?"

Captain King rested a hand on my back, his touch cool against my skin, though the effect was a burning zing that went straight to my gut. We might have broken up, but it wasn't due to a lack of chemistry. The chemistry between us was enough to set the Necromancy Lab on fire—especially when we couldn't act on it. At least when we were burning up the sheets at night, we got a reprieve from the sexual tension between us. *This* was unbearable.

I stepped away from him, and King's lips tightened. He dropped his hand and marched forward. "No, Detective, I'm afraid your slice will have to wait."

Chapter 3

While Nash hung back with the bodies to supervise the techs and the evidence sweep, Dani and Matthew made their way down to the motel lobby. Matthew dropped back, letting Dani take the lead as she ran a hand through her brilliant, waist-length blond hair and stepped into the office. Matthew admired her as he always had, but today the admiration was clouded by concern.

The weight of this case hit like a hammer with the first call to the station. Matthew had been at home preparing a solitary dinner for one when the urgent Comm had pulled him from his feast of synthetic blood. Nash had arrived at his door minutes later, insisting they get his sister involved with the case.

Matthew had agreed, for the sole reason his hands were tied. A dead mayor found in a potentially compromising position with a Goblin Girl would be a borough-wide nightmare, if not more. The ramifications of cases this size often bled over into New York, and whether the humans were aware of it or not, the consequences rippled across society.

The faster the precinct could close this case, the better for everyone. And the ticket to closing this case would be her, of course. The bane of Matthew's existence and the love of his life. Legend said that vampires could only truly fall in love once. If that were the case, Matthew King was a hopeless soul. He'd found and lost his love, which made him destined to be alone.

"Are you talking to him, or should I?" Dani asked Matthew. "What sort of badge will I be getting, by the way? I don't want some stupid placeholder; I want the real deal."

"What kind would you like?"

She considered, her mouth tilted in a thoughtful pout. "Honorary Detective," she said with a shrug. "Might as well stick with what I know."

Matthew's nod was confirmation, and he jotted down a note to have Felix get her that badge, stat. Knowing Dani, she'd poke her nose around whether she had a badge or not, and a civilian asking questions into the mayor's murder wouldn't reflect well on the department. The sooner Felix could get her official, the better.

"I'll let you take the reins on the questioning," he said. "Keep things light if you can. Donny's a, *ah*, friend of the department."

Dani rolled her eyes. "Yeah. He's a sleazy sometimes-snitch and a liar. He addressed my breasts when I first arrived at the motel. I don't think *friendly* is in the cards."

Matthew couldn't blame Donny all that much for his interest in Dani's figure, seeing as Danielle DeMarco was the most beautiful woman Matthew had ever laid eyes on. But he'd never admit that aloud these days, or Dani would squeeze the non-beating heart right out of his chest.

"Right," Matthew said instead, his tone light since he trusted Dani to make the right calls. "Then let's try to keep things civil."

With a snort, Dani gave a shake of her head. The former detective rapped her knuckles against the door to the inner office and didn't wait for a response before entering. That's how she worked—ask forgiveness, not permission.

"Can we have a minute?" Matthew asked the officer in charge of watching Donny. "You can wait outside."

The officer—a half elf—gave a succinct nod and moved outside. Dani ignored the whole exchange, perching a hip on the desk and studying Donny.

Donny's head was tilted down and his eyes were focused on Dani's body. Matthew spoke some harsh words in a voice that was a hint too growly to be professional, and Donny's eyeballs popped right back into his head. He paled as he brought his gaze to Dani's face.

"I'm honorary Detective Dani DeMarco," she said, wasting no time putting her new title to use. "I'm going to ask you some questions. Don't lie to me, Donny, alright? I want us to understand one another."

Donny gave a sneering smile. "Sure thing, honey-bear. Say, if you ever need a room around here, I can hook you up with a discount and a special offer."

Matthew prepared to launch himself across the room at Donny. The urge had nothing to do with professionalism and everything to do with protecting what was his. Matthew was able to restrain himself for only one simple reason: Dani was no longer his.

Matthew's fangs pressed through, sharpening in a primal reaction, but he kept his mouth shut. Dani would hate if anyone stepped on her battle. Since the day she'd joined the force, she'd taken pride in standing up for herself. Matthew had always wondered if that was a quality groomed from growing up with a household of brothers.

"Listen here, scumbag," Dani said. "I have a special offer with your name on it. I'll rearrange whatever joke you've got down here for free." She gestured to his lap. "If you come onto me again, take one look at my chest, or lie to my face, you'll need a surgeon to pull the stick out of your ass. Understood?"

Donny's face paled even further. "Yes, uh, lady. Ma'am. Detective, Your Honor."

Dani gave a thin, but not satisfied smile. She didn't delight in taking others down a notch; it was simply a hazard of the job. And as a woman on the force, unfortunately, she'd had to toughen up early in her career.

"Great. Glad we can be friends. So," she said, easing back and adopting a lighter tone. "Who rented room 309 tonight? Start from the beginning and give me everything you've got. We have all the time you need."

"Well, uh," Donny said, shifting his eyes toward Matthew, who offered only a bland stare in return. "I don't really, uh, know ma'am."

"Isn't it your job to know who rents the rooms here?"

"I just work the desk."

"I imagine you keep logs." Dani glanced around her for evidence of some sort of bookkeeping system. Technology of the human variety was rarely found in Wicked—all the magic zipping through the air made the products essentially useless. "Who signed in?"

Donny shifted with discomfort. "Charlie Bone."

Dani's eyes narrowed. "And you believed that was his real name?"

"Look—lady, your honorary whatever. This is the Motel Sixth. We don't exactly have prime real estate in Wicked, so we do what we can to stay afloat." Donny gestured behind him. "The casino's two blocks away. We've got Goblin Girls coming back here two, three different times a night, each time with a different guy. You understand what I'm saying? Nobody around these parts puts their real name on the paper, and we don't require identification. That's the way these parts roll, in case you're not familiar."

"I didn't grow up in the Golden District," she said lightly. "I know exactly how these parts work, Donny. Tell me—did this Charlie Bone come here often?"

"Never seen him before."

"How about a little more. You know what I'm looking for, so don't make this difficult. Distinguishing characteristics?"

"The dude was about as tall as you." Donny's gaze roved over Dani for a second, a split second's hesitation on her breasts before he jerked back to attention and averted his eyes. "Kind of reddish hair, but not that real vibrant shade of ginger, you read me?"

"I read you. What else?"

"That's it. He checked in. A little weird because usually dudes don't come in here without a Goblin Girl at that hour of the night."

"What hour is that?"

"He walked in here around eight p.m. It ain't that late, but after a long day at the casino, sometimes a guy needs something for dinner that ain't food, if you read me."

"Donny, I read you loud and clear. We all get it. But if he didn't have a woman with him, what does that mean?"

He shifted uncomfortably once again. "Well, sometimes people use this place as a meeting spot."

"There was a pretty big SpellHash deal that went down last night in Room 309. I don't suppose you were on duty when that happened, were you?" Dani treaded lightly, but her threat was clear. "Got anything you want to share?"

"Fine. If a dude comes in the motel alone, he's probably got some darker business to attend to—but it's not *serious*. At the Motel Sixth, we don't get the big stuff—you know, the moneymakers. The Void—none of that."

"The Void?" Dani's voice hitched. "What made you think of that?"

The Void is a term locals use for the black market sale of magic. Certain spells, and more often curses, are illegal. But like all illegal substances, there's a place to find them. In the Sixth Borough, that place is The Void. A dark, shifting sort of mass that is never quite tangible and all too elusive.

"I'm just saying the stuff that happens in these rooms ain't the sort of busts that make a cop's career." Donny spoke almost apologetically. "It's like, SpellHash deals and shit. Nothing important. Pennies, really. No cop's gonna make chief because they broke up a little party in the Motel Sixth."

"What about Charlie Bone was different than the normal dealers that come in and out of here?"

"He was..." Instead of looking surprised at the question, Donny seemed to think it was a good one. "He was polished. Soft spoken, not the usual thug looking to have a good time or to make a quick buck. I sort of wondered if he'd gotten the lines of communication crossed with his partner or whoever and ended up here on accident."

"Did you ever see a partner? Did anyone enter the building after Mr. Bone?"

Donny thought. "We had one dude and a Goblin Girl come in here—a Mr..." Donny paused, glanced over the chicken scratch list of names signed into his log. "Mr. Long."

Dani rolled her eyes. "What did he look like? He a regular?"

Donny snickered. "Yeah. He's in here twice a week. According to the girls, he lives up to his name."

Dani looked a bit like she might gag, which was impressive, seeing as her stomach was one of the strongest in the precinct. She had worked some of the most gruesome cases the borough had ever seen. Matthew allowed himself the slightest of smiles at the irony.

Donny wiped the smirk from his face when Dani sent him a scathing look. "Where might I find Mr. Long?"

"He's upstairs with the girl. They should—ah, be finished by now. He checked in around eight thirty. He usually stays until midnight, but I can't imagine he keeps her busy the whole time, if you know what I mean."

"We know what you mean, Donny!" Dani flicked her hair over her shoulder in frustration. "Which room is he in? By the time I get back downstairs, I want a list of everyone who's been in and out of here in the last week."

"Room 412," Donny said. "It's at the end of the hall. Say, what do you think is going on here? Usually they don't bring out the vamp for nothing."

Matthew's lips curled inward, and his fangs began their descent once more. He could try to fight it, but it wouldn't work; some aspects of him were too natural, too animalistic in nature. Fighting who—or what—he was would be useless. He'd come to terms with that a long time ago.

"Shut up," Dani said. "His name's Captain King."

Donny raised a hand in apology, though he seemed relaxed, as if he somehow knew he'd passed the interview. Dani glanced at Matthew as she stood, and her eyes flitted toward his mouth expectantly. She twisted away when he caught her staring.

"Officer..." Dani started, as the door opened and the half-elf leapt to attention.

"Dwight," he said. "Officer Dwight, Detective."

"Dwight—get a list of all the visitors from Donny and go over them one by one. I want to know who they are, what they look like, what they were doing—or who they were screwing—and then what they were *really* doing here. Understood?"

Dwight nodded, took a clipboard and a pen, and stepped into the office. Danielle left, giving a wide berth as Matthew held the door open for her. As she brushed past, he caught the familiar scent of her: honeysuckle and sugar, with a hint of sunshine.

Sure, there were the added smells of rising dough and melting mozzarella and Italian herbs, along with hints of fresh basil, tomato sauce, and a whiff of red wine that clung to her shirt.

As a vampire, Matthew could dissect even the faintest, the most exquisite of scents, yet his favorite in the world was that of Dani. The way she smelled fresh from a shower, free from perfume, from lotion, from anything that might mar her natural pheromones, was absolute perfection.

"Thanks," she said once the two reached the hallway. "For that."

"For what?" Matthew raised an eyebrow in question.

"For letting me handle Donny in there." Dani brushed a strand of hair from her face, which unleashed a new wave of scent that hit

Matthew straight in his gut. "I know you probably wanted to step in, but I appreciate you letting me handle him by myself."

Matthew gave the faintest of laughs. "Even I wasn't feeling like stepping between the two of you tonight."

She laughed too, but it was dry and businesslike. "We didn't learn a whole lot from him, unfortunately. We've got an unknown dude strolling in here with a fake name. As far as we know, he wasn't meeting anyone, nor was he accompanied by a partner. How did he get the bodies to the third floor?"

"I don't think Donny was looking for Invisibility Incantations," Matthew pointed out. "Our mystery man could have floated them in through the front door for all we know."

"True enough." With a disappointed grimace, Dani shook her head. "I tried to look at the Residuals around the front door, but there are over a hundred Cloaking Spells from the last twelve hours alone. The people who come here don't want to leave any proof behind. Things are too diluted around the front desk to determine whether Charlie Bone cloaked himself or used any sort of invisibility spell."

Matthew reached out a hand, despite his better judgment, and rested a finger on her cheek. As usual, she felt warm, vibrant, filled with life—some of the many qualities he missed dearly from his days next to her. The movement was tender, and Dani closed her eyes, leaning against him for the slightest of moments before her sigh broke them apart.

"I suppose we should get upstairs and interview Mr. Long and his girlfriend before they head out." Dani checked her watch, noted the time was around 11:30, and then led the way to the fourth floor.

Matthew followed her, swift and silent in his movements, and together they ascended the stairs because the elevator wasn't functioning. When they reached the door, Dani extended her hand to knock, but Matthew reached out and clasped her wrist before she could move.

"Thank you," he said. "For coming back to help. I know it's hard."

She tilted her head to the side. "It's not so bad."

Matthew pulled his hand away from her, the absence of warmth singeing him like dry ice. Dani didn't seem bothered by it. She rapped her knuckles against the door and waited.

Eventually, a man opened the door, and Dani groaned at the sight of him. "I did *not* sign up for this," she said, and then stepped inside.

Chapter 4

I made sure Matthew heard my mutterings as we stepped through the door of 412 in seedy Motel Sixth. I hadn't signed up to see *this*. I'd signed up to deal with dead bodies and criminals. Not naked men.

"Put some clothes on," I said to the nude man I could only assume was one Mr. Long. I didn't stare long enough to verify. "Now. I'm Detective DeMarco with the Sixth Precinct, and this is Captain King."

The man didn't seem inclined to move at all, and in fact, seemed quite proud to be on display. "What's this about?"

I focused on the man's face, raising a hand to shield the worst bits from view. He was fair-haired and blue-eyed—with a shimmer of amusement on his face. I instantly disliked him.

"I *said* put some clothes on," I repeated. "Why would you open the door in the buff?"

He gestured to the bed behind him. "I was occupied. The knock sounded important, so I figured I'd answer."

I scanned the rest of the room and spotted a Goblin Girl in bed—also naked, though she'd had the decency to cover herself with a sheet. I could tell she was on the younger end of the spectrum because her skin was the lightest shade of green. Not quite as pale as the young woman found with the mayor, but close.

She had maybe a year or two on the dead girl downstairs, which would put her somewhere between twenty-three and twenty-five, if I had to guess. Purchasing time with newer Goblin Girls was more expensive than the older models. Luck must have been on Mr. Long's side at the casino this evening.

I strode past the couple to the bathroom and grabbed a towel from the shelf. I threw it at Mr. Long with enough force that he flinched. "Wrap this around your waist."

He draped the towel casually over his hips. I ignored the fact that it didn't hide very much at all. When I instructed Mr. Long to sit on the bed, he did so with a smirk, letting the towel slip to the floor in the process. He gradually retrieved it and rested it on his lap in what felt like slow motion. The cocky idiot was playing games with me, and I did not appreciate it.

Matthew stood back in the doorway, not quite watching Mr. Long, but aware of every detail. He must have known that if he asked me back as a consultant, he'd have to give me the freedom to do things my way. I appreciated his thoughtfulness, albeit grudgingly.

"What time did the two of you arrive here tonight?" I asked Mr. Long. I jotted down his response, an answer that corroborated Donny's story. "Okay—you rolled in here around 8:30. Did you see anyone else? Hear anything?"

Mr. Long shook his head. "Not that I remember. What's this about?"

"Are we in trouble?" The Goblin Girl's artificially long eyelashes trembled, her voice quivering. Becoming a Goblin Girl walked the gray zone between legal and not. But it appeared this girl was still too new to the profession to be jaded against law enforcement. *Give her time*, I thought—*she'd grow to hate us.*

"Did you do anything that might cause you to get in trouble?" I gave the girl a firm stare, figuring I'd push while she was nervous. She shook her head, convincingly enough, and began to cry. "Then no, you're not going to be arrested, so long as you're honest with us. We're looking for a man with light-red hair, a little taller than me. Did you see anyone who matched that description?"

"You don't have a name?" Mr. Long asked.

"I'll give you his name the minute you give me yours," I said. "Feel like handing over your identification?"

Mr. Long shut up. He had the look of a businessman that wouldn't necessarily appreciate word about his activities at the Motel Sixth being made public.

"Great. Then we'll keep this as anonymous as possible so long as you give us something to go on." I hesitated, doing a brief scan of the Residuals in the room. Aside from some odd enchantments with a sexual overtone to them, there wasn't much for me to dissect. There was the lingering scent of SpellHash, and though I could tell it was likely from the previous tenant, they didn't know that. "If you're not interested in sharing, however, I'd be happy to collect that ID I mentioned and bring you in on some Hash charges. I can smell it in the air."

"We didn't take any!" the Goblin Girl cried. "I'm not into illegal substances. I swear to you."

"Then tell me what you heard. Something you saw. I need something," I pressed. "*Now.*"

Mr. Long shifted uncomfortably. "The description you gave us could fit a lot of people, Detective."

"Fine. Get started listing them. While you're at it, how often do you come around here?"

Mr. Long glanced at his girl, almost sheepish. As if he didn't want to admit the truth in front of her. But one glance at Matthew's silent, hulking figure in the door, and Mr. Long's face lost most of its blood.

"Two, maybe three times a week on average. Give or take," he said softly. "I don't usually talk to anyone except for Donny."

"You usually come up here with her?"

Again, his eyes flicked behind him, then refocused on me. "No. We just met for the first time tonight. I usually..." He hesitated to clear his throat. "I had a good night at the casino."

"She's a little pricy for you on a normal night," I said, deducing easily what he'd meant. "Fine. You use the same girls normally?"

"Use." He flinched at the word. "I *see* some of the same girls from time to time, yes. But more often than not, it's whoever is...available."

"Lovely," I said icily, my voice giving away exactly what I thought of his practice. "The man whose description I gave you: I want names."

"Lady—er, sorry, Detective, you know we don't do names around these places. There are two people I can think of who I've played MagiCraps with at the casino that *might* fit. But don't quote me on it—I didn't see them around here tonight. They're called Joey Jones and Lucas Fitz."

"Where might I find these gentlemen?"

"Gentlemen." He snorted at that, which I thought was interesting considering his own present state of undress. "Yeah, sure. You'll find them at Table 13 on any night of the week. They should still be there now if you need to talk to them that badly."

"What is this about?" The Goblin Girl asked. "Something bad happened, didn't it?"

"I wouldn't be here if it was anything pleasant," I said, then crooked my head toward Matthew. "Neither would he. So, you didn't see Joey or Lucas here tonight?"

Mr. Long appeared to be deep in thought. "I don't think so—I don't recall seeing anyone here tonight except for Melinda—" he nodded toward the girl—"and Donny."

"Fine." I took a card out of my pocket and prepared to hand it over. However, I realized it was a card for DeMarco's Pizza—not my most professional move on the job.

Before I could turn to Matthew, he'd already crossed the room and handed both Melinda and Mr. Long one of his cards. "Get in touch if you remember anything else. Doesn't matter if it seems insignificant; it might not be."

Even after two years of dating, his quickness still sent my heart racing. He could cross rooms in the blink of an eye, and it just wasn't fair. Then again, I suppose that's what others thought about my ability to see Residuals. We all had our strengths, and Mr. Long's was an alarming lack of inhibition.

Matthew and I had barely made it out of the room before the towel came back down and sloppy sounds resumed, echoing through the thin walls.

"Getting his money's worth, I guess," I said with a frown. "Pig."

Matthew made no comment. He knew better than to get involved when I was in a mood—even if he agreed with me.

"Do we know how the bodies were discovered?" I asked as we walked back down the hall. I felt itchy from being in this place and wanted a shower. "Who called the cops?"

"Donny called, though reluctantly," Matthew said. "We have the record on the Comm system if you need, but it doesn't say much. He asked for the Sixth Precinct badges to check into a room."

"I get the feeling Donny normally checks on things himself," I said. "Keeps the cops out. What was different this time?"

"Charlie Bone only rented the room for an hour. After two hours had passed, Donny was getting anxious."

"Donny must have smelled something fishy about Charlie, or else he would've busted down that door himself. Unless he's holding out on us and knows more."

We'd reached the front office again. Officer Dwight was still grilling Donny. Judging by the annoyed look on the latter's face, the cop was doing a fine job. I left them to it.

"You should get some rest," Matthew said, reading the tiredness in my face correctly. "I'll fill you in tomorrow. We've got officers canvassing every full room in this place, and Nash will be here until morning to monitor. If we find anything, I'll let you know."

"You're going to interview Joey and Lucas." Before I finished speaking, Matthew's quick blink and crooked nod confirmed my suspicions. "Great. I'm going with you."

"Danielle—"

"Detective DeMarco," I said swiftly. "The Residuals clock is counting down, and we need to find that crime scene or we'll have no clue who—or how—someone did this, let alone why."

Chapter 5

Matthew and Dani crossed the short distance between the Motel Sixth and the casino. The land where they walked toed the line between Goblin Grid, the troll and gnome residential areas, and the ogre and orc stomping grounds. In the distance light gleamed from the prestigious Golden District belonging to the elves, shiny and glittery above the dirt and grime of the slums. The biggest dichotomy in the borough, aside from the Outer Regions.

Matthew moved at Dani's pace, quickly and silently, both of them lost in thought. Matthew watched the frown form on her lips and wondered what had put it there. He suspected it might be the death she'd seen this evening, or possibly the return to a career she'd tried to escape. Or maybe, she was just frustrated by the lack of Residuals she'd been able to read.

Dani looked tired, but he knew she wouldn't agree to rest until he did. The tiredness in her gaze wasn't that of physical fatigue, but the sort that showed her exhaustion with the world. The never-ending cycle of death and violence, of darkness and despair, no matter how much she tried to outrun it.

Matthew hated to draw her back into the cycle, but the truth was that he needed her. They all did. And until they could find Lucia or another Reserve with even *half* Dani's talent, their options were limited.

"Lucky table thirteen," Dani muttered as she pushed the door open to the casino. "What are the chances both men have vanished?"

"High enough," Matthew said. "Word travels fast around here."

Dani gave a nod, obviously remembering how quickly folks around these parts scattered at the first mention of the cops. As she and Matthew entered the casino, she gave a shudder, as if she could feel the hope slipping away when the scents grime and desperation swarmed them like a noxious cloud.

They wound their way through the casino, Matthew doing his best to keep Dani close without letting her sense she was being *protected*. She hated that, but she'd have to deal with it on his watch. As Captain, Matthew took the job of watching over his men and women seriously. Though Dani had never technically reported to him—Reserves were floaters around the Investigative Division, never attached exclusively to one unit—he still considered her his responsibility.

As Dani and Matthew reached Table 13, Matthew signaled to Dani that he would be taking the lead on this one. He stepped forward, resting against the MagiCraps table as he scanned the paranormal folks cringing at the disruption.

An ogre leered from one side, and a group of three elfin women gave him plenty of space as they curled against the opposite corner to watch. A spellslinger held dice in his hand and waited for the round to start. He was one of the flashy sorts of men who'd bought his magic with gold.

Spellslingers used magic like witches—casting spells and brewing potions, but the majority of them weren't innately gifted with powers. They purchased spells and magicks from select stores, and sometimes The Void. When trained well and armed with appropriate hexes, a spellslinger was almost indiscernible from a witch or wizard. The one at this table, however, wasn't all that harmful. Annoying, maybe, but that might be due to the fact that he wore a purple cape and a lopsided crown and bellowed for luck as he blew into his palm.

"We've got a winner," intoned the gnome officiating over the table. He had a stool that reached two thirds of the way up the table and a stick longer than his entire body to pull the dice toward him.

"Another win for Mr. Royal! The man is on *fire* tonight, ladies and gents."

"Speaking of fires," Matthew said, as he discreetly flashed a badge to the gnome who had a name tag that read Alvin. "Nobody moves. I'm looking for Joey Jones and Lucas Fitz. The sooner someone gives me their location, the sooner I pretend there's no SpellHash around this table."

Alvin's eyes narrowed. Gnomes were notoriously bad with magic and had a horrendous sense of smell. "Who's got the Hash?" Alvin snarled. "You think just because I can't *smell* I won't kick out whoever's packing? Y'all know the rules."

"We'll forget all about it," Matthew said evenly, "for a little information. We hear these two boys frequent the table."

"Pretty much every night of the week," one of the elf girls supplied. "They usually buy a round of drinks for the table around midnight. That's why we're here—we want our free drinks."

One of her friends nodded in agreement. "I thought I saw Lucas leave about an hour ago, but I don't know where he went—or why he'd leave. He's here all the time. I'm sure if you come back tomorrow, you'll find him."

"I'm not so sure about that," Matthew said. "It's imperative we find them both quickly."

"What're they running from?" The spellslinger on the end put a hand on his hip and leaned against the table. He was tall and fit, his body probably accentuated with some sort of Body Buffer to blow up his muscles and tan his face. "Joey didn't even show tonight. Do Lucas and Joey know each other outside of the table?"

Matthew ignored him. "Anyone know where they live? Where they might be? I'm guessing those aren't their real names."

"Joey is his real first name," one of the elfin girls said with a giggle and a blush that gave away exactly how she knew that. "Jones isn't, though. I don't know his real last name."

"Lucas doesn't say much," Alvin supplied from his perch on the stool. "He shows up, plays, leaves. Tips well if he wins, mild if he loses. Never had a problem with the guy."

"And Joey?" Dani asked. "He gives you trouble?"

Alvin squinted, cocked his head in thought. "I wouldn't say trouble, but he's a character. In a good mood, he's the most fun guy you'll ever meet. In a bad mood..."

The silence around the table spoke volumes.

"Were they here tonight?" Dani asked again. "What times did you see them—exactly?"

"Lucas was here eight to eleven-ish, but I don't think he stayed put the whole time." Alvin frowned. "He went to refill his drinks a few times or something—not sure what. Joey didn't turn up at all tonight. It's not totally unheard of, but it's unusual. Usually means he's got a new squeeze at home."

"You might want to try the Sorcerer's Square apartments to find Lucas," the spellslinger suggested. "I thought I saw him headed in that direction once. And he knows how to use magic, but he's not a spellslinger."

Matthew nodded his thanks but didn't make eye contact. He focused his next question on the giggly elf. "And Joey?"

She rolled her eyes. "I think his dad's a shifter. Joey's not, but he gets along with them best out of all the species. I'd head toward the Howler and ask around."

Dani bit her bottom lip in thought. Matthew noticed the movement in his peripheral and flinched. He hated when she did that. It reminded him of the last time they'd been together; the moment he'd ruined everything.

"Detective." Matthew spoke the word so sharply Dani flinched. "Let's go."

She looked confused as Matthew managed a nod toward Alvin, then stormed off at a pace that had Dani jogging to keep up.

Matthew didn't bother to explain, instead brushing through the casino with such force pixies and faeries and the like scattered in his wake.

"Where are we going?" Dani asked, breathless as they stepped outside the casino. "Do you really think Joey and Lucas would just go *home*?"

He shrugged. "Hard to say, but we need to follow up."

"Did I say something to offend you?" There was no apology in Dani's question. "I didn't mean to step on your toes back there."

"You didn't."

"Fine, then..." she sighed. "Be mad. We'll walk in silence."

Matthew turned to her, spun on a heel as he reached the street corner. The torch above their heads burned directly on them like a flashlight. Matthew reached roughly for Dani's arm and tugged her into a darker alleyway, into a dimmer, more private corner of the world.

"I'm sorry," Matthew said, his eyes flashing dark gemstones against the moonlight. "I hate that I dragged you into this. You've been on the job for only a few hours, and I can already tell it's tearing you apart. You're exhausted—"

"I'm fine, Matthew."

"It's hurting you to be back." He let his statement hang, offering her a chance at a rebuttal, but she didn't take it. "I wouldn't bring you into this if I didn't have to—if I knew any other way."

"I know," she said in a whisper. "I could have said no."

"I knew you wouldn't say '*no*' if I offered you The Hex Files."

"That's my choice."

Matthew stepped forward, entering an odd dance with Dani as she stepped backward, her spine pressing against the wall of the brick building. "Try to forgive me."

"Matthew, there's nothing to forgive. You offered me a job with fair payment, and I accepted."

Matthew raised a pale finger, one that looked like marble in the moonlight. When it connected with her cheek, however, it was no more weight than a breath of air. "Then don't let it break you. If this—any of it—becomes too much, let me know."

"Sure," she said, though they both knew that wasn't any sort of promise. "I say we stop by Sorcerer's Square first, then hit the Howler on the way back to the station."

Matthew blinked, though the movement was unnecessary for his kind. It was no more than a practiced reaction meant to make him appear more human-like. "Fine."

He backed away from her, noting Dani's racing heartbeat, the erratic gait of her breath. With a frown, Matthew wondered when she had become afraid of him.

Matthew and Dani arrived at Sorcerer's Square in silence. Dani looked to him for guidance, but Matthew tilted his chin toward her, offering her the lead. Dani wasted no time in searching through the listing of names, and to her surprise, she found Lucas Fitz listed there. It was either his real name, or a well-constructed alias.

Matthew and Dani were buzzed in without being asked for a name. After climbing to the second floor, they quickly located Lucas's door. Danielle gave two succinct knocks, then waited.

The door eventually opened to reveal Lucas Fitz in his bathrobe, a bowl of popcorn in one hand. He looked wildly innocent—too innocent. His eyes were a murky green, his hair the light-reddish color that Donny had described, and even his height was accurate at just a few inches taller than Dani.

Lucas crooked an eyebrow at the sight of us. "The head vamp," he said. "What'd someone accuse me of doing to get a visit from you?"

"What were you doing at the Motel Sixth tonight?" Dani launched straight into her attack. "I'm Detective DeMarco, and you're obviously familiar with Captain King, so let's not waste time. We have eyewitness accounts of you there."

"I wasn't there, Detective." Lucas's voice was smooth sailing. "I was at the casino. Table 13, but I suppose you've already checked there."

"Nobody could verify you remained at Table 13 the entire evening," Dani said. "Where were you, Lucas? Where'd you go? Did you kill them, or were you just doing the dirty work moving the bodies?"

Lucas's eyes widened ever so slightly. Despite his cool-as-a-cucumber attitude, Dani suspected it was true surprise. "Detective, I've never killed anyone—ever. I have my flaws like anyone, but helping murder along in any capacity isn't one of them. Now, if you don't have anything to arrest me on, I'm going to bed."

"Lucas—"

"Warrant?" That eyebrow raised again, and like most good crooks in the business, he knew his rights. "Goodnight, officers."

Lucas closed the door tightly and left Matthew and Dani alone. "He didn't kill them," she said. "A hunch, but I think that was genuine surprise."

"I agree," Matthew confirmed. "Let's find Joey."

"I think..." Dani stopped, rested a finger against her lip in thought. "I think we also need to find out who ratted on us. How'd Joey and Lucas know to scram so quickly?"

Matthew's jaw tightened. "Either someone saw us at the Motel Sixth, or someone on the inside gave a tip."

"Whoever it is better enjoy their evening because when I find them..." Dani trailed off, shook her head in dismay. "I hate rats."

As they set off toward the Howler, Matthew suspected her disgust for snitches stemmed from her past caseload. He wondered as they walked if the answers would be in The Hex Files—and if that's why she wanted them so badly.

Or maybe, it was something more.

Chapter 6

The Howler sits on the east side of the borough. It's located outside the edge of a dense forest known as The Depth—named aptly for the darkness under its canopy of trees. The woods are mostly reserved for frightening monsters—and those who transform into them at night.

While The Depth is home to a wide variety of magical creatures—not *all* of them are monsters. The forest floor undoubtedly belongs to the shifters, but the treetops belong to the fairies and wood nymphs, the phoenixes and the creatures who soar. It's a mixed bag inside the trees, and one doesn't tend to venture much deeper into the arena than a stone's throw—because death is always close in The Depth.

The Howler is considered the last 'safe' establishment on the perimeter of the woods. It lurks just out of reach from the waving treetop shadows and acts as a trading post, a center for gossip, and a home base for the shifters in their human form.

I've spent more than my fair share of time at the Howler—and not always for pleasantries. I've had to arrest more than one werewolf for transforming too early in public—the equivalent of a drunk and disorderly or indecent exposure for the human NYPD. It's always a good time.

Then, there'd been the half-shifter I'd dated a while back—we'd spent an evening or two at the Howler. However, things had never progressed past a third date. Call me shallow, but I could never get over the fact that he had hair *everywhere*. That, and there'd been no chemistry.

I'd never had chemistry with anyone in the same way I did with Matthew. Whatever zinged between us was unique—vibrant and dangerous and addictive. However, we wouldn't be revisiting those memories, especially because we'd resumed working together. It was simply too dangerous and not worth the risk.

I hesitated, remembering our last night together. The first—and last—time his fangs had pierced my skin. The night that had ended all hopes for a future between us. The night he'd caved to his basic nature. While it wasn't his fault per se, Matthew had seen that moment as a failure. Ultimately the pleasure of that night had been beyond belief—wild with the primal nature of it—but the terror had also been real. He could have killed me, and we both knew it.

"Danielle?" Matthew murmured softly.

I shook my head to clear the fog and glanced at the vampire I used to love. It was obviously not the first time he'd said my name, and as I took in the surrounding scene, I realized we'd made the cross-borough trek and arrived before the Howler.

"Are you alright?" His hand reached out, then hesitated. As if he knew the exact thoughts that had been flitting across my mind. "It's late. Are you sure you don't want to go back home, get some rest? I can fill you in tomorrow morning."

"Don't be ridiculous." A shudder racked my body—delayed, I figured, from my reminiscing. "What are the chances Joey's inside?"

Matthew shrugged. "If he's anything like Lucas, he'll be home and scouring his list of friends for a manufactured alibi."

"Speaking of alibis," I said, "we'll need to find two of them. One for the actual time of the murder, which I would guess to be around six this evening, and one for the time of movement—around nine tonight."

Matthew nodded thoughtfully. "We need the connection between the mayor and the Goblin Girl."

"You don't think it was sexual in nature?"

"We'll have to wait for the reports. I've seen plenty of sex crimes, and usually the victims are in some stage of undress," he said. "Both of them were fully clothed. From the way they were found on the ground, the bodies look dumped together, not as if they'd been intimate just prior."

"It was a staged scene. Why there?" I pictured the room in my head—the nondescript space, upset only by the presence of one public figure and a woman on the other end of the social ladder. "They would obviously be found there at one point or another no matter what. The maids would've stumbled on them in the morning, so why *there*? If trying to dump the bodies, why not go to the river? The Depth? There are so many places that lend to concealing bodies much easier than a hotel room."

Matthew gave a faux-shudder. "It's so romantic to hear you talk about disposing of bodies."

I broke into a dark grin. "Come on, let's go find Joey and let it percolate. I think the location is some sort of clue or message, though I can't say what. It could be nothing more than convenience, but even that is something."

Matthew nodded toward the bar. "Shall we?"

I tilted a head. "I can't imagine you're a well-loved figure in there. You can wait outside, if you'd prefer."

He gave a rare bark of laughter. "I'm in a mood to stir things up."

"A VAMPIRE AND A WITCH walk into a werewolf bar," I told him. "This can't end well."

"A vampire with a *badge* and an honorary detective walk into a bar..." Matthew corrected. "We'll be okay."

The bouncer was a large man whose hands, even in human form, resembled massive paws. Perhaps it was the tattoos running the length of his arms, or the sheer bulk of him, but he was one man I didn't want to annoy this evening. Even the animal-type grunts he made as he allowed us inside with a flash of our IDs were gruff and intimidating.

Matthew and I decided to forego our badges and attempt to fit in as casual patrons... but 'fitting in' was a lost cause the moment we stepped through the door. Between Matthew in his expensive suit, and my all black ensemble, we stuck out with or without our shields.

Every shaggy head in the place turned to face us the second I took a breath. I calculated quickly and realized the full moon was only days away. Tensions would likely be rising. Nobody wanted to be on duty *anywhere* the night of a full moon—sometimes the precinct paid time and a half just to prevent max amounts of sick calls flooding in during the hours before sunset.

One cursory glance around the place told me that anyone here might be Joey Jones. Without an obvious target to approach, I nudged Matthew in the direction of the bar so at the very least we could sit and try to blend in somewhat.

There were one or two non-shifters sipping ales and chatting with bowed heads, though the vast majority of bar patrons could easily be linked to the Sixth Pack—an alliance between shifters and their families. While intelligent on the shifters' parts to band together, the laws of the Sixth Pack often made things difficult for law enforcement trying to work in shifter territory. The main rules of the pack weren't much different than those of mobsters: hear no evil, speak no evil, see no evil. Nobody ever saw nothin' in the pack, which didn't leave me with a lot of hope for our evening's agenda.

We sat on barstools. Matthew automatically ordered a red wine for himself and a sparkling water for me. He wouldn't touch his wine, as usual, and I'd inhale the bubbly. It was our old song and dance from the days we'd worked homicide cases together and sat through many a stakeout.

The drinks arrived, and Matthew left a generous tip.

"Any chance Joey's here tonight?" Matthew asked in his silky, seductive tone.

The female bartender, whose nametag read Lorraine, leaned over the counter. She wore a low-cut white tank top, thin enough to expose every detail of the red bra she wore underneath. Plenty of bust spilled over the edges, and a large paw print sat atop of each breast. To Matthew's credit, if he noticed the cleavage, he didn't show it.

She continued to size him up. "Who wants to know?"

"A friend," Matthew said. "We met earlier tonight at Alvin's table."

Lorraine frowned. "You hang at the casino?"

"Joey and I go way back," Matthew lied easily. "I borrowed some money from him earlier tonight. Won a helluva lot more than he gave me, and I figured I owed him a round of drinks."

It was to Matthew's advantage, physically and mentally, to keep her engaged in a conversation as long as possible—his voice had its own magnetic pull to it. I knew this from experience. He could sweet talk the pants off the police chief if he wanted, and the man was a happily married orc.

"I can vouch for the vamp," I said, trying to join in the banter. Apparently, I was all awkward turtle in this situation, and my ploy didn't work. Both Matthew and Lorraine turned to me with a frown. Matthew's work on her unraveled before my eyes. "I'll shut up," I offered.

"Lorraine." When Matthew used names, it added intensity to his persuasive magic. "We don't have any business with him except to deliver some winnings. But if he's not here, I'll see him tomorrow." Matthew gave a light laugh, almost dainty. "If there's anything left to give him by then."

Lorraine weighed the pros and cons of giving up information on Joey, with Joey's probable desire to get his hands on potential prize money. With a sigh, she wiped her hands on her apron, her eyes darting up and down the counter, checking to see if anyone was listening.

When all customers appeared to be enticed by their own beverages and discussions, she focused on Matthew. "He's over in the corner. Look, you're not gonna arrest him, are you? I think he's a little...dazzled."

Matthew's grin widened. "We're not here to arrest anyone."

That was the end of the conversation. Lorraine swept away from us. Talking too long with strangers in a bar was cause for alarm. Plus, Lorraine had gotten her generous tip. She'd snitched on her pal. All three of us had known we weren't here to toss winnings in Joey's lap. I assumed it was only because Joey wasn't part of the Sixth Pack that Lorraine had spoken to us at all.

Matthew left his wine on the counter, I grabbed my sparkling water, and together we made our way across the room. We kept to the dark outer edges and gave wide berths to the shadowy tables lining the walls with even more shadowy figures whispering beneath cloaks.

"Joey?" Matthew continued with the lead as he eased into the booth that Lorraine had pointed out. "It is Joey, isn't it?"

I sat next to Matthew, watching with concern as the man across from us swayed in his seat. This particular booth was wedged in a corner. Joey appeared to have been sitting here alone in a sweatshirt, the hood pulled up so the edges covered his eyes.

His hands, however, rested on the table, and I spotted a dark pawprint tattooed on the back of his left hand. A symbol of the pack, though not the markings of an official member. I remembered the elf-girl telling us that she suspected his dad was a shifter, though Joey wasn't. I wondered briefly why he hadn't joined. It might have saved him from getting snitched on tonight at the very least.

I pointed it out to Matthew, but he barely acknowledged me save for a flutter of his eyelashes. He'd already seen it.

"Well, this is fun and all, but the Residuals clock is still ticking, and I don't think our friend is waking up." I murmured a brief Wind Whisper incantation, and the small breeze that emanated from my fingers lifted Joey's hood from over his face and flung it back against the wall. One or two shifters looked my way, then quickly turned back to the beverages.

Matthew and I studied the man before us. He was handsome, and I could see why the elfin girl had turned all giggly and red when discussing Joey with us. If there had been life in his features, I could've seen his smile being charismatic, his eyes being lively in their light blue shade.

As it was, he stared ahead at us—his eyes dead, his breath coming in robotic, even gusts. It was eerie the way he looked straight at me, but through me. It was as if he couldn't actually *see* a thing.

"What do you think he took?" Matthew leaned forward. "I'd say SpellHash, but this has got to be ten times stronger."

"Anything new in The Void lately?" I asked. I shifted my weight around to the other side of the table and slid into the booth next to Joey. "Oh, shit. Matthew, come look at this."

I moved again, making way for him to take my place next to Joey. I pointed out his eyes—and what I'd found in them. With his face impassive, Matthew studied Joey's face with keen interest.

There, in his bright blue irises, danced a golden light. A small sort of beam with a shimmering tail that played like a game of pong across his eyes—bouncing off one side, pivoting to the next, rebounding and rebounding in an infinite loop. Both eyes had the same golden comet shooting through them, though they appeared to move freely from one another.

"What in Hades' name is that?" Matthew whispered. "I've never seen it before in my life. Any Residuals on him?"

I'd quickly scanned him for Residuals when we'd first sat in the booth, as had become habit ever since I was a little girl. When I was young, I hadn't realized it was strange for me to see Residual magic. I had used it in my own way—for simple things, and as a safety measure. It had come naturally, and I had assumed everyone else did the same.

By the time I was seven, I'd realized that I was indeed a strange duck, and that not everyone had the same abilities. That was when I learned to keep my mouth shut. It wasn't until the Sixth Precinct discovered my talents and recruited me that I began studying my skills and capitalizing on them in earnest.

My initial scan of Joey hadn't turned up anything alarming. There was the usual mess of magical Residuals around him as with most supernaturals—even those who didn't use spells. Magic clung to us, to everyone, and seeing that Joey spent a lot of time in the casino, he had a boatload of washed off spells lingering on him. I wrinkled my nose as I deciphered a few of them, and eventually shook my head.

"He's not our guy," I said. "No evidence of Moving Magic on him anywhere."

"And Lucas?"

"He had some around his hands, but I'm not convinced it was enough to move two bodies. He could've used it to call his keys or something."

"Why didn't you question Lucas about it?" Matthew turned from Joey to look at me. "It might have shaken him."

"It might also have tipped our hand, and we can't have that with a case this size," I said. "Also, you know as well as I do that it's completely unreliable to use Residuals on a person's body as evidence. There are too many ways to wash off or dilute residue, or for someone else to force them—even unknowingly—onto another person's body. Watch."

I raised my hands, muttered universal words to invoke Moving Magic, and watched as ribbons of light invisible to everyone else shot from my fingers and wound themselves around Matthew's hands. His sleeves flew up his arms exactly as I'd intended.

Satisfied, I sat back in my seat. "Hate to say it, Captain, but you're swimming with Moving Magic residuals. You're glowing as pink as a teenage witch's bedroom."

Matthew noted my explanation, nodded, and turned back to Joey. "Then what the hell is wrong with him?"

"He's laced," I said. "If I were you, I'd have Lieutenant Abbott from Narcotics take a look into The Void if he can. Something new is bound to be hitting the black market if it's not already there."

"This is nothing like SpellHash," Matthew mused. "If it is a drug, it's dangerous. Are you positive it's not a curse?"

I gave a one-shoulder shrug. "Not all curses leave Residuals on the outside—and if he's been cursed for more than a few hours, they'll be fading anyway. I seriously doubt it, but I can't say for certain."

Matthew nodded. "Let's bring him in for Detox."

"You're making an arrest in a shifter bar?" I winced. "Maybe I will head home a little early."

"Coward," Matthew said with a thin smile. "No arrest. I say we march him out the front doors—the Sixth Pack won't want someone dazzled in their bar for too long. If the wrong cop turns up and tries to arrest him, it'll be a showdown."

I rolled my eyes, stood, and held out my arms. "Which side of him are you taking?"

Matthew heaved Joey to his feet, took one arm and offered me the other. We marched out of the bar, silence following us as heads turned. The only person who didn't watch us go was Lorraine. I had a feeling she didn't want to be involved in the slightest.

We only made it a few steps outside of the bar before a swift figure cut in and blocked our forward progression. We didn't want to start trouble, so I kept my magic under wraps and Matthew kept his fangs tucked away, but I could feel the discomfort radiating from him. Neither of us wanted to be standing outside a shifter bar in the middle of the night, hauling in someone close to the Sixth Pack for illegal drug use.

"To what do we owe the pleasure of your visit?" A tall, unfamiliar man stood before us, a slight smile crooked on his face. "Detective DeMarco, Captain King—" he nodded to each of us. "Do you need some help with Jones?"

"Who are you?" Matthew purred his answer, just on the edge of a growl.

I glanced at Matthew in surprise. I hoped my glare told him to back off—the way he was talking would pick us a fight, and I wasn't looking to roll up my sleeves and tussle with a werewolf. Judging by the looks of our new friend, that's exactly what we were dealing with.

The man introduced himself simply as Grey—and I had no idea if that was a first name, last name, or nickname. He had a shaggy mop of brown hair that lightly curled at the edges, and two paws tattooed on the backs of his hand.

Definitely a member of *some* pack, even if not the local Sixth Pack, I realized with a quick glance. More tattoos—solid bars—climbed up his arm signaling his rank. I swallowed—he had to be close to the Alpha, if not the next in line. Even so, I suspected he wasn't from around here—or else I would have recognized him.

Even with my Stunner and Matthew's fangs, we'd be in for one helluva fight if things went south with this strong of a shifter. In his human form, the man looked like he belonged among statues of Greek gods; I imagined his shifter form was even more incredible in size and strength.

Grey wore a black t-shirt despite the chill in the night air and jeans that molded over long legs bulging with muscles underneath. He was oddly handsome in a purely raw, male sort of way, and I found myself tiptoeing the edge of fear and admiration.

"We don't want any trouble, Grey," I said gently. "We're helping your friend Jones out. Looks like someone laced his Hash with a little something extra, and we need to get it out of his system."

"They don't bring out the vampire for a SpellHash overdose," Grey said smoothly, his sharp, moon-drenched eyes landing on me with something that felt like curiosity. "What's Jones suspected of?"

"Get the hell out of our way," Matthew said, a hint of a hiss in his voice. "We're on official business, wolf."

"Matthew," I snapped at him, watching in awe as his lips curled back and he bared his fangs. "Captain King, get a damn hold on yourself!"

Grey landed a pleasant smile on me. "It's fine, Detective. Nothing I can't handle. I just figured I should warn you that the full moon is days away, and I'd keep some distance between yourselves and the Howler. We don't get many vamps around these parts, and the wolves hanker for a fight when the clouds roll behind the moon..."

I finally took a step back and watched the two men face off. Something was happening here that was distinctly male, and I wanted no part of their pissing contest. I was already annoyed at having to hold up Joey Jones's heavy ass without the help of magic, and Matthew's little showdown with the werewolf wasn't helping.

"Captain, I'm going," I grunted, rolling up my sleeves in frustration. I shot a jolt of Moving Magic underneath Joey's armpits. It made him about half the weight as before, and I sighed and stretched in relief. "Are you coming with me or not?"

My indifference finally drew Matthew's attention, and he fell in line beside me, his fangs gradually retracting with each step we took toward the station and away from Grey.

As we neared the end of the block, Matthew let out a low, snappish growl for seemingly no reason, and I chanced a look over my shoulder in surprise. Grey stood there, his eyes following our every move, his ginormous figure outlined by the moon as he waited and watched.

"What was that all about?" I demanded when we finally turned the corner. Matthew distinctly relaxed. "It is extremely unprofessional to call someone a *wolf* on the clock. And what happened with the fangs? Come on, Matthew—this isn't a game."

"He looked at you," Matthew snarled. "And I didn't like it."

"Oh, gee whiz." I exhaled a huge, exaggerated breath. "Let's arrest him. He looked at me. Guess what? He looked at you, too, and you looked at him. So did I. We all looked at one another."

"That's not what I mean."

"Well? Get ahold of yourself."

"He showed an interest in you."

"You're full of it. There was no interest anywhere; he was just protecting the pack. It's their natural instinct—and you, my friend, know all about natural instincts."

Matthew hesitated, a look of horror and sadness winding across his face. He looked as if he wanted to apologize, then couldn't find the words.

"I'm sorry," I said. "That was out of line."

"No. You're right; I acted like an idiot back there. It's just sometimes..."

"I know," I said softly. I'd felt it too. "I think we have to keep our personal interests and history out of this if we're going to be successful working together."

Matthew gave a nod, and that ended the conversation.

We got Joey into Detox by the time three a.m. rolled around. Matthew and I combined efforts to fill in the paperwork and left instructions for the clerk to hold Joey until someone could return the next day and interview him for an alibi.

If Joey had been dazzled all evening, that was as good an alibi as any. Matthew and I watched him from behind bars. The bars on the

detox cell were magical, created from bright beams of electrical current that hummed with the constant effort of restraint. As I watched
Joey, I felt something resembling pity. The man couldn't have formed
a sentence, let alone murdered two people with complex runes and
dumped their bodies in a Motel Sixth room.

I sighed. "We're no closer than when we started."

Matthew turned away from the clank and gestured for me to
move outside before discussing the case. We stopped at the bottom
of the stairs outside the station under the clear night sky, moonlight
piercing through the blackness with sharp little stabs.

"That can't be further from the truth," Matthew said as he turned
his gaze on me. Even though he was attempting to be casual, not a
thing in the world could dim the intensity of his gaze. "We know
that the bodies were staged, or at least dumped at the Motel
Sixth—not killed there. We know Joey and Lucas are unlikely to
have moved the bodies, but that they might resemble the man called
Charlie Bone." To himself, he muttered, "Need to get Donny with a
HoloHex artist."

"It's fine, Matthew. You don't have to cheer me up. I just wish I
could've been more assistance on the Residuals. If we don't find the
crime scene by tomorrow, I'll be no help whatsoever."

Matthew watched me with lidded eyes, his expression severe.
"They didn't recruit you solely for your Reserve skills. You're a damn
good investigator, Detective. Don't sell yourself short." He cleared
his throat, seemed to declare the pep talk portion of the evening over,
and continued. "If you're disappointed about The Hex Files, don't be.
So long as you offer your help on the case to the best of your abilities,
I owe them to you whether we close it or not. That's not on you, De-
Marco."

My anger flared. "This isn't about the files—this is about doing
the job I was hired to do."

"Danielle—"

"Detective DeMarco," I snapped. "Where to next?"

"Get some rest. I'll meet you at the station in the morning."

"Captain." I raised a hand in a 'stop' gesture. Matthew froze, standing as still as only vampires can. "Convenience. Proximity."

"What are you talking about?"

"What if that specific hotel room was used because it was close to the actual crime scene?" My head jerked upward to meet his gaze, which finally wasn't prying into my soul and was instead focused on the case. "What if the runes were used in one of the adjoining rooms, and then the bodies moved a short distance?"

Matthew looked conflicted. I could tell he didn't want to ask me to scour the rooms. It was the middle of the night, and he'd already torn me away from the grand opening of my pizzeria. Now he was stealing my sleep, too.

"Let's go back," I said. "It won't take long to pop into each of the rooms, but we will probably annoy a ton of guests."

"We can go in the morning," Matthew ventured weakly. "There are plenty of officers scouring every room and making certain there's nothing else relevant to the crime scene. The guests will have already been disrupted."

"Then let's disrupt them again, King. Tick, tock."

Chapter 7

The sun was rising as Matthew watched Dani let herself into the front door of the pizzeria. He imagined that one of her brothers had restored the wood from shards with the help of magic while Dani had been away. Considering the mood she was in, it was a wonder she didn't crack the panel in half all over again.

Even from across the street, Matthew's perceptive hearing picked up the angry click of the lock as she slipped it into place. Matthew still didn't move once she was safely inside. He stood, perfectly still, waiting until the light clicked on in the second-floor apartment above her shop.

He watched for another hour maybe—time felt elusive just before dawn, as if it was neither early in the morning nor late at night. He had nowhere to be at times like this, so he merely waited: thinking, processing, considering. It helped him to feel less alone.

When an acceptable hour rolled around, he headed to the station. Matthew was seated at his desk by five thirty waiting for the chief to arrive. Though Chief Newton's office was three floors up, Matthew picked up the unique sound of the chief's gait a few minutes later. With a heavy sigh, King stood. Newton would be bellowing for him in minutes, so he might as well get a head start. Better if Matthew beat him to the punch.

At the office, Matthew didn't bother to keep his intense speed under wraps. Whispered about, admired, hated—he was many things within the walls of this building, but the only one he cared about was being a damn good captain for the Homicide Unit.

"Kin—" the chief got out the first sounds before Matthew opened the door and stepped inside. The chief looked up, impressed. "Not bad, King."

"Sir," Matthew said. "Good morning."

"Doesn't feel like morning. Feels like the middle of the goddamn night. Didn't sleep a wink, not that you know anything about it." The orc looked up at Matthew. "What do you have for me?"

Matthew stared into the face of his superior. He had nothing but respect for his boss. After all, the two had many things in common. Both were the only one of their kind on the force, and both had shattered glass ceilings as they rose through the ranks. However, to call them *friendly* would be overly generous. The chief hadn't gotten to the big corner office by making buddies.

"Sir, we have—"

"You're stalling, King. Don't bullshit me."

Matthew blinked again—another imposed human trait that had become a natural habit. Mostly because Dani had told him it "freaking creeped her out" when he stared at her without blinking for long periods of time.

"We've got nothing, sir," Matthew said honestly. "We've got a dead mayor whose body was tossed out with a young Goblin Girl. No obvious reason the two are—or should be—connected."

The chief looked down his long, crooked nose at Matthew. "Sex?"

"Not that we can tell, sir," Matthew said blandly. "Though we can't rule out the possibility. They were dumped at the motel, not murdered there, and they were fully clothed. We'll get the reports back from Sienna soon enough that will confirm one way or another."

"The Goblin Girl—do we know anything about her?"

"I have officers running down leads, but you know the nature of the business." Matthew gave a disheartened shrug. "Mostly street girls looking for a way to get on their feet. Fake names, families who disowned them—it's not easy to chase down any meaningful identities among them."

"That's why I hired you, King, so you would do the hard work."

"I understand, chief."

Matthew took the note of disappointment to heart because at the bottom of it, the chief had a point. Though Matthew's status as captain had been earned and well deserved, not every chief would have trusted a vampire on the homicide team. After all, he was still a vampire, and his nature had a way of rearing its ugly head. Homicide often involved blood. Nothing more needed to be said.

"What else?" The orc turned back to some paperwork on his desk, mostly disinterested. "It's an election year, King. We've gotta work fast on this. It's a relief you don't need sleep. I hope you don't plan on taking a breath until this case has been wrapped."

"We have recruited Detective DeMarco to work as a special consultant on the case." Matthew ventured into the territory lightly. "I'd like to request that Felix grant her a temporary badge with all her credentials and access reinstated."

"Dani DeMarco agreed to come back?" The chief looked up briefly from his paperwork. When Matthew confirmed with a nod, he gave an amused smile. "The badge ain't happening."

"But sir—"

"I'll grant her a pass alright, but access to anything confidential outside of this case is denied. In the buildings, she'll need an escort. The pass is only for conducting business and assignments from you."

"Thank you, sir." Matthew withheld the smile. He'd discovered long ago that the chief always needed to have the final say on any idea that wasn't his. So Matthew made a habit of asking for more than he needed—such as the all-access badge—in order to get what he wanted, which was merely a pass.

"You're the babysitter. Shit hits the fan with DeMarco, and you're biting the official bullet, got it?" Newton reached into his desk and pulled out a cigar. He flicked on a lighter and started puffing away. "Can you handle it?"

The question was layered with meaning. It hadn't been a secret that Matthew and Dani had a history. A ripe, colorful history that had been both beautiful and terrible, light and dark, warm and cold. Ice cold.

"Yes, sir. I think she'll be imperative to the success of the case. She's already cleared the Residuals from the Motel Sixth, and it was Dani who determined the murders were merely staged in Room 309. We followed up on a few leads together, and she'll be returning to continue this morning. I'll have the full report on your desk by seven a.m."

The chief nodded. "Find the crime scene, King. And the connection. I've got reporters breathing down my neck, and if you can't wrap this up in a nice tidy bow, heads will roll. You know what happens if you cut a vampire's head off, don't you?"

"Noted, sir."

Matthew managed to swallow without his fangs descending, though he felt the pull of them as a natural reaction to the threat. He could only hope the chief didn't notice. The orc wouldn't take kindly to being hunted in his own office, even if Matthew didn't intend to act on his instincts.

Matthew turned instead, let himself out of the office, and reappeared downstairs seconds later. "Helena!" He yelled for his assistant in the front office. The poor, haggard old ogre responded with a squeak. "Yes, Captain King?"

"I'm going to give you my notes. Write them down, will you?" He stood, paced back and forth. "Has the new shipment of synthetics come in yet?"

Helena looked down at her notepad. "No, sir—the blood is scheduled to arrive this afternoon."

"Thank you. Now, I'll start at the beginning."

Chapter 8

I woke a few hours after I'd tumbled into bed to the sound of my door breaking in half.

Seconds later, my eyes flew open to find New York's most ineligible vampire standing over my bed, his fangs descended.

"What the hell, Matthew?" I scrambled from bed, but the sheets twisted over my legs and I ended up flopping halfway over the edge of the bed in a most ungraceful way. I overcompensated for my awkwardness by pulling my Stunner on him by the time my feet hit the ground. Thankfully, not all my training had been forgotten.

Matthew raised his hands slowly, a grim smile on his face. The fact that his fangs hadn't yet ascended only made his smile darker and more intense. "At least your reaction time hasn't suffered—much."

"What are you doing in my apartment?" Now that I was semi awake, I lapsed back to my detective days. My fingers rested steady on the gun, my eyes leveled on his, and I mostly pushed away the pull of attraction that seethed in my gut at the sight of him. "I don't recall you getting a warrant."

Matthew gave one of his rare laughs. Then he looked around, gestured for me to drop the gun, and sat on the edge of my bed. "Your security around here is abysmal."

"Um, yeah. The door is supposed to need a key..." I crossed my arms. "But wood is hardly a match for stone."

Matthew stiffened. Though accurate, he tended to not appreciate references to stone. It reminded both of us that he was both superhuman, and not quite human. It had always bothered Matthew to know his heart no longer beat. As if somehow that made him less than the rest of us.

"Sorry, Matthew, but come on—you can't put a fist through my door and think that's okay. What are you doing here, anyway?"

"Apologies, Detective." Matthew stood, his arms stiffly by his side as an air of professionalism returned. "I simply came to deliver this."

I glanced at the proffered temporary badge. "Special Consultant?"

He shrugged. "It was the best I could get. You want your detective title back? Talk to the chief."

"No, of course not." The sight of a badge without its familiar detective label on it stung, though I couldn't admit it aloud. I'd voluntarily stepped down from my job. "It's not an all access pass."

"We both knew that wasn't happening. Take what you can get."

"Excuse me?"

"Dani—you quit on the precinct. They didn't quit on you," he said. "You want full access, you want the detective title back, you know what you have to do."

"I don't, I can't—"

"It's not your fault." Matthew was at my side in a second, his dark eyes roving over my sleep-streaked face. "You couldn't have known. I hated him for other reasons, for personal reasons, but even I had no idea what that man was capable of."

"I should have known," I said fiercely. "There's no excuse."

"Love is blind," he said, and the word seemed to pain him. He gritted it between his retracting fangs as if every syllable tasted like sand. "That's why we don't take personal cases."

My hand shook, descended slowly, the Stunner dropping from my fingers onto the bed. I watched as Matthew turned on a heel and strode for the empty doorway.

"Matthew," I called after him as he stepped across the rubble. "Wait."

He hesitated, glanced down at the debris. "I'm sorry about the mess. When you didn't answer my knock, I feared..."

"Matthew," I repeated, my voice barely audible across the silent apartment. "He's not coming back."

He watched me, his eyes indiscernible as they processed. Without another word, he turned and stalked away, disappearing into the chill of morning.

I stood perfectly still for some time—not as still as Matthew, but as still as a living, breathing witch could be. Only when the downstairs front door shut and the sight of Matthew's long, loping stride disappeared down the dusty road, did I move.

I first cleaned up the door with a quick repairing spell, righting the wood properly in its frame. There was a bit of a lopsided tilt to it because of my frustration, but seeing as it closed and locked, I'd focus on the aesthetics later. Then, I faced my furniture.

"What's wrong with you guys, anyway?" I shouted toward an empty apartment. "I thought you were supposed to help me!"

When nobody responded, I walked toward the kitchen and flicked on the coffee pot. "I'm talking to you, Mrs. Coffee. And you—" I kicked the door of the fridge. "What are you good for, huh, Fred? And Carl—" I spiraled over to the sofa and gave it a nudge with my foot. "I thought you were supposed to be my friends!"

I felt rightfully crazy for a full minute when none of my furniture or appliances responded. I even preheated my oven, Owen, to five hundred degrees to get him all hot and bothered before I got a response from any of them.

"You didn't let us get to bed until this morning!" whined Mrs. Coffee. "We were exhausted!"

"Your skinny ass fell asleep on me," Carl, my couch, said with acidity. "I was sleeping here peacefully when you flopped down at an ungodly hour this morning. You know I get crabby if my REM cycles are interrupted."

"You're a freaking couch," I said, sitting on Carl with a huff just for revenge. "We had an intruder in the apartment, and none of you even blinked an eye."

"I might have," chimed in Fred, my fridge, "but you open and close me so damn much I have to conserve every bit of energy I have. And anyway, Matthew isn't an intruder."

"He broke down the door!" I gestured to the splinters of wood in the gaping hole of a doorway. "Anyone who doesn't have a key, you may consider an intruder."

"Oh, darling..." Marla, my coat rack, purred in her luxurious, French-tipped voice, "Matthew is certainly not an intruder. I think I speak for the rest of the inanimates when I say we've seen *very* intimate details of the captain."

Carl grunted from beneath my folded legs. "Don't remind me."

"Oh, shut up. Shut up." I waved my hands at the mess of furniture that had come to life after a spell gone horribly wrong years ago—and wished for the millionth time that it was a reversible one. Unfortunately, I'd never figured out exactly how to reverse it, and therefore, I was left with a lusty coatrack, a bitter fridge that cursed like a sailor, and the laziest couch known to humanity. "I told you not to repeat any of that."

"I don't need to repeat it," Carl quipped. "The horrors I've seen between the two of you—right here on top of me—let's just say I can't wash my eyes of them."

I leapt off Carl and gave his cushions a violent plump before I stomped to the kitchen and threw open Fred's door. "What do you have?"

"Same damn things you had last night," he said. "It's like you think things will magically appear every time you open me. Spoiler alert: I'm not magic."

"The hell you aren't," I said. "You think normal refrigerators give their owners this much sass? You're *welcome* for not throwing you out on the front stoop."

Fred remained silent as I grabbed the cream cheese from the door and slammed him shut. I threw two pieces of bread in the toaster and pressed Tammy's buttons with a flinch.

She jerked to life, perky as ever. "Morning! Morning, Detective! How are you today?"

"Can't you just toast the bread?" I asked with a sigh. When she glowed red with frustration, I decided I'd better be nice to the only appliance who seemed to like me—and who had the capacity to burn my apartment down. "Good morning, Tammy," I said reluctantly. "How are you today?"

"Great! Great!" she said, a small, almost dreamy face appearing on the side nearest me. "It was wonderful to see Matthew again. Will the two of you be getting back together?"

"Nope."

"Aw, but it's true love! I'm part psychic, did you know that? And I see the two of you together."

"Part toaster, part psychic?" I murmured, heavy on the skepticism. "Why do I find that to be a stretch of the imagination?"

"Your *toaster* talks," Carl said from across the room, "and you think the weird part is she used to be a psychic?"

"Shut up before I donate you to a pillow fight!"

"Put me out of my misery," Carl said. "It's not like there's any rest for the wicked around here. You use me like I'm going out of style."

"Matthew still loves you, you know," chirped Tammy. "I can tell. The way he stormed in here all upset this morning..." She heaved a huge sigh, which was echoed with a dreamy one from Marla across the room. "It was magical."

"What are you talking about?"

"Oh, he is so handsome," Marla said in that velvet voice of hers. "When you didn't answer after the first few knocks this morning, he just blew through those doors like they were nothing. A knight in shining armor coming to save his queen." She said the last part with a hint of bitterness to her voice, as if she'd give anything to be in my place. "If only I could turn human. I'd love that man right."

"You don't understand," I muttered. "It's not that simple."

"You're right. I don't understand," Marla said. "He's the most gorgeous male specimen to walk this earth. Deadly, too—he's got that dangerous thing when his fangs come down, and *whoooo*-mama. He obviously cares about you—fiercely."

"She's right," Tammy agreed. "He was ready to murder someone this morning when he thought you were in danger. Poor Doorknob—rest in peace."

I glanced toward the door, once again finding it curious at the way the other appliances seemed to have a special fondness for the silent knob now resting on the floor. Apparently, Doorknob had inherited a voice like the rest of the objects in my apartment, but I'd never heard him speak before. The others simply referred to him as Doorknob. I often wondered if the appliances were just playing a joke on me and the handle wasn't enchanted at all. One could never tell...

"Here you go! Here you go!" Tammy dinged, positively shivered with excitement, and shot two pieces of toast toward the heavens. "Perfectly golden with a hint of burn, just the way you like them."

"Thanks, Tammy." I grudgingly moved through my apartment in relative silence as I nibbled at the toast, dressed for the day, and listened to the inane chatter of my furniture.

They're pretty good about keeping quiet when I have guests, but the second I am alone in my apartment, they start up. It's like having a permanent radio turned on at a low volume all the time. On a more depressing note, I'm rarely lonely.

Maybe someday, I'll find the counter curse to shut them up for good. In the meantime, I'd grown used to them and, some might say, almost fond of them.

"I'm going to send Jack up to straighten out my door. While I'm out, can you guys please keep an eye on this place?"

"If Jack's around," Marla drawled. "My eyes will be focused on something else."

I ignored the coat rack and left the apartment with one last glare before taking the stairs down at the end of the hall.

My living quarters take up the entire second floor above the pizzeria. It has two bedrooms, though one is miserably unfurnished, along with an open kitchen, a living room, and a tiny Juliet balcony off the master. One and a half baths round the space out into a cozy home. A fire escape perches outside of the living room window, though it's hardly necessary at only two floors up, and I am fairly certain the window to it is stuck shut.

The door to my apartment leads into a narrow hallway, the wooden floorboards old and creaking—normally loud enough to alert me to the sound of visitors, except for Matthew. The man moved with no more footprint in the world than a light breeze.

At the end of the hallway is a skinny spiral staircase that rounds down to the back of the pizzeria's kitchen. I often keep it locked during business hours to prevent random guests from traveling upstairs in search of the restroom.

I let myself into a small room meant for employees to lock up their possessions, then pushed through the swinging door to the kitchen. At this hour, all surfaces, pots, and pans gleamed spotless and quiet. I mentally thanked my brother for seeing the party through and leaving this place looking flawless. The party seemed to have been a complete success.

I eased out of the kitchen and made my way into the dining area, finding my youngest brother, my all-important Director of Operations, snoozing head down in a booth by the window. I moved closer to him, noting his nose had faceplanted just inches from a half-eaten pie. I was magnificently unsurprised.

What did surprise me was the beauty of the parlor at sunrise. Matthew had barely waited until normal witching hours to wake me—an hour I hadn't seen since I stepped down from the precinct—and the stunning stillness of the world rendered me silent.

Light filtered in, washing the room in a vibrant array of pinks and oranges and yellows. The sparkling tables and stools stood empty, a sight that wouldn't last when the pizzeria clicked into high gear for the lunch hour. Just last night, this place had been filled to the brim with all varieties of species, all flavors of pizza, all different beats and hums of Jack's eclectic soundtrack. This morning, the silence was golden.

Until Jack gave a snore I'd have suspected from a troll. I nudged him with a light tap to the back of the head. He hardly reacted, merely shifting his head deeper into his arms and lapsing back to sleep.

"Jack, what happened?" I pinched the skin just above his elbow. I'd try to be nicer, but nothing short of a trumpet to the ear could wake my brothers. "Why didn't you go home? Did you get evicted again?"

Jack shook himself from his haze, peering through one bleary eye at me. "No, I paid my rent."

"Then what are you doing sleeping in my booth?"

"Dougie dared me to eat a full pizza."

The mention of my twin brother had me rolling my eyes. Where Jack was 'pretty and dumb' of his own admission, my twin was 'nerdy and brilliant' by all accounts. Whether out of jealousy or boredom, Doug never seemed to leave Jack alone. I ran interference when I could, but sometimes...watching over Jack felt like a full-time job.

"I couldn't quit," Jack expanded, a look of reproach in his eye. "A DeMarco never backs down from a dare."

"Yeah, but this is just stupid. Why couldn't you take the pizza home and finish it there?" I gestured my hand to show the empty room. "Nobody else felt the need to stay and watch over you."

Jack watched me blankly for a second. "Didn't think of that."

"Right."

"I could have done it too, you know," Jack argued. "If I hadn't eaten seven pieces during the course of the evening."

"Something to be proud of." I clapped him on the back. "Say—I know you're scheduled for the afternoon off, but is there any chance you could stay?"

Jack surveyed me. "Will I get paid?"

"Uh, yeah. Of course."

"Then yeah, I can stay all day," he said happily. "I told you a half-truth right there about rent—I only paid half of it. So, I could use the extra hours."

"Tell you what," I said. "I'll give you enough for the next two months of rent *now* if you help full time at the pizzeria for the next two weeks."

"What's the catch?"

Sometimes Jack wasn't as dumb as he claimed to be. I hated those moments. "Something's come up, and—"

"Something? Or some*one*?" He gave me a look that said this was one of his more perceptive moments. "I saw Matthew and Nash last night at the door. What's going on?"

"There's this case that's come up, and they need my help."

"What about the new chick? The hot one you trained."

I smacked my brother's head again. "Lucia is a very intelligent, capable woman."

"Yeah, and she's smoking hot. What happened to her?"

"She's..." I exhaled, unsure how much was public knowledge. "She's unable to help on the case, and they need my expertise."

"I dunno, Dani—I don't like the sound of this." For all of Jack's flaws, he had the most gigantic heart out of any of the DeMarcos. Loyal to a fault, he was a teddy bear that we all tried to protect—even though he often ended up watching over the rest of us. "You quit for a reason—a very good reason."

"I didn't quit, I retired."

"Sure, whatever," he said. "You stepped away because you couldn't handle it anymore."

"Jack—"

"Look, Dani, it's not a weakness." Jack pushed aside the pizza and rose to his full height. He was two years younger than me and six inches taller. Due to his massive caloric consumption, he had more muscle than a grizzly bear. "You have seen some weird shit, and none of us blame you for taking a step back. It's not going to help if you run right back into the precinct at full force."

"The borough needs this case solved, and—"

"Would you have done it if anyone besides Matthew asked you to come back?"

His eyes leveled on me, and I hated that they cut through my flimsy excuses. He could see that my feelings for Matthew hadn't gone away. I didn't have to *like* Matthew to still be in love with him in a peculiar sort of way. There was a connection between us that ran deeper than attraction, deeper, maybe, than love. We had counted on each other, pulled one another out of dark times, and that bond had yet to be severed despite the distance we'd put between us.

Jack shook his head in dismay. "The vamp's using you."

"Captain King asked out of respect—Nash was there too. It's not just *the vampire*. I'm damn good at my job, Jack. How quickly you forget."

"I've never doubted that, *Detective*," he said, leaning on the last word. "But more than an officer, you're my sister—and I don't like seeing you hurt. That's the only way this is going to end, Dani. Nash didn't see you when you were at your worst—he was too busy dealing with his own problems. I was there for you."

"No, it's different this time around. It's just one case."

"You'll end up hurt—if not physically, then heartbroken." Jack averted his eyes, looking almost ashamed. "I'm not watching you go through that again. I love you, Dani, but you're picking up the pieces this time. I can't do it again. Consider this your warning."

"Fine," I snapped. "I've been warned. Thanks for your consideration."

I reached into the travel belt I always carried when on duty, not having realized how natural it had been for me to slip back into my role as detective. I had on dark leather pants and a black tank top, my belt along with a Stunner, potions and antidotes strapped to it, and my badge. It stalled me for a moment, and I wondered if Jack was right. Was this such a horrible idea?

Yes, I decided—it was a bad idea to return to the precinct. But there was nothing I could do about it, either. Lucia was missing, and Wicked needed me. Once a public servant, always one. If Captain King needed my help, I'd be there to serve.

The Hex Files were just a bonus, I told myself, though the little voice in my head wasn't entirely convinced. I felt particularly snarly at the thought as I pulled a drawstring pouch from my belt and threw some money toward Jack.

"Rent," I grunted. "Have the shop open by eleven to be ready for the early lunch crowd. Make sure you get rid of the pepperoni stuck to your cheek before it opens."

"Dani, wait—"

I spun around, watching as Jack stared forlornly at the coins on the table. It was more than he'd need to cover rent for the next six months. I could tell his fingers itched to reach for it, but something held him back.

"I know why I'm doing this," I said quietly. "I don't like the situation any more than you do, but I need to do it. Trust me."

Jack watched my face for any sign of a lie, any sign of weakness. He studied me in the honest way that nobody else in the world could, and eventually, he must have approved of what he saw. Snatching up the coins, he nodded at me.

"Don't worry about the pizzeria," he said. "I don't have anywhere I need to be, and I'm happy to help."

"Thank you, Jack," I said. "For everything."

Jack watched as I left, his eyes on my back even after I locked the door and headed down the street to find Matthew. His eyes followed me through the window, but I didn't look back to meet his gaze. If I had, I might have turned around. I might have thrown out this case and refused to help, but I was too weak to do that.

Whether it was the pull of the case, the need for order in the borough, or the effect Matthew King had on me, I couldn't say no. The desire for justice ran deep through DeMarco veins.

If I repeated it over and over again, I could just about convince myself.

But even I knew better.

The Hex Files were not just a bonus.

They were the only hope for me to heal.

Chapter 9

As Matthew had promised, my badge wasn't all-access. It wasn't even half-access, if I were to be honest. I showed up at the precinct flashing the special consultant photo at the front desk, and all it got me was a stupid Comm up to Matthew's office.

The goblin receptionist told me to 'have a seat, the captain will be right with you', but I remained standing. It never took Matthew long to arrive.

Right on time, he appeared a few seconds later dressed in his Monday best. He must have gone home and changed after he'd scared the sheets off me this morning. He'd traded the black jeans for more official looking attire.

He wore a severe, exquisite suit. It enhanced his already powerful aura and brought out the depths of his eyes and the pale tint to his skin. His hair looked different, as if he'd showered and run his fingers through the dark strands before they'd dried. To polish the look, he'd planted a fresh smirk on his face that said I didn't look nearly as put together as I'd hoped.

He studied me for a long moment, and while he did, the lobby fell intensely still. Not a soul breathed. The receptionist didn't shuffle a paper, the Goblin Girl who'd been sobbing in handcuffs froze, and the set of overweight spellslingers bumbling through the front door stopped in their tracks.

My skin burned as Matthew's eyes raked over me, taking in my significantly more informal uniform. My relaxed attire had been the butt of many jokes between Matthew and me before, but it was easier to laugh about our choice in clothing when we'd been in the middle of taking them off.

As his eyes settled on my face, his lips quirked into a remembrance of his older smile—the one that glowed only in private when the two of us were alone—when we'd been wrapped around one another, the secrets between us bound by our embrace.

"The badge looks good on you."

"How's Joey?" I asked as Matthew gestured for me to join him on a walk. My brother's earlier comments returned in full force, reminding me of the dangers, not only of the physical nature, involved with the case. There were also the complications of the mind to consider, and now I wondered if there could be complications of the heart, as well. Because of this, I stuck closely to a professional script. "Did he come out of the daze?"

"Yes, he's in an interview room. Not feeling well, I'm afraid, but that's to be expected." Matthew's brow furrowed. "He doesn't seem to remember much."

"You questioned him without me?"

This time when Matthew's eyes flicked to me, they belonged to that of a captain, not a friend. "Though it's none of your business, no—we didn't. He was mumbling and entirely confused when we took him out of holding, however."

I nodded. "You think he could've accidentally gotten dosed?"

"There's always a chance. Tricky to say—it's been used as a defense so often with druggies it's impossible to know who's lying to get out of charges and who's telling the truth."

"Jones doesn't have the characteristics of a recreational drug user," I said with a frown. "When I checked his Residuals yesterday, there were none of the usual signs: Scent Sweepers, Drug Deducers, Sanity Boosters—nothing that the usual suspects use to cover up their tracks."

"He was picked up once for illegal purchase of a Goblin Girl," Matthew said. "Often, the crimes one is picked up for is tenfold less than what they've actually committed."

"Illegal purchase of a Goblin Girl?" I raised an eyebrow at him. "Do you think it could be related to the body we found in 309?"

Matthew shook his head. "It was an underage soliciting attempt. He was seventeen, and the legal age to engage with a Goblin Girl is twenty-one. The files are technically sealed on Joey, but..."

I understood what wasn't said. Matthew had power, status, and the skills to unlock things meant to stay hidden. I dared not press him further since the topic was too close to my heart. After all, The Hex Files wouldn't unlock themselves.

"Here we are." Matthew stopped in front of a two-way mirror. "He hasn't moved for an hour."

Behind the glass sat Joey Jones with his head in his hands, looking as if he had the mother of all hangovers. He barely looked alive, save for the uneven breaths he inhaled every few seconds.

"Let's go," I said. "Keep this brief—I don't think he's our guy, and we can't waste time on drug charges when we've got a double homicide waiting for us."

Matthew nodded to the witch who sat in the surveillance room. She pressed a few buttons, muttered an incantation, and the door opened with a hiss. Matthew and I had barely stepped foot into the room before it clanked shut behind us.

"Hi, Joey," I said. "I'm Detective DeMarco, and this is—"

"The vampire," he groaned. "I know."

"Captain King," I corrected. "We're here to ask you a few questions."

I knew it bothered Matthew to no end that no matter how proficient he might be at his job, or how much he'd given up to defend the city, he would always be known as *the vamp*.

"Can I get some water?" Joey croaked. "I'm dying here."

"You'll be dying more if you don't give us information," I said, but I gestured for the witch behind the mirror to pass a glass of water through the door. Once I'd handed it to Joey, I sat down, folded my hands in front of me, and resumed. "What happened to you last night?"

"I don't know, man." Joey stopped to suck down the glass of water in a noisy gulp. "I don't know *what* that stuff was, but it knocked me on my ass—I can tell you that."

"Yeah, I know—we saw. Carried you here myself, actually," I said. "Start from the beginning. Talk fast and don't lie, and we'll see what we can do about the drug charges. One wrong step, and you'll be behind bars faster than you can say Hash."

"It wasn't SpellHash," he said, immediately defensive. "I mean, I'm not saying I know what Hash is like..." His eyes shifted between us, saw stone in our gazes, and then broke. "Fine. I'm a recreational Hash user—but I never overdose, and I'm always at home. No way I'm wandering around the borough on Hash—I'd get caught in a heartbeat, and I can't go to prison. I'm too pretty for prison."

I tried not to flinch as he said it, but I couldn't help it. Joey had a certain appeal to him, I supposed, for the right sort of girl—like the elf from the casino who'd drooled over him. To me, he looked like a slicked back broom salesman with a little more polish than a thug. Sitting across from Matthew, he couldn't even be called handsome.

"Fine, I'm not a looker like the vamp, but how can I compare to a true supernatural?" Joey shrugged. "My dad's a shifter with the pack. I'm a peripheral member, but nothing important. I'm not bound by blood, none of that crap. I make my money at the casino, and I spend most of my nights alone."

"When's the last time you sought the company of a Goblin Girl?" *Alone my ass,* I thought. The man had spent at least a night with the elf. "Before you answer, let me remind you what I said about lying."

Joey sighed and put his head flat on the table. I rested my fingers there for a moment, felt the coolness of the marble, and realized it was the equivalent of a wet washcloth for him. If magic weren't blanketed in interview rooms, I would've refilled his water glass, but at the moment, my patience was lacking.

"We've got Hangover Helper waiting for you if you get talking," I said. "It'll help the headache and aches and pains. No truth, no hex."

"Last Goblin Girl I saw was probably six weeks ago. She was middle-aged," Joey confessed, "and all I could afford at the time."

I nodded. "How often do you normally see them?"

Joey shrugged. "I stopped seeing them just over a month ago. Before that, I'd find one whenever I had a good night at the casino. Usually once a week."

"Why'd you stop?"

"I met this elf," he said, looking a little sheepish. "She was a fun time. I figured, why pay for the green girls if I got myself a real elf?"

"Lovely," I said under my breath. It wasn't loud enough for Joey to hear, but it drew a wry smile from Matthew. Louder, and feeling sorry for the elf, I continued. "So, you met the elf at the casino. Anything special about her?"

Joey gave a cheesy sort of grin and looked straight to Matthew. "Sure, but nothing I'd want to say in front of a lady."

"Anything that doesn't involve the bedroom?" I clarified. "We know you enjoy your evenings with her."

"Oh, not only evenings, Detective," he said with a leer toward me. "Those elves are insatiable, I'm telling you—"

"Joey—" I snapped. Matthew coughed, which I suspected was to cover up a laugh. I ignored him and continued. "I'm talking about the Hash—did she use or sell? Is she the one who got you into this mess?"

"No way, she's a good girl. Innocent, really. She's just a casino groupie. She's clean. I swear the elf isn't involved in this at all."

"If I didn't know any better," I said smoothly, "I'd say you're developing feelings for her."

"Not a chance," Joey said, though his eyes didn't follow through. "She's...whatever. Leave her out of it."

I nodded, letting the win sink in for a moment while Joey fumed at his transparency. When he was thoroughly steamed, I changed tactics. "Do you sell?"

"Me? No. I'm not smart enough to sell much of anything."

At least he wasn't lying so far, I thought, glancing at Matthew to see if he agreed. He gave a nearly unnoticeable nod—the signal to continue.

"What did you take last night, Joey?" I leaned forward, begging him to know the answer. "What was in your system?"

The deeper we got into the questioning, the more I wondered if Joey hadn't been mere collateral damage. As much as it pained me to be no further in the investigation, I just couldn't see Joey Jones as the mastermind behind a high-profile double homicide.

"I don't know," he said. "I went to the Howler like I usually do to pregame for Saturday night at the casino. I must've gotten there at three in the afternoon."

"You like to start early," I said wryly. "What happened then?"

"I ordered my usual—Wolfram Whiskey on the rocks—and then sat down in my normal booth."

"Where's your normal booth?"

"The one in the corner, last row—straight line of sight to the bar. Lorraine's got a great rack. I like an unobstructed view."

"Your girlfriend is so fortunate to have you," I snapped. Then took a deep breath and focused back on the case. "Was that the same booth where we found you?"

Joey stared straight at me. "Lady, I don't remember ever seeing you before. No offense—I mean, I'm sure I would have remembered if I had seen you..." His gaze traveled suggestively downward until Matthew cleared his throat. Joey's head whipped up so quickly I wondered if he'd feel it the next day. "I just mean—I don't remember a thing after I took a sip of that drink."

"Who served you the drink?"

"Lorraine."

"Did you talk to anyone else?" I pressed, tapping my fingers against the table. "Did anyone besides Lorraine touch your drink?"

He shook his head. "Obviously, she's my favorite bartender since the rest are dudes. I tip her well, so she always jumps to help me. She poured the drink, and I watched her make it. You know, she shakes the ice and the whiskey, and everything's all bouncy and..." He abruptly stopped. "The answer to your question is no."

"Are you sure?"

"I swear on my life. She handed me the drink, which she poured straight from the bottle, and then I took it over to my booth. Nobody came over to talk to me. I saw people I recognized, but I didn't talk to any of them. I had a few sips and *whoosh*." He signaled over his head. "Next thing I knew I woke up behind bars. You have to understand, Detective—I'm not one of the pack. Nobody particularly likes me in that bar; they just accept me because it's against pack law to kill the descendants of a blooded wolf."

I nodded, well aware. And unsurprised that Joey wasn't a popular figure there. "But that would mean your drink was poisoned—or something."

"He couldn't have been cursed?" Matthew murmured it as a question, but it was more of a statement. "It's possible to curse without touching the targeted individual."

"Not a hint of any magic in any of his Residuals. He was almost entirely clean."

I preferred to keep my peculiar talents under wraps whenever possible, since I never quite knew how someone would react. I kept my voice low enough so that Joey couldn't hear, which was one of the benefits of working with a vampire—and also the downfall. There was no such thing as a whispered secret around the captain.

Matthew nodded to show he understood. Then he asked his first question to Joey of the morning. "Did you give Lorraine any reason to doctor your drink?"

"No. Of course not."

"So, you didn't perhaps *stare* at her body day in and day out?" I asked, glancing skeptically at Matthew and tried to shut my mouth. It didn't work. "I'm just saying, I might've cursed him too."

Joey narrowed his eyes at me. "That's not very professional, Detective."

"Neither is you speaking to my bra," I said. "Do you think Lorraine poisoned you somehow?"

"No. I mean, I know I can get carried away, but I swear—I didn't ever pressure Lorraine into anything. We had a good banter, and I always tipped well. I knew that messing with Lorraine would get me kicked out of that bar faster than a wolf howls at the moon."

"He does have a point," I admitted, to both myself and Matthew. "If Lorraine had an issue with him, she would have told us. Or, more likely, she would've had the wolves ban him long ago."

"If Lorraine didn't poison you," Matthew said, speaking with the distinct, old-English form of enunciation that arrived when he was too distracted to change his speech patterns to more modern ones, "then someone might have poisoned the bottle."

"Yeah, right," Joey said. "You said you found me zonked? Well, the Howler goes through a bottle of Wolfram Whiskey in an hour—it's the signature drink there. You would've found a bar full of zombies if the bottle was poisoned. I'm telling you, I couldn't move a muscle."

"I know," I said dryly. "You weren't much help walking back to the station. Listen, Joey—I'm going to go out on a limb here and say that I believe you. Everything you've told me adds up, and frankly, you said it yourself—you're not sly enough to deal."

"Agreed." Joey sounded too proud of that fact, but in this case, it worked in his favor. "Someone had it in for me, but I don't know who. I swear I haven't pissed off anyone in the last few weeks."

"What a gentleman." I moved along too fast for him to respond, though the sarcasm amused Matthew again. "So, what do *you* think happened?"

Matthew appeared surprised by my change in tactic, as did Joey. The latter sat back and bit his lip in concentration. "That's a good question, Detective."

"She's good at her job," Matthew said. Though he didn't look at me, his words were weighted, as if there was additional meaning behind them.

I ignored him. "Speculate, Joey. Think outside of the box."

He took his time thinking, his eyebrows knitted together. Under the slick exterior, I could see a hint of what the elf had found in him. A youthfulness, a sense of innocence covered by a well-worn cape of bravado and charisma, and the genuine way he seemed to want to help.

He blew out a huge sigh and turned to face me. "I am sorry, Detective, Captain. I really wish I knew. All I can say for certain is that whatever knocked me out—I've never seen it before. Never heard its name whispered on the streets. And, I have to say, I never want to see it again."

Chapter 10

"What'd you make of him?" Matthew asked as he left the building with Dani close behind. "Do you believe him?"

Dani was too lost in thought to respond. After a few paces in silence, she gave a distracted shake of her head. "I don't know," she murmured. "My gut feeling says he's telling the truth. I'll know better after we talk to Lorraine."

Matthew gave a firm nod of agreement, pleased with the ease at which the two still communicated on the job. If only their personal lives could have gone so smoothly, he thought, as their feet pounded in sync down the road. Neither spoke, yet they both knew they were headed back to the Howler.

In daylight, Wicked was a beautiful place—save for the certain areas that mothers warned their children to avoid when they first learned to walk. Certain land: the casino area, Goblin Grid, and of course the necromancy regions—along with the Otherlands, were often avoided at all costs.

Today, however, the darkness had pervaded the borough. Matthew and Dani walked south of the market, past the hustling and bustling portion of the borough that drew tourists from around the globe to its quirky, cobblestone strewn streets and unique magical culture. Wicked Way remained one of the most densely populated magical streets in the world and had been since the Salem witch trials caused people to flee toward the hidden borough for safety.

With stores piled over three hundred stories high and proper shopping only accomplished on a broomstick, every vendor in Wicked flocked to peddle their wares. Both Matthew and Dani avoided the market as much as possible. Between the two of them, they'd arrested too many people. There was no way they could make it through the markets without running into someone they'd locked up who still had a chip on their shoulder.

They veered down a dirt road winding just north of DeMarco's Pizza. Dani seemed lost in thought, but Matthew was reluctant to let precious time alone slip through his fingers.

"How's retired life treating you?" he asked as they rounded the pizzeria. They watched through the windows as Jack grinned brightly at a customer and slung her a slice of fresh pizza.

She frowned. "The idiot is flirting with her. Twenty bucks Jack doesn't charge her for the slice."

"I know your brother too well to take you up on that bet." Matthew smiled delicately. "I see a different set of issues comes with owning a business than it does with the detective life?"

"You could say that." Dani pulled her gaze from the window, glanced at the dust swirling around their shoes as they continued down the street. "It's quieter, but it's good. The only destruction I have to worry about is the occasional customer having too much vino or Jack burning the crust."

"The quiet doesn't always help," he said knowingly. "They catch up to you, you know."

"What does?"

Matthew glanced at her, averted his eyes. "The demons. The memories, the screams, the smells of dead bodies. It's normal if you're struggling with any of that, Danielle."

"Well, I'm not."

"You have to let the past go."

"I have, Matthew. It's my business what I do with my own past, so stay out of it." Dani picked up the pace as the Howler came into view. "I'm fine."

Matthew stopped in the middle of the road, adjusted the tie he wore with his suit. It had cost him more than most people made in a year, but then again, Matthew had more money than he could ever use. He didn't need much: he didn't eat, didn't sleep, didn't have many vices—besides Dani.

His money had to go somewhere, and he enjoyed the feel of the exquisite fabrics against his skin. His senses were so hyper aware that anything less than the best felt itchy and constricting. Dressing well was one of his only luxuries.

"If you were fine, The Hex Files wouldn't matter."

"That's different," she said. "You know that has nothing to do with everything you just said."

"The past is—"

"The past is the past," Dani interrupted, her eyes darkening to a murky shade of violet. "For me, The Hex Files are not yet in the past."

Matthew had never figured out how or why, but when she was angered or drunk with desire or scanning Residuals, the detective's eyes turned a shade of purple he'd never seen in anyone. Maybe it was something to do with her talents, the fact that she was a Reserve, or maybe it was just her. Either way, Matthew lived to see the violet.

He swept to her, closing the distance between them, his hand landing on her cheek as he took in her irresistible scent. Throwing professionalism out the window, he planted his mouth on hers, and he took. He stole from her a kiss that burned the very stone of his skin, the blood in her veins, the current between them.

Dani's eyes lit from murky purple to an electric violet. Her body reacted, and she leaned into him, her eyes closing as she began to take in return. Matthew broke the spell first. He stepped backward, both of them breathing heavily. He could feel the blood pounding through her veins, the increase in her body temperature, the skittish way her heart raced.

"What was that?" Dani snapped. She turned, shielded her face, and launched into a march toward the Howler. "Professionalism my ass!"

"You wanted it as much as I did. I felt it. I could hear it, see it, smell it." Matthew said, catching up to her. "I'm sorry. I just—I can't resist you."

"We are not together any longer. I'm not—I don't date, and I'm certainly not dating *you*." Dani sounded surprised at her own declaration. "I'm meant to be alone."

"That's not true."

"It is. After *him*..." She trailed off, shuddered. "Never again, Matthew. Swear you won't kiss me again."

"I can't make that promise." He spoke in that soft, satin tone that calmed her, another skill vampires had at their disposal. Along with persuasiveness, Matthew could influence moods, often in a calming sort of way. Historically, these traits had been used to lure humans into a sense of trust. Matthew had found the same tactic worked to bring Dani down from a cliff, from a rage that would otherwise consume her alive. "I'm sorry—I wish I could, but around you, I don't have control."

"You know this will never work."

"If you don't let The Hex Files go, they will be the death of you." Matthew spoke with a certainty that sent a tremble across Dani's skin. "I'll try my best to protect you, but—"

"I don't need protection."

"Exactly." He gave a nod that indicated a point to Dani. "You don't want my protection. You'll go it alone, and even if you did let me in, I'm not sure I could protect you from all you'll find."

"Do you know what's in them?"

"I know enough to warn you away." Matthew's eyes were inky black, deeper than the depths of the ocean, darker than the blackest night. "To hear you talk..."

Dani's hard exterior softened just the slightest amount. For the one made of stone, Matthew often found it harder to crack Dani than she did him. She must have sensed a change in him because she met his eyes, pursed her lips in thought.

"What is it?" she murmured.

"That was the last one—the last kiss," he said. "I swear I will leave you be... until you ask me to kiss you again."

"Until I ask you." Her eyes shifted, still a hue of brilliant violet. She laughed. "Sure."

"It's not funny," Matthew said. "If you do not let The Hex Files go, that *will* be the last kiss we ever share."

"Matthew—"

"I swear I'll not say another word after this, but I owe you a warning. Please, Danielle, reconsider."

"I've had over eight months to consider." Dani's mouth fell into a straight, narrowed line. "I am done considering. This isn't your problem, Matthew, it's mine. Are we going to talk to Lorraine, or not?"

While they'd been speaking, they'd been moving, and had swiftly reached the Howler.

Matthew could only bow his head and hope the locked files wouldn't be the death of her. "After you."

MATTHEW COULD FEEL Dani's emotions festering just under the surface. He'd promised to let her take the lead as much as possible. However, he wouldn't let her do it when she wasn't thinking straight. Doing so could risk everything.

"Lorraine," Matthew said, effusing the silk into his voice—whether for the bartender's sake or Dani's, he couldn't quite say. "May we have a word for a moment?"

Lorraine wore her usual uniform: tight dark jeans and a low-cut tank top. She dressed for tips more than comfort, he suspected, though the style fit her personality well. Her auburn red hair rolled in bouncy tight circles around her head, and with the addition of heavy makeup, she looked almost like a caricature.

"What about?" Lorraine's eyes seemed trusting of Matthew. Ironically, it was Dani she glanced at with concern.

Matthew reached for Dani's shoulder and rested a hand there. "This is Detective DeMarco, and I'm Captain King—we were in here yesterday and spoke briefly to you," Matthew said easily, lightly, his voice lilting with an ancient accent. The language of seduction. "We need just a moment of your time."

"What's her problem?" Lorraine wasn't so affected by Matthew's persuasiveness that she didn't notice the clenching of Dani's fists or the eerie violet that lingered in her eyes. "The detective looks like she wants to bite my head off."

"It's a difficult case," Matthew said, so far relieved the media hadn't caught wind of it. "And upsetting. If we could have your help, it'd be greatly appreciated."

Just after he'd arrived at the crime scene and seen the mayor's body, Matthew had requested and received approval for a magical ban of silence over the case that would last until noon. After that, the feeding frenzy would begin, and everyone would go wild. Tip lines would be flooded with losers and hopefuls, paranoids and well-intentioned. They'd have to run down all the leads no matter how far-fetched. It was always a race against time to see how fast the officers could work through a case before the media ban broke. The hours were ticking down.

"I don't have anything to tell you." Lorraine put a hand on her hip. "I swear. What do you need an alibi for? Or when?"

"We don't need an alibi," Matthew said, though Dani started to argue. He raised a hand to stop her. "You're not a suspect, though it is a murder case. We think you might have information that could lead us to the murderer. We believe he might have even been here."

"It's okay, sweetheart." The voice was familiar. It came from behind Matthew and Dani. "I had the pleasure of meeting these two yesterday," Grey smiled as Matthew and Dani whirled around. The werewolf moved his hulking form with a silence and grace that came solely with supernatural skills. "You can talk to them, Lorraine. In fact, I encourage it."

Lorraine looked to Grey as if his word was law. Eventually, she shrugged under his gaze. "Don't know what I can do to help. I don't have anything to hide, nor do I have any information to offer."

Grey loped around behind the bar. His shoulders were wide and broad, and his height matched that of Matthew's plus some. Matthew stood stiffly, annoyed he hadn't heard the approach of the werewolf. For one of the first times in his life, Matthew discovered he may have found a worthy opponent; in a physical battle, it would be hard to predict who might win—the *vamp* or the *wolf*.

The bars tattooed on Grey-no-last-name's arms moved as the muscles flexed underneath, and even Matthew couldn't deny the raw appeal of the man before him. He recognized one of his own—a loner, an alpha of sorts, one who enjoyed being in control.

Matthew's fangs started to descend in reaction to the dog. He caught a whiff of power, of the nonchalance that came from Grey's comfort in his own skin—from a sheer, dumb confidence bordering on invincibility. Grey might not be handsome in the traditional sense, but he turned the head of every woman in the bar from sheer presence alone.

Matthew sensed the subtle pulls toward Grey. Even Dani was affected, though she might not realize it or understand it, and Matthew knew why. Like most women, Dani was drawn to the dark of power, to the mystery behind Grey, to the magnetic draw of his gaze as it fell on hers.

"What are you doing here?" Matthew murmured, using everything he had to keep his fangs from descending, his teeth from gnashing at the wolf. "Lorraine can talk on her own."

The sense of false calmness that'd descended on Lorraine from the satin lilt in Matthew's voice disappeared in a snap. Her eyes focused, the haze that'd swirled there seconds before now painfully vacant.

"No," she said. "I want Grey here. Anything I say, he can hear. I'd tell him the second you left, anyway, so it's useless to try and keep this private."

Matthew's eyes raised to Grey. He was vaguely aware of the women's gazes following the two as they stood in a standoff similar to last night. What Matthew found in Grey's expression surprised him: curiosity more than challenge, and pity more than fear.

Grey's next move had Matthew exhaling a sigh of relief. He rested a huge hand on Lorraine's shoulder and pulled her too close to signal of friendship. The kiss that followed was anything but cordial, and both Matthew and Dani turned away.

When Lorraine pulled back from Grey, she gave him a salacious smile that sent dirty thoughts to anyone within a stone's throw of the couple. Though their outward displays of affection made Matthew uncomfortable, he couldn't deny the relief that washed through him at the pairing. Matthew could rest easier knowing that for now, at least, the werewolf had his sights set on the pretty bartender, and not on the love of Matthew's undead life.

When he spoke, Matthew's voice left behind any sense of the ancient lilt and sounded downright cheery for once. "Fine—any chance someone can cover for Lorraine so the four of us can grab a booth?"

Lorraine again looked to Grey for an answer, their gaze a shared sizzle that again caused Dani to roll her eyes in impatience. Matthew hid his own smile of relief.

"Sure," Grey said. "Hey, Liesel—take over for a minute, will you? We'll be in Ten."

The werewolf led the rest of the party through the dimly lit room. Both cat and doglike gazes watched their movements from the corners. Shadows prowled around the edges of the bar, and Matthew's senses leapt to high alert, unable to process every little detail that made his skin crawl. The place smelled like dog, like cat, and like...Danielle.

He focused on her floral, honeysuckle scent as they made their way to the back of the bar. When they reached a door cloaked in darkness, Grey slipped his arm around Lorraine and led the way. Matthew followed, holding the door open for Dani before stepping through himself.

Once inside, Matthew realized that Ten must be shorthand for the servers when labeling their tables. In the darkness beyond the main bar, this small room, containing only a circular table, provided privacy from the rest. Old smoke from expensive cigars hung in the air, and a dusty shelf of amber and opaque liquids wrapped in crystal decanters sat with shiny glasses next to them.

The four of them took seats in high backed black leather chairs. Matthew found himself wondering idly what sorts of deals had gone down here in the past. It was the sort of place with blood on its hands. Targets named and eliminated, treaties signed and broken, spies made and destroyed.

Dani hid her discomfort well, but it was no surprise that a witch and a vampire trapped in the back of a shifter bar would be anxious. It was their natural instinct to flee.

"Thanks for agreeing to talk," Matthew said, surveying the room. "As you both know, I'm—"

"We know who you are," Lorraine said. "What do you want with me?"

Grey leaned back in his chair, watching through eyes that matched his name. His irises looked like windows into a misty forest, the fog there alluring and mysterious. He traced circles on Lorraine's bare shoulder with his finger, and the motion seemed soothing to her.

"Yesterday, we were in here looking for Joey Jones." Matthew leveled his gaze across the table. "When we found him, he was in bad shape."

Grey gave an interested nod that signaled he remembered the body the vampire and the witch had carried between them. "What had he taken? I didn't recognize the smell."

"Neither did I," Matthew admitted in a moment of bonding. "We still don't know what was in his system, but we believe he encountered it here."

"That's impossible," Lorraine said. "He didn't talk to anyone. As usual, he came over to me, took a good long gander at my boobs, and then tipped a boatload because I caught him looking. It's our usual song and dance."

"That's what he said, too." Matthew focused directly on Lorraine and allowed the lilt to seep back into his voice. "He said that you—"

"Shut up," Grey snarled. He leaned forward, menacing. "Talk to her like that again, and I'll have you by the throat."

Matthew turned calmly toward the werewolf, relieved, for once, to be in control. "What are you talking about?"

"That stupid—the glamour," he said. "Knock it off or we're done."

Matthew cleared his throat, stifled the smallest of smiles while both women looked on in confusion. It had been so subtle that neither of the women had noticed the accent, the ancient lilt. In retrospect, Matthew realized he might've done it just to egg on the wolf, *knowing* he'd be the only one in the room to see through it.

"My apologies. Sometimes my, *ah*, peculiarities just slip out. Nature—I'm sure you understand." Matthew watched Lorraine but spoke to Grey—the meaning of his words clear. No matter what, every full moon, Grey would morph into a werewolf if, indeed, that was his true form. In some ways, nature would always win. No amount of control could quench a werewolf's thirst for the moon or a vampire's taste for blood.

"You said Joey didn't talk to anyone else." Matthew focused intently on Lorraine. "Are you absolutely positive? One hundred percent certain? We're looking for even the briefest of interactions. It takes but a second to slip a capsule into someone's drink."

"I'm sure," Lorraine said quickly, but then she paused and considered before giving a nod of confirmation. "I watched him walk over to the booth and sit down. I remember because it wasn't long after that he got all spacey and dazed, and I wondered why. But the Howler isn't a place one asks too many personal questions."

The end of that statement was pointed.

"I'm sorry," Matthew said, "but there's been a murder, and it will be out from under wraps soon. We need to follow every lead we can before the public gets wind of it."

"This is the borough." Grey leaned forward, eyes squinted. "Why is it important if someone talked to Jones? Spells, curses, runes—magic can be used from across a room. Across the world."

"Not without a trace." Dani broke the silence. "His Residuals were clean."

Grey's eyes lit with the revelation. "You're a Reserve."

Dani's eyes flicked briefly toward Matthew, but she held his gaze. "I'm a detective on the case. Captain King is correct—the public will be getting wind of the murders soon, and all hell will break loose after that. We need to finish up here as fast as we can. Are you sure there's nothing you can add?"

"Murders," Grey said, latching onto Dani's slip. His eyes went toward King, the obviously higher ranked officer of the two. "Who? Why did they send a Reserve and the vampire to a shifter bar over a murder?"

Matthew hesitated, but eventually buckled. "I suppose you'll find out soon enough. Whatever I tell you here doesn't leave the room—understood?"

Grey nodded and Lorraine's eyes grew wider as she mumbled an affirmative.

"The mayor was found dead with a companion," Matthew offered. "We don't know the connection between the two deaths, but being that they were in the same location, we're imagining they're somehow related."

"And how does Joey play into this?" Lorraine wrinkled her nose. "He's dumb as a box of rocks. Sorta pretty-looking, but...I mean, come on. He ain't a murderer."

"No, but something was off with him," Dani said. "He doesn't remember taking anything illegal, doesn't remember any magic hitting him. Neither of them—" she gestured at the vampire and the werewolf—"recognize the scent of it. It's not SpellHash."

"Not even close," Grey muttered. "Jones stank from here to the high heavens of something new."

Matthew nodded. "We are trying to find out where it came from. We have an eyewitness who saw someone resembling Joey at the hotel around the time in question."

"Joey ain't a murderer," Lorraine said. "I'm telling you; you're going after the wrong guy."

"Who should we be looking at, then?" Matthew's eyes flicked to Lorraine's, his voice full of natural venom. "Because from what I can tell, Joey Jones walked into the bar expecting to have a normal afternoon. He was to have a few drinks, head to the casino, and find a nice elf or Goblin Girl to cozy up to at night."

"Instead," Dani continued without interrupting the flow, "he got served a drink from you. He didn't talk to another soul, nor does he remember a thing after that."

"So, you'll have to excuse us for being curious," Matthew said, sinking into the easy repartee he had with Dani, "when I ask: What the hell did you put in his drink?"

Lorraine's lips zipped shut, her green eyes glowing like gemstones. "I didn't do nothing."

Grey stiffened in his chair, a fact that didn't go unnoticed by Dani or Matthew. "Talk to them," he encouraged Lorraine. "You've got nothing to hide, and they're not here to arrest you. Cooperation's only going to get us the answers faster."

"I want a lawyer," Lorraine said, defying her boyfriend in an unexpected flash of stubbornness. "Ain't that my right?"

Grey sat up quicker, then blinked and forced himself to remain calm. "She wants a lawyer," he said, recovering quickly. "That'll be all for today."

"In the spirit of full cooperation," Matthew said, leaning across the table. "Would you mind if I took the bottle of Wolfram Whiskey from which you served Joey?"

"I don't know if there's any left," Lorraine said. "Plus, you gotta pay for it. Shit's expensive."

"Take whatever you need," Grey said. Though he didn't work formally at the bar, Matthew got the feeling that his word was law in this place. "It's on us."

Matthew stood, nodded, and proceeded to the door. Resting a hand on the knob, he paused to glance over his shoulder and address the couple. "Just a fair warning, this case will rip the borough apart. There's no telling what we'll have to dig through to find the murderer, but rest assured, we'll find him or her."

"Is that a threat, vampire?" Lorraine pushed herself to her feet, her knuckles gripping the table as she snarled across it.

Matthew didn't want to engage, but he wouldn't be threatened either. Leaning toward her, he spoke in a low voice. "I don't need to threaten you, Lorraine." King's eyes leveled on hers, piercing so deeply through her she seemed to lose her breath. "If you're involved, we'll know. A lawyer..." He smelled the fear, heard the hitch in her breath, and felt the tips of his fangs descend ever-so-slightly. "A lawyer most *certainly* can't save you now."

Chapter 11

Matthew and I left the bar before someone could throw us out. He'd obtained the bottle of Wolfram Whiskey from Liesel at Grey's instruction, and then we'd moved at near-lightning pace down the dirt road and away from The Depth and the Howler.

I considered all we'd learned and struggled to make sense of it. "Lorraine is hiding something."

"I don't think she's a murderer," Matthew agreed, "but I think she saw something, and she's not telling us."

"Do you think she's afraid?"

Matthew bit his lip in thought, the last remnants of his fangs poking through the sharp incisors as they slowly retracted completely. "It's hard to say. I think either someone paid her to pass along a spiked beverage *or* she realized something had happened and was covering for someone."

"And if it was the latter, she's worried about being implicated because she didn't say anything when she noticed." I sighed. "And if it's the former, she's guilty anyway. Though she did have one good point."

"What's that?"

"You have *got* to control those fangs." I glanced at Matthew, disarmed by the sight of the sharpness there. "It's going to get you in trouble. You're not supposed to use your *affinities* as a form of intimidation."

"I wasn't intimidating anyone," he said good-naturedly. "She asked for the facts, and I gave them to her. Like I told Grey—some things, natural things—can't be helped."

96

My blood frothed under the surface in reaction to his fangs. My mind clicked mentally to the last night we'd spent together, the night we'd fallen apart as a couple. It was the first time he'd tasted me—my blood.

I shuddered at the thought and pushed it away. *No distractions.*

"Retract them," I instructed, though that was as effectual as telling someone to hold in a sneeze. It just wasn't possible.

Matthew took pity on me and closed his mouth entirely, hiding the fangs from sight. Though he looked more than a little amused at my obvious reaction to them.

With his senses, it was nearly impossible to hide my thoughts from him. My blush of remembrance was a dead giveaway of the pull I still felt toward him. He'd warned me a long time ago that he could be a form of addiction. There is a sort of magic, an ancient lore, that states once a person has been bitten, their reaction to vampires is heightened to new levels. I now knew this to be true.

I feared it would never go away.

"Did you know Lorraine and Grey were seeing each other?" I turned the conversation to another interesting subject—one that had seemed to set Matthew both at unease and at peace.

"No, I didn't," he said. "I shouldn't be surprised; they're a good fit."

"What do you mean by that?"

Matthew gave me some serious side-eye. "You were there. You felt the chemistry."

"They practically burned the place down."

"Do I sense jealousy?"

I gave him a serious round of the stink eye. "Jealous? Of what—the bartender dating the wolf? No. Never."

We walked in silence, this time taking the path north of the pizza parlor. The dusty road was empty, a sleepy little path through neighborhoods neither rich nor poor, but filled with average families, well-worn herb gardens, and rusted cauldrons sitting on the curb with *FREE* signs spray painted on them.

"Were we ever like that?" I asked quietly, unable to resist. "Like Grey and Lorraine. Where you could just feel the passion radiating out of them."

Matthew gave me a crooked look. "Were you *there* when I kissed you this morning?"

I rolled my eyes. "That doesn't count."

Matthew held out a hand—his palm pale in the sunlight. He pressed it toward me and waited until I, too, raised my palm. I moved it against his, mine flushed and warm while his remained smooth and stony.

We didn't touch. We merely held our hands inches apart, and the sheer proximity of it had my body on the verge of combustion. Combined with the glimpse of Matthew's fangs, I was ready for him to forget all about his promise to leave me alone and demand he take me back. If he asked me to be *his* now, I'd be powerless to refuse.

"That's what I thought," he whispered, his voice barely audible.

He pulled his hand back and shook himself from the daze. I followed suit. If nothing else, Matthew was a vampire of his word, and he would leave me alone until I asked—demanded—more from him. I couldn't do that yet. Not until the past was truly in the past.

"Give me that," I said, switching subjects. "The bottle of Wolfram."

Matthew was still flustered enough to hand the bottle over without argument. "What are you planning to do with it?"

"Well, I know what *you're* planning to do with it," I said, uncapping the bottle and taking a quick whiff of the liquor inside. It smelled like burnt rubber. I wasn't a fan of alcohol, though I could appreciate a fine wine or a well-crafted ale. To me, drinking Wolfram was as appealing as downing straight-up human gasoline. "You're planning to send it to the lab."

"For testing," Matthew said. "We'll have the results back in a few weeks."

"Exactly." Before he could argue, I raised the bottle to my lips and took a swig.

Matthew's eyes widened in horror, and despite his quick reflexes, even he couldn't stop the liquid from sliding down my throat. He grabbed the bottle from my hands, capped it, and shot a hand to the front of my shirt.

With a grasp stronger than a gargoyle's, he bunched the fabric there and pulled me too him. "What the hell were you thinking? Not only is this evidence, but it's potentially dangerous! Deadly!"

If I hadn't been so disgusted by the burning of werewolf whiskey in the back of my throat, I might have appreciated the hard length of Matthew's body pressed against mine. I'd always admired the way I fit against him—my head to his shoulder, his chest to mine, my legs wound tightly around his...

"That's filthy," I said, wiping my mouth with the back of my sleeve. I fought against Matthew's grasp, and he let me go in a wave of surprise. "But there's no foreign substances in the liquor. At least nothing I can taste, and nothing that's been enchanted—Residuals are completely transparent save for a quick Vanilla Snifter spell for flavoring. Though frankly, it might taste better without that garbage."

"Danielle—" Matthew slipped, using my full name, and it took a long moment for him to recover. "That's entirely unprofessional and completely dangerous."

"Yeah, okay." I stomped forward, leaving him to catch up. "It's also unprofessional to lock lips with your Special Consultant while on duty. And what about showing your fangs?"

"You're reckless. I will throw you off this case if I can't trust you to make logical decisions."

"Look, Captain." I spun to face Matthew. "We both knew there was nothing in that bottle. If it had been tampered with, the entire bar would've turned into the zombie apocalypse. The pixies in the lab would've taken weeks to tell you the same thing, so there—I did it for you. The whiskey is clean. That means, without a doubt, that someone slipped something into Joey's drink. Either Lorraine drugged Joey, or she knows who did. My money's on the second option."

Matthew paused in his fuming for long enough to consider my point. He probably realized that the harm in my calculated guess was already done and let it go. I'd come to a valid conclusion, and he knew we needed to keep moving.

"I agree," he said finally. "I'll get a unit out to follow her tonight. We'll see if she meets anyone; we must have spooked her. Hopefully into action."

"While we wait for her to crack, we have to get moving on the mayor," I said. "The Residuals at the crime scene will already be weak. If we can't get there before sunset, my abilities will be useless."

"I have an appointment with the mayor's wife in an hour," Matthew said. "Would you like to accompany me? If we can find out where he went last night, follow his footsteps, we might catch wind of something."

I nodded. "If you have any extra men, get a unit on Lucas. He seemed too slick for me to write off—he'll lawyer up, which makes him tough to reach. Same with Lorraine. The only person I actually believe right now is Joey, and he's clueless."

"What about Grey?"

"Grey?" The question surprised me, and I thought back to the werewolf. "What about him?"

It'd take a dead woman to not appreciate the features of the man, the wolf—whatever he might be. He oozed raw sexuality, and though I wasn't looking for anything in the way of romance, it would have been impossible for me not to notice the way he'd looked at Lorraine with complete devotion. I had wondered if I would ever find someone who looked at me in that way.

One might argue I'd had it before.

And then lost it.

"Do you believe him?" Matthew asked, an edge to his voice. "He's obviously close to Lorraine. He could have her covering for him. Maybe she saw him spike the drink, and—"

"No," I said flatly. "I don't think so."

"And what makes you say that?"

"He loves her—you can see it in his eyes. The infatuation, the care for her. He wouldn't use her in that way."

"Love can make people blind."

"You think I don't know that?" I turned to Matthew. "You asked for my opinion, and I gave it. Plus, he seemed surprised when she snapped for a lawyer."

Matthew nodded, looking annoyed even as he agreed. "Lorraine might be hiding something from him."

"Well," I said darkly. "Let's find out. In the meantime, we follow the mayor's last steps."

Chapter 12

The mayor's home is on Summit Avenue—the oldest street in the borough. It cuts through a territory called Sorcerer's Square that's located northeast of the market and just far enough south of the casinos to be considered safe from goblins. The Golden District touches the northwest corner of the territory and the orcs and trolls are off to the east.

Sorcerer's Square is considered the most politically neutral place in the city. For ages, the sorcerer species has been the most neutral of all witches and wizards. They tend to be lonely creatures, lost in the magic within themselves.

They don't form packs by blood like the werewolves, nor are they inclined to fall for the tricks of the goblins. They keep a peaceful distance from the necromancers and respect, rather than abhor, the magic of the dead. They are the only ones who travel freely into the Otherlands, and even then, they go only when absolutely necessary and take nothing more than they offer.

That was the reason the mayor's mansion had been built inside the square. To sorcerers, politics were nothing more than a circus. Magic was their only ruler. The square was thought to be the safest place for the mayor to live, but even that hadn't been enough to protect Lapel.

"I'll bet that nobody saw *nuthin'* around here," I told Matthew as we entered the district after a brief detour to grab a SandWitch from the hunched little lady on the edge of the marketplace. "Either the sorcerers are completely oblivious, or they don't want to get wrapped up in the investigation."

"I don't plan on asking around," Matthew said in agreement. "That will waste time. But the mayor's widow might have some thoughts. While we're there, keep an eye on the Residuals for the staff. You never know."

I didn't bother to nod my approval. For me, keeping an eye on the Residuals was like telling Matthew to listen carefully. It was as much a part of me as breathing or having a beating heart—there was no way to turn it off.

"I only see the usual spells," I muttered as we came up to the gate that would allow us entry into the mayor's mansion. "It looks like we've got the antibody to Lock Lifters. We have Shifter Sensors and VamPirates." I shot a look at him—the last was protection against vampires. Ironically, the only vampire in the borough was the one who kept peace in the community. "But your badge will get you past that."

Matthew nodded, his lips pursed. All law enforcement badges had a golden shimmer around them—permanent, ever-changing Residuals. The badges protected the officer when on duty from the most basic of spells. It wouldn't prevent a full attack, but it'd blow right past a few cautionary VamPirate hexes.

We reached the gate and Matthew flashed his badge at the peep-hole. Two wooden doors stood before us well over ten feet high. They were thick and strong, and were fastened onto huge metal poles.

Beyond the doors stretched thick rows of enchanted hedges that glowed yellow with a Siren Spell to loudly alert guards of intruders. Within the hedges lived a set of Guarden Pixies—pixies who offered their services to live in gardens and hedges and lawns and chase off intruders.

"I take it you see the Guardeners," I mumbled to Matthew as the gates creaked open. "Over us we've got a Sky Spell that'll keep out all minor flying creatures."

Matthew gave a quick nod as the small pixie behind the gates hovered at eye level. The Master Guardener, I presumed.

"We have an appointment with Mrs. Lapel," Matthew said somberly. "We are incredibly sorry for the loss of the mayor."

The pixie ignored the well wishes. His kind didn't much care for emotions or loyalty, though they cared boatloads for money. So long as a pixie was getting paid to protect, that pixie gave their services without question. Should the money stop, they'd vanish.

"You're good," the pixie said to Matthew. "But who's the witch?"

"She's a Reserve," Matthew said smoothly. "Special Consultant. We have pulled out all the stops on this case."

The pixie again ignored Matthew once he got the information he needed. He turned to squint at me. "A Reserve?"

I was getting a little tired of this. One thing I hadn't missed about retirement was explaining my peculiar talents to those who didn't believe such a thing existed.

"Yes," I said with a sigh. "You're going to want to refresh the Oak Scraper you have over there." I nodded toward a tree positively tingling with green Residuals. "It's burned out. The Sky Searcher? Yeah, that's a load of crap." I shrugged. "Your Sky Spell is okay, but...the Searcher won't be able to pick out a flying elephant coming right at it."

The pixie flinched. "I'll have you know—"

"I know you think you're wearing a Cloaker," I said, noting the red fireworks bursting around the pixie's head, "but it's about as useful as closing your eyes and pretending people can't see you. If you want the Cloaker to work properly, you can't use the cheap silver. You've got to fork it over for the real stuff."

"I did!" The pixie recoiled at my honesty. "I paid top dollar for this Cloak!"

"Where, the marketplace? The Void?" I asked with a snort. "Whoever sold you that was pulling the wool over your eyes. Now, may we pass?"

He waved us in, disgruntled.

"Just warms the heart when you do that," Matthew said with a dry smile. "I've missed working with you."

"Oh, shut it, King," I said, barely hiding a laugh. "I can see you bought a lavender Spell Splash and let me tell you—it's not relaxing."

He stared at me.

"Yeah, even magical perfumes have Residuals," I said. "If you're interested, your cologne is purple."

That silenced him, and we made it to the front gates without further interruption. I took advantage of the walk to study the beautiful landscaping around us, the fountains bursting with real, flying fish and the whispering hedges craning to catch a glimpse of the visitors. Flowers bloomed that must have been imported from exotic lands—The Isle, perhaps—and a small grove of citrus trees dripped with fruit and burst with tropical flavors.

Matthew knocked, and we were greeted quickly by a butler dressed in the usual green jumpsuits worn by those who worked in the service industries. The demure creature, a possible half elf, showed us to a living room and offered us lemon elixir or a Caffeine Cup.

I took the caffeine, Matthew took the lemon, but I knew it was only out of politeness—he wouldn't touch it. By the time our drinks arrived, the mayor's wife could be heard down the hall, talking quietly with another woman. The two ladies stepped into the room seconds later, stopping their conversation at the sight of visitors.

"Hello, ma'am." Matthew stood and addressed the women with a bowed head. "I'm Captain King, and this is Detective Dani DeMarco. We are terribly sorry for the loss of your husband."

I followed suit, wishing my condolences on them in soft tones. I watched the ladies closely for their reactions; sometimes, the slightest hint of alarm at meeting with law enforcement could be telling. Then again, with Matthew being a vampire, half the time a person's alarm came from mere proximity to him. And that, I could understand.

"Thank you." Mrs. Lapel stepped forward and shook each of our extended hands. "This is my sister, Lilian. I hope you don't mind I've brought her to sit in with me—she's been next to me since we heard the news. I don't think I can bear to go through this alone."

"Of course," Matthew said graciously. "We apologize for the intrusion during these difficult moments. But as you know, time is of the essence in our line of work. We want to find whoever did this to your husband and bring justice to them."

Mrs. Lapel gave a grateful sniff. "Thank you, thank you. I see Elvira brought you drinks?" When we both nodded, she wrung her hands together and glanced at her sister. "Then I suppose we can get started."

As Matthew launched into the questioning—covering all the basics from how long they'd been married (twenty-three years), to how long they'd lived here (six years), to the state of their marriage (very good)—I watched Mrs. Lapel for any sign of contradictory expressions to the words that came out of her mouth.

Aside from the basic Spell Splash—a perfume-like substance that acts as a light protectant to ward off simple spells, hexes, and the like—Mrs. Lapel was free of Residuals. Her sister, however, had a more in-depth makeup of glowing particles around her hands. I tried not to stare, but it was nearly impossible as I struggled to tease out the Residuals dancing around the mayor's sister-in-law.

"Tell me about your husband's last term in office," Matthew was saying when I tuned back in to the conversation. "Did he make any enemies? Any friends? Anything in between?"

"My husband was well liked," Mrs. Lapel said. "I can't think of anyone he'd consider an enemy. Except, perhaps, Mr. Blott. But my husband wouldn't consider him an enemy. Just, ah, healthy competition."

"You're referring to Homer Blott, the candidate running against your husband for mayoral office?"

She nodded. "Obviously we knew this year was coming—elections for all political offices are every seven years, so we shouldn't have been surprised. Still, it was a shock to actually see Homer's advertisements sneaking up on us. My husband was so focused on doing his job that he'd nearly forgotten to campaign for reelection."

"Have you met Blott in person?"

"Multiple times." Mrs. Lapel frowned as she considered. "Charity events, galas, all of the formal events. Of course, they'd had a few small-scale debates."

"Did either man have ill will toward the other?"

Mrs. Lapel shifted uncomfortably in her seat. "It's a bit complicated. They were in competition with one another, as I mentioned."

"Honesty is appreciated," Matthew reiterated. "It's the only way we can find out who killed your husband."

"I obviously can't speak for Homer, since I don't know him," Mrs. Lapel said with a quick, furtive glance at her sister. "My husband never spoke ill of him. In fact, he rarely worried about Blott at all. If he did talk about him, it was to admire a campaign strategy he was using."

"Did your husband feel threatened by Blott's campaign for mayor?"

"I suppose *somewhat*," Mrs. Lapel said with a hint of annoyance. "Only one mayor will be living here after the election, and Blott has raised huge amounts for his campaign."

"Now, Blott is almost a shoe-in." Matthew spoke too quickly to realize the insensitivity of his statement, and when he did, he back-tracked. "Apologies, Mrs. Lapel."

Mrs. Lapel devolved into tears. "I-it's true. I lost my husband, I'll lose my house..."

Mrs. Lapel leaned against her sister. Her eyes were red, her coiffed blond hair mussed from its usual perfect bob. Lilian hugged her close, ran her hand in soothing circles over her sister's back.

"I know it sounds so crass of me, but it's so much change all at once. Where will I live? I hate to talk of such things when my husband's been murdered, but..." Mrs. Lapel let out a wail. "He took care of me. Who will take care of me?"

"You'll live with me, sweetie," Lilian told her sister. "Don't worry about anything except taking care of yourself. Okay? It's going to be okay—we'll get through this together."

I swallowed, feeling intrusive in the moment. Matthew sat still as a statue, and I could tell he didn't like it any more than I did.

"I'm truly sorry," I said, chiming in while Matthew seemed frozen with discomfort. "We hate having to ask you these questions, and I promise there will only be a few more. They'll be difficult, but there's no way around them. I'm going to need to ask you to be strong, Mrs. Lapel, for your husband."

She wiped her eyes, then gave a grateful smile to her sister. "Go ahead—let's get this over with."

"You mentioned competition with Blott," I said. "You also mentioned the fact that your husband was well liked. Do you think Blott might have been worried he'd lose the election?"

"Of course." Mrs. Lapel paused, offered a strange little smile. "My husband was smart. Friendly. Good. He was a truly good man, Miss—"

"Detective DeMarco," I supplied. "I believe you. I never had a bad word to say about him myself."

The personal tidbit seemed to help. She smiled again. "So yes, I suppose my husband would be considered competition."

"Did your husband ever mention any disagreements or arguments with Blott?" I asked. "Anything that might have gotten Blott angry?"

"Plenty of times, but that's the nature of politics," Mrs. Lapel said. "My husband always stands up for what's right. Blott..."

I frowned, leaned closer. "What about Blott?"

She gave me a tense smile. "I think he'd rather *win* than be fair, but that's just my two cents. My husband didn't say a bad word about him personally, but I found him frustrating to be around and incredibly rude. Even when he was trying to be friendly for media photos, it was forced. My husband said I was biased and imagining things, but I wasn't."

"Do you think Blott would have murdered your husband over the mayoral office?" I asked. "There is a lot at stake with this year's election."

"What sort of person would kill another over political office?" Mrs. Lapel sniffed harder. "Only a monster. I don't have any love lost for Homer, but I don't think he'd kill for it."

I nodded, although I wasn't sure I agreed, and jotted down a few notes. I highly suspected that things would be rough going for the borough if Blott took over office. He had a name for being ruthless and bullheaded, and somewhat of a jerk. Mayor Lapel had been genuinely well-liked, and he had been the heavy favorite of the people who knew him to win another election.

However, Blott's campaign was permeating the borough, making the polls indicate the results would be closer than they should. I wondered if Matthew was thinking along the same lines, and after a quick glance his way, I knew we'd be following up on Blott later.

"You said the state of your relationship with the mayor was 'very good'," I quoted, moving along. "Can you expand on that?"

For the first time, she shifted uncomfortably. "It was very good. I supported him, and he supported me. We loved one another."

I tried not to give anything away, but the gears in my brain were churning. That wasn't exactly a passionate cry of love over her deceased life partner. "I see. There hadn't been any...bumps in the road recently?"

"Nothing out of the norm for any marriage," she said, her smile faltering. "I know what you're getting at, Detective. He was found with another woman, wasn't he?"

"A Goblin Girl," I said, taking a chance on the truth. "They were found in a motel room together."

She flinched, but her expression remained strong and her eyes dry. "He wasn't having an affair—"

"Mrs. Lapel—"

"I don't care what it looks like. It wasn't an affair. I don't know if he was meeting the...the Goblin Girl or not for business reasons, but I can guarantee it wasn't romantic."

"How?"

"Because," she said fiercely. "Despite our *bumps*, we loved each other. He is—was—a good man. I'm certain of it."

Something wasn't quite adding up, but I couldn't put my finger on it. The only option was to dig deeper, to let her statements sink in while my subconscious churned away and dissected the facts. "Where was your husband supposed to be last night? Did he keep a calendar?"

"He had dinner reservations. A business meeting," she said, waving her hand. "I'd planned dinner with my sister because I knew he'd be absent. For more specifics, you'll have to check with his assistant."

I made a note to do just that. "Can you give me the exact outline of what happened last night?"

"Detective, are you asking me for an alibi?" Mrs. Lapel murmured. "Because it sounds like—"

"She's asking the questions that need answering." Matthew leaned forward, his face severe. "In the interest of time and of helping your husband's case along, I suggest you answer to the best of your ability."

The sharpness to his words surprised everyone in the room, but it seemed to do a world of good for Mrs. Lapel. She snapped to attention, wiped the offense from her face, and looked at me with determination.

"I had a hair appointment yesterday until five p.m.," she said. "I came home shortly after, changed from my errand attire into my evening clothes and left the house again. I took a carriage to dinner—I'm sure you can ask the Master Guardener for the specific time, since he tracks all that, and you can find the carriage driver as well to verify. I met my sister at the Spritely Broomstick at a quarter after six. We had drinks in the bar until seven when our table was announced ready. We dined until..." she hesitated, glanced to Lilian.

Lilian bobbed her head back and forth in thought. "I sent for a carriage back around quarter to eight. You likely arrived home just after the hour."

Mrs. Lapel nodded. "That's about right. I changed into my nightgown and prepared for bed. I read for over an hour, maybe closer to two, and then the doorbell rang. I thought it odd since my husband always comes in without knocking, of course. But it was about the time he was due home, so I figured..." She shrugged. "I went to the door and there were two officers who explained they'd found my husband dead."

"I'm so sorry," I added, as her eyes teared up once more. "When was the last time you saw your husband?"

"I kissed him goodbye that morning," she said with a watery smile. "He stayed at the office all day. We talked once on the phone at lunch—as we usually do—to go over evening plans. All seemed well."

"Nothing seemed off with him?"

"No," she said after a pause. The pause caught my attention, and Mrs. Lapel realized her error and sighed. "Okay, he did seem very busy lately—coming home later than usual, lots of business dinners, the like. But I assumed it was all related to the campaign for his re-election."

"It wasn't—"

"I'm sure it wasn't *personal*," she said. "I know my husband better than anyone in the world."

"I think we're done for today," Lilian said. "My sister is tired, and she's lost her husband. Any non-urgent questions can wait."

We stood, thanked both sisters again and wished our condolences on the family. Matthew and I huddled next to one another in the hall as Lilian shuffled her sister away, presumably to rest elsewhere. Lilian returned alone several minutes later looking polished and brisk.

"I imagine you want to talk to the staff?" she asked without fanfare. "You already know my alibi. I met my sister for dinner, then I went home and read as well. Alone. I was asleep by eleven and woke in the middle of the night to my sister's Comm."

Matthew gave an appreciative nod. "The staff?"

"This way." As we walked through the hallway, she gave a sharp inhalation of breath. "I must warn you, I don't think you'll learn anything helpful. You're wasting your time."

"Why do you think that?" Matthew asked. "The staff saw Mayor Lapel every day."

Lilian snorted. "Sure. That's exactly the problem—they *didn't* see him every day."

"What are you trying to say?" Matthew asked. "That your sister lied?"

"No—that my sister is a sweet soul, naive and innocent." Lilian's eyes flashed with frustration. "That *bump* she mentioned? My sister and her husband have not been sleeping in the same room for months. The long hours at the office? He'd sleep there three nights a week."

"So, you're saying marital issues aren't out of the question?" I asked. "You think something might have been going on, and Mrs. Lapel was oblivious?"

Lilian raised an eyebrow. "He was found dead in a Motel Sixth with an expensive Goblin Girl. I'll let you draw your own conclusions."

Chapter 13

We strove to keep our interviews with the staff short, but it took over an hour before we'd concluded even a precursory meeting with most of them. That spoke to the number of staff at the mayor's mansion, rather than the thoroughness with which we spoke to them. Other cops had already questioned them briefly, and still more would follow in the coming days as the mayor's case blew wide open.

After an hour and a half, we concluded that Mrs. Lapel had an airtight alibi. At least three different members of the staff recalled seeing her before dinner and after her return. While we still had to follow up with the restaurant where she claimed to have eaten dinner, I suspected she was in the clear.

"Can you give us a rundown of what the mayor's day looked like?" I asked the personal assistant to the Lapels. "Minute by minute if you have it. Oh, and we'll need a copy of that calendar."

The assistant glanced at her clipboard. "I already told you he didn't have anything out of the ordinary scheduled yesterday. He had breakfast at home with his wife—that's quite usual for him. Sometimes it is the only time they have together all day, what with his re-election campaign and the long hours at the office."

"Will the cook be able to verify this?" I asked. "And are you suggesting the mayor normally took dinner out?"

Andie Smite, the well-kept assistant, gave a polite blink. "It depended on his schedule, which I'll give you a copy of," she said before I could ask. "For example, this week he was only scheduled to have dinner at home once."

"Starting with breakfast yesterday," I prompted, "give me a run-down of his day."

"Breakfast, then a walk to the office," Andie said, scanning down the list. "He held a few meetings after he arrived, though you'll have to talk to his secretary for specifics on those. I just have times blocked off in red—which means mandatory work obligation."

"Fine," I said, jotting down the times and a note to speak with the secretary. "Meetings throughout the day. Any plans for lunch?"

"It was open." She frowned. "That's unusual. He nearly always has meetings over meals."

"Any particular buddies or friends with whom he might've grabbed a quick bite?"

"You'll have to talk to his secretary. Nobody that I know of—the mayor didn't keep many close friends except for his wife." The answer sounded a bit too rehearsed, and I made a special notation in my notebook to follow up with his secretary to see if their answers matched. "What types of people was he meeting over meals?"

"Donors to his campaign, worried political figures, even citizens," she said. "He was always taking a pulse on the political climate of Wicked."

"Was he well-liked by these acquaintances?"

"Incredibly well-liked. If you ask me, it was Mr. Blott who should have been concerned." Andie lowered her voice. "Then again, I'm biased. If Blott takes over, of course, I could very well be out of a job. Every seven years the newly elected mayor is allowed to choose his own staff."

"Were you offered the job by Mayor Lapel?"

She shifted uneasily. "Yes. Assistants are very personal, and we often turn over with the mayor's office. I haven't spoken to Mr. Blott, so I can't tell you his intentions, but I suspect I would have been let go at the change in office. Now, I suppose," she said wonderingly, "it's inevitable that I'll lose my position."

"I'm very sorry, Ms. Smite."

"Nature of the job," she said briskly. "I have business to attend to, so let's finish up, if you don't mind. After lunch—which appears open on my calendar—he was in meetings most of the afternoon. Small break around five. Dinner and drinks scheduled for six."

"Do you know where?"

"No, I only handle the household items. Anything business related is the responsibility of Mayor Lapel's office secretary. Now, may I pass you off to the chef? I must check on Mrs. Lapel to see how she's holding up."

I thanked her, and Matthew and I followed behind Ms. Smite through sweeping hallways decorated with heirlooms from mayors past. Paintings from Wicked's early eras lined the hallways, the home feeling part residence and part museum.

We swept behind Andie and listened carefully as she explained useless bits of history and fun facts that weren't fun at all. By the time we reached the kitchens and she introduced us to Chef Lollabridge, we were ready to be rid of her inane conversation starters.

"Chef Lollabridge, just a few questions." I spoke to the thin, dark-haired female under the tall white hat. She was pretty, in a severe sort of way, and almost painfully slim—ironic for a chef, I thought. "Can you briefly give us a rundown of a normal day in the kitchens?"

"I start at four every morning," the chef said crisply. "Food prep. I have kitchen help who I'm sure you've already interviewed, but if I want something done right, I must do it myself."

"I understand."

"Around six I begin preparations for breakfast—Mrs. Lapel prefers biscuits, a very specific variety and freshly baked, with her tea. On mornings the mayor eats at the office, he has an egg white omelet here to hold him off." The chef paused for a smile. "That's what he'd order, at least. What he'd *actually* grab on the way out the door was a fresh, warm chocolate croissant. Doctors ordered the omelet, but he preferred the baked goods."

"Which did he have yesterday?"

She thought back. "He had a croissant brought up to his room."

I glanced at my notes. "Does he not normally take breakfast with Mrs. Lapel?"

"He used to," she said. "Recently—I'm not sure if it's due to the upcoming election flurry of activity or something else, but he hasn't had the time to dine in the breakfast nook. Mrs. Lapel normally takes tea by herself before her morning walk."

I battled back a frown. Seemed to me Mrs. Lapel wasn't doing a great job hiding the issues between her and her husband—and the rest of the staff hadn't coordinated their stories to match. "Alright, thank you. I'm assuming lunch is just for Mrs. Lapel?"

"It's almost always been that way, though in my early tenure here—an assignment that began with the current mayor six years ago—the mayor would come home for a sit-down lunch with his wife on Wednesdays. Wednesdays were long days for me in the kitchen," she added with a shy smile. "But that stopped about six months ago. Recently, the only sort of formal lunch I've prepared is afternoon tea for Mrs. Lapel and some of her female acquaintances. Her sister has been present for most of them as the two are very close."

"Any idea why the mayor stopped coming home for lunch?"

"Longer days at the office? I suppose you'd have to check with his assistant. I'm not privy to his schedule except to know how much food needs purchasing and cooking."

"I plan to ask." I smiled. "After lunch?"

"Dinner lately has been a rare occasion. In terms of something grand, I mean," she hurried to amend. "When dining alone or with her sister, Mrs. Lapel tends to keep things simple—salad, charcuterie board, a coffee and chocolate for dessert. It doesn't take much prep."

"The mayor hasn't been eating at home much?"

"No. Although he did have me pack him hearty suppers to take with him to work. He brought a lunch pail, though I had to use a Spoiler Spell to prevent everything from going bad. From my understanding, he often snuck dinner at the office in between calls."

"And yesterday—"

"Including yesterday," she said. "I packed him supper in the morning and sent him on his way. Speaking of which, I never did get the pail returned. I hate to be crass, but if that turns up and isn't needed, I wouldn't mind having it back."

"I'll see what we can do," I promised. "Did he take supper whether he had dinner plans or not?"

She shook her head. "If he had dinner plans, he'd let me know that morning and his food would be fair game for the staff." She gave a wry smile. "I've never seen meatloaf disappear so quickly at seven in the morning."

"Yesterday?"

"Like I said, he took supper yesterday. As far as I know, that meant he planned to work straight through dinner at the office. On late nights—which have been the norm lately—I was gone by the time he returned home. I left the mansion around four yesterday afternoon because neither the mayor or his wife required my services for dinner, and I'd gotten an early start on my day."

"Thank you so much for your candidness," I said, scanning over my notes. "We'll let you know if any other questions come up."

She gave a succinct nod. "Can I tempt you into a croissant?"

I glanced at Matthew who, of course, gave a subtle shake of his head. "I'll take one," I said, reaching for the basket behind her on the kitchen counter. "Thanks. Do you know where we can find Marta Tchaikovsky? She's the last person on our list."

"Sure. She'll be upstairs. Let me show you."

Chef Lollabridge led the way through her gleaming workspace up a nearby staircase that circled to a second level. We climbed, listening to the chef explain that this passage was rarely used except for the staff to run food to and from the bedrooms. Which explained the drab nature and precarious state of the stairwell.

The chef left us on the second level where the drabness gave way to a bright and glittering hallway, a sort of regal coziness settling into the private quarters. She pointed out a dark-haired woman with a watering can in hand who'd just emerged from the bath at the end of the hall.

"Marta?" I asked. The woman looked up, gave a shy smile, and nodded. "Can we talk to you for a second? I'm Detective DeMarco and this is Captain King. We have a few questions for you."

"Um, sure," she said. "What can I help you with?"

The chef took her leave as Matthew began questioning Marta, his voice gentle and easy on the ears. She visibly relaxed the moment he began asking questions.

"How long have you been working for the Lapels?" he asked. "Did you begin after the last election?"

Marta shook her head, black wisps of hair falling to either side of her pretty face. She had features like that of an Eskimo—big, round eyes and darker skin. Her hair trailed over her back in a long, thick braid, and though she had dark hair like Chef Lollabridge, where the chef was all slim lines and staccato clips, Marta was soft and sweet-faced and curvy.

"My mother began working here..." She hesitated, her thick eyelashes fluttering over pink cheeks as she spoke. "It must be four election cycles ago? About twenty-eight years past? You could say I practically grew up here. I was hired two election cycles ago and Mr. and Mrs. Lapel kindly kept me on when they got the job."

"What are your responsibilities at the mayor's mansion?" Matthew asked.

"I clean, water plants—" she lifted the pail with a grin. "I take care of the personal quarters for Mr. and Mrs. Lapel. I do what needs to be done. I report to Ms. Smite."

"Is it possible to take a quick tour of the personal quarters?" I interrupted Matthew to ask. "We won't interfere with anything, but it would help us to get an understanding for how the mayor lived."

"How is that relevant to the case?" Marta looked skeptical. "I think I would need permission from Mrs. Lapel."

"Trust me," I said. "Every little bit is helpful. We won't touch anything. Just a precursory glance, and it will save us a lot of time and paperwork—we need to work fast to catch the murderer."

"I guess it's fine," she said doubtfully. "As their personal quarters won't belong to them much longer anyway. The mayor technically doesn't live here anymore." She glanced at us with a sudden realization. "Excuse me, that sounded incredibly crass and insensitive."

"Not at all," I said gently. "You do have a point. Though the mayor might be gone, we can bring him justice by finding the killer. Time is ticking, and we're desperate for anything that could direct us toward the person who wanted him dead."

Matthew gave a displeased frown at my candidness, but it worked.

"Come on, a quick look can't hurt." Marta's posture grew stronger as she led us to the first room in the hallway. "The master bedroom."

"This is where both Mr. and Mrs. Lapel slept?" Matthew asked.

The question wasn't supposed to be a trick one, but Marta hesitated. "They lived here together. These are their private quarters."

Her answer was an equal dodge. I didn't give any sign I noticed, and neither did Matthew. Instead, we focused on surveying the room for anything that could give us a lead on the mayor's murder.

The bed was large, grand—only one side rumpled. The room contained many of the same qualities as the hallways and sitting rooms—a sort of historic slant to their modernity. The space was grand and bold, lined with a unique mixture of old wooden chests and antique candlesticks. Precious few photographs or personal items sat out on display.

I poked my head into the restroom across from the foot of the bed and paused. Something felt off, though I couldn't put my finger on what. As Matthew quietly questioned Marta in the entrance to the master bedroom, I leaned against the doorframe and studied the bath.

A large, claw-foot tub sat against one wall. The vanity was a quaint old thing, sparkling clean, but tarnished in ways only age and use could bring. There was a distinctly feminine tilt to the room, and as I soaked in the base Residuals, I noted pastel pinks and light blues, bright purples with splashes of yellow and hints of springtime green.

It was obvious what was missing. I glanced over at Matthew for confirmation. Though I'd teased him for it earlier, the cologne he wore had a deep violet shade to it, an almost royal tone. Around his chin I studied the faintest hint of bold red—the aftereffects of a Shaver Spell he'd used just that morning. Spells that were distinctly masculine. There were none here.

"Thanks for showing us this space," I said, returning to where Marta and Matthew had lapsed into silence. "Now where's the other one?"

"Excuse me?" Marta's eyes flicked toward the bed. "The other what?"

"Where did the Mayor keep his things?" I asked. "We know that he and Mrs. Lapel have been leading somewhat separate lives as of late."

"They weren't leading separate lives," she burst. "They loved each other."

"Fine, but they haven't been sleeping together," I said. "So where did the mayor sleep when he was home?"

Martha gave us a reluctant gesture to follow her from the master bedroom. She walked stiffly ahead of us to another door further down the hall. "I meant what I said about them loving each other. You could tell they truly cared for one another. It was sweet."

"But?"

"But about six months ago, the mayor seemed different." She hesitated. "He became defensive, almost...fierce about his privacy."

"He was keeping a secret from his wife?"

"Yes, I'm sure of it." Marta paused in front of a closed door. With a sigh, she pushed it open and led us inside. "But I don't believe it's the kind of secret you're thinking."

This room positively burst with male Residuals. Reds and violets and dark, forest greens snaked across every surface the mayor had touched over the last few months. A slight dusting of white, sugar-sand Residuals over the bed told me he'd used Sleeper Spells quite often.

Though active, single-use Residuals faded within twenty-four hours, that wasn't the case with spells that saw repeated use over time. It was like a marble staircase: one footstep onto the stairs left them virtually untouched—just like one use of a spell allowed Residuals to fade completely. But after enough footsteps pass by, eventually the marble becomes grooved, and the footprints are impossible to eradicate.

"Hey, look." I moved into the bathroom and picked up a bottle of cologne. "The mayor's Spell Splash is blue."

Matthew frowned. "Marta, you say Mayor Lapel's secret isn't what it seems?"

"No. He hid something from her, but I don't think he had a choice. It almost felt like he was distancing himself as a way to protect Mrs. Lapel."

I returned to the bedroom and focused on Marta. "Protecting her from what?"

Marta shrugged. "I don't know. I've told you everything I do know, and I think it's time for you to leave. I have two bedrooms to clean..." she faltered. "Though I suppose there's no rush to do this one."

"Thank you." I rested a hand on Marta's wrist, and though she pulled away, I could see a flash of gratitude in her eyes. "This has been really helpful."

"Will it assist you in finding the mayor's murderer?" Marta's huge, beautiful gray eyes pooled with tears. "Whatever you think about politics, the mayor was a good man. He didn't deserve to die."

"Yes, I hope so. Now, before we go, I have two more questions," I said. "Don't take either of them personally."

"If you're looking for an alibi, I have one," she offered. "I worked here yesterday until Mrs. Lapel retired to her bedroom after dinner. Then I returned to the staff quarters where any number of people can vouch that I showered, ate leftovers from Chef Lollabridge, and then fell asleep. My room is shared, so I was never alone aside from the shower, and that was brief."

"Thank you," I said. "And lastly..."

"You're wondering about the girl," Marta said, once again perceptive beyond belief. "The poor Goblin Girl found with the mayor."

"Yes."

"I just don't see it," she whispered. "I don't believe there was anything going on between them. If I had to guess, I think the mayor was trying to help her somehow. Do you know her name? What she was doing with him?"

I hesitated to answer. "No, not yet. She hasn't been identified."

"I'm going to give you a suggestion, which I'm sure isn't warranted" she said with a smile. "But I think that finding out what the Goblin Girl wanted from the mayor will be the key."

"We're working on it," I said. "Thank you for your insights."

"Detective, Captain," Marta said as she led us from the mayor's bedroom and closed the door tightly behind her. "I know most people think politics is a charade, or a circus, or a play. And probably, it is most of the time. But Mr. Lapel meant what he said when he got elected—he truly does love Wicked and the people in it. If that Goblin Girl was in trouble and came to him asking for help, he would have given it." Marta nodded firmly. "He wouldn't have turned her away."

"What are you trying to say, Marta?" I asked. "That she's the reason he's dead?"

"I just think it's worth looking deeper into the girl. Find the connection between the two, and you might find some answers."

Matthew and I waited until we were outside, past the Guardeners and beyond the hedges and the gate, before we spoke.

"I think Marta's onto something," I said. "We need to find out how the mayor and the Goblin Girl are connected."

"Let's check in with Felix," Matthew said. "The HoloHex of Charlie Bone should be ready. We can show it around the casino and see if any of the other girls recognize him."

"We should get a sketch done of the girl, too," I said. "If we find the girl, we may find the killer."

Chapter 14

Matthew heard the chaos before he saw it. He kept the warning to himself, however, because it annoyed Dani to no end that his senses were more perceptive than hers. Dani preferred to see, hear, and experience the world on her own.

Except when that meant trouble. And the commotion around the corner was trouble.

As Dani swung around the edge of the building, Matthew threw his arm out and blocked her path. She glared at him, furious, until she paused long enough to see the gathering for herself.

"Oh, no," she breathed, the fury leaving her with a sigh. She glanced down at her watch. "I really thought we'd have until lunch."

"It's a big case; the ban can only do so much." Matthew surveyed the swarm of reporters hovering around the steps to the station. Media wasn't allowed in the actual building or on the property, but the dusty path before the precinct was fair game.

Matthew melted silently back into the shadows, bringing Dani with him. One thing he hated more than the rest—and there were many things he hated—was the spotlight. And with the media came spotlight.

"The hologram of our mystery man will have to wait," Matthew growled. He turned and moved in the direction from which they'd come, heading south toward the Dead Lands. As he walked, he raised his wrist to his mouth and spoke into the Comm. "Felix, you got the HoloHex waiting for us?"

Felix grumbled a reply. He was the grumpy, magical version of a computer tech. He dissected spells, ran the Comm system, and was the Brainiac behind every weird magical investigation in the borough.

"It's a frenzy outside, so we'll be back for it later. Can you also get me a HoloHex of the female vic, too?"

"You have the vic's body," Felix snarked loud enough for Dani to hear as she caught up. "What do you need a hologram for?"

"We want to show her face around a few places. We'll be back to pick them up late this afternoon."

"You think I can pull HoloDiscs out of my ass?" Felix snarled. "I've got other cases besides yours, you know. I'll need more time."

"This afternoon. Top priority."

Felix signed off with a few choice words that made Matthew smile. "He'll have it," Matthew assured Dani. "In the meantime, I vote we pay our respects to the dead."

Dani fell in line behind Matthew, and together they walked toward the morgue. Sienna, the necromancer in charge of the lab, was simply the best in the business. If anything was left on the bodies that might be of use in the case, she'd find it.

For Matthew, a visit near the Dead Lands always toyed with him like a sick game of cat and mouse. Vampires, the undead, never quite fit in with the necromancers. They also didn't quite fit in with the living. And as the only known vampire in the borough, Matthew King didn't fit in with anyone at all.

Vampires had chosen collectively years before to avoid interaction with the living. It's said some of them still live in the Dead Lands. Others migrated to damp, dark corners of the earth and formed small colonies where they could live mostly in peace. The vast majority, however, existed in singles and doubles, living in sewers and drains in large cities, feasting on inhabitants that wouldn't be missed.

Matthew's fangs had never killed. He'd bitten exactly one living, breathing entity, and she walked beside him now. A shudder came over him at the thought of what would have happened if he hadn't found the patience, the self-control, to stop. Vampires couldn't be changed recklessly through a bite—despite what most legends said—but only through careful, cautious consideration and planning. Only then could a vampire change a human to join their kind.

The sight of the Dead Lands approaching sent a chill over Matthew as he walked. A murky mist hovered over the lands for no scientific reason known to man. It was as if the very earth sensed the death and destruction there and cast down tears to cover the surface.

Matthew stopped the moment the dampness touched his skin. "You don't have to join me."

"Excuse my crassness, Captain," Dani said, "but I dated the undead. I think I'm fine at the morgue."

He allowed a small smile, then continued onward. After flashing their badges and following the familiar sign-in procedure at the front desk, Matthew and Dani waited for the bored looking monster named Ursula to alert them that the necromancer was ready.

Neither Matthew nor Dani had ever quite figured out what sort of creature Ursula was, and they hadn't asked. She had a scar running across her face and strange, almost opaque purple skin. She must have immigrated from a monster camp some time back, and over time had assimilated as a staple in the community. It was considered very impolite to talk about one's species in public with anyone except close friends.

Finally, Ursula pushed a thick set of glasses over her odd skin. She opened a huge mouth and called for *the detective and the undead guy* to approach the bench.

"Sienna will see you now," she said when we stood before her like we might a judge. "You know the drill. Don't touch anything. No holograms or notetaking will be tolerated. You want an official report, you request it from me."

We grabbed our temporary passes and moved beyond the desk to find Sienna waiting quietly for us in the background. Unlike the big, busty Ursula, the necromancer didn't offer any sort of greeting.

Sienna had viciously pink hair, dyed by a spell, and wore headphones over a pixie-tiny head. The necromancer came up only to my shoulder and couldn't have weighed more than eighty pounds soaking wet. Still, neither Matthew nor Dani would want to meet her in a dark alley.

Sienna stomped back toward the lab in heavy black combat boots. Tight jeans were ripped up and down her legs as if she'd let a werewolf try them on, and her thin shoulders were covered by flimsy tank top straps underneath a cropped leather jacket. She was the epitome of flashy, trendy, and terrifying all at once.

When we reached the cool, refrigerated room, Sienna didn't bother to give instructions. We'd all been here before. She slipped into her gloves and lab coat, leaving the leather jacket outside, and showed us to the table on which the mayor rested.

He looked older, pale, a tinge blue thanks to the chill in the air and the fact that he was dead. Sienna stared down at him for a long moment, bobbing her head to the beat of the music thumping in her ears. Dani and Matthew knew better than to interrupt.

When the song crashed to a close, Sienna snapped her fingers and the headphones disappeared. She launched immediately into an explanation with neither a preamble nor a greeting. "Cause of death: ancient runes. Time of death: seven-forty-two p.m., though there was movement around nine eighteen. That'll be the moment they were tossed in the Motel Sixth."

Matthew nodded, making mental notes as all three surveyed the body. He watched carefully as Sienna's eyes trailed over the mayor's figure. She walked in close proximity to the body and brushed a hand gently down his arm, ending with a few taps against the veins protruding on the inside of his elbow.

"Blood is frozen," she said, looking thoughtful. "Helluva painful way to die, if I had to guess. Obviously, I can't and won't be asking him, but I can infer from the look of horror on his ugly mug."

Sienna was both highly intelligent and brutally honest. Even when death claimed a victim and brought them to Sienna's table, she didn't censor what she said. In her words, *an asshole alive is still an asshole dead, just a silent one.* Apparently, an ugly guy alive made for an ugly guy dead.

As to her comment about raising the mayor to ask—well, that was an impossibility. Necromancy was outlawed in the borough and in most places around the world. Necromancers were allowed to live near the Dead Lands on the condition that their form of magic was never used. Never. Usually, even Sienna didn't joke about it.

"If I had to guess at a species type for the killer, I'd say..." She hesitated, thinking. "I'm going to say sorcerer, witch, or wizard. Possibly a very talented spellslinger, but I'm talking someone who's already magically inclined, not some Joe Blow who picked up a magic kit at the marketplace."

"Have you ever seen this before?" Dani asked. Matthew was impressed with her nerve—Sienna frowned upon questions before she'd finished her summary. "The rune magic, I mean."

Sienna's sharp eyes cut to her, but she deemed the question worthwhile by answering it. "No. I remember each body I've examined, and this is a new-to-me technique."

"Where did it come from?" Dani asked. "How is this magic getting into the borough?"

"Do you think—" Matthew faced Dani. "Do you think this could have something to do with Joey?"

Dani shrugged, then explained to Sienna. "We've been encountering a few strange symptoms lately."

"Drugs?" Sienna caught on quickly. She saw the officers' looks of surprise, and she rolled their eyes. "I know Joey Jones. He's harmless, but he dabbles."

Dani allowed herself a nod.

"This is purposeful. Painful. I would venture a guess that it was meant to torture," she said, then winced. "Blood doesn't freeze in an instant. It's a painstaking process that feels like an eternity. The time of death that I quoted you—that's just the end of the process."

The room sank into silence at the gruesomeness of it all. Dani's stomach churned, but she fought back a reaction and swallowed mightily.

"I did find myself wondering if the killer was trying to cover up the murders," Sienna wondered aloud. "Theoretically, if the bodies had been left long enough to thaw—and realistically, that's possible since they wouldn't start to stink until the decomposition set in—the cause of death would've been impossible to pin down. Sure, I would've seen some ruptured veins, but I would never have guessed..."

She trailed off, shaking her head.

"What about the other body?" Dani asked. "Can we see her?"

"The Goblin chick? Sure. Over here." Sienna led them to the opposite side of the room and pulled open a drawer. "I processed her already—didn't think you'd care to see her."

Even as she opened the drawer, Dani wondered if the girl would be the key to everything. The murderer would never have expected law enforcement to focus on her—to so many, Goblin Girls were seen as disposable creatures. But not to Dani, and not to Matthew. The mayor might have been the question, but the answer might be buried with the girl.

"Why didn't you expect we'd want to see her?" Dani asked, though Matthew supposed she already knew the answer. Dani was agitated and hankering for an argument. "She's part of the case too."

"Exactly. That's why I processed her first, in case there was a reason for me to *make* you see her." Sienna put a hand on her hip, glanced coolly over at Dani. The temperature in the already chilly room went down a few more notches. "Usually, those high up on the totem pole ignore those down below."

"Excuse me?" Dani's eyes narrowed. "Our entire careers, and therefore our lives, are centered around bringing justice to the dead—rich or poor."

"Then you happen to be the exception, Detective DeMarco." The ME's tone was dry and sarcastic. "Good job to you. Is that what you want to hear? Maybe a pat on the back?"

"I don't want to hear anything," Dani shot back. "What's your problem?"

"My problem is this." Sienna gestured furiously toward the wall of boxes before her. After a split-second pause, her fingers moved like lightning as she pulled open a series of refrigerated drawers to reveal seven different bodies. Most of them were shades of light green, all of them female. "All of these women died within the last month."

Dani's eyes processed them with scientific precision. She cleared her throat. "Looks here like we have a strangulation case, two Spell-Shots—that is not good, Captain—and four questionable causes of death. Why are you showing me these, Sienna?"

"Because they're still here." Sienna looked down at the open drawer nearest her side. Her face changed, the sharp pinks of her hair and blacks of her eyeliner fading to the background as edginess gave way to sympathy. "These girls all had one thing in common: they were poor. Worked in the casinos, on the streets, etc. Their deaths were never investigated."

"I'm sure there are officers assigned," Captain King said. He watched, interested, as the tough, hardened ME reached down and gently stroked the deceased woman's cheek with her finger. The gesture was almost loving, almost as if Sienna was trying to comfort the girl. "We investigate every homicide. I can get you names if—"

"I don't need names," Sienna said, and then she sent the body and its drawer back into the wall with a distinct metal clang, her face losing all sympathy and reverting to stone once more. "I saw the cops assigned when they stopped by—well, most of them. This one, whose cause of death was overdose and likely not self-administered, didn't have any visitors. Not even the cop assigned her case."

King's jaw tightened. "I'll find out why."

"Great, you do that," Sienna snapped. "And then you can sit on your throne at the NYPD and gloat about it. Maybe get an award for all the good deeds you've done."

"Watch it," Dani warned. "You're talking to the captain."

"I'm talking to a vampire, an equal—another being, just like me," Sienna said. "That's the problem. The mayor gets murdered? They get the Reserve and the vamp on the case. If it weren't for this poor girl's body being dumped in the same room as the mayor, would the two of you have shown up to bring justice to her murderer?"

Matthew and Dani remained silent. The answer was no—neither of them would have. They could have made excuses: not enough time in the day, other fish to fry, etc. But the truth remained that some cases received special treatment.

"In my morgue," Sienna said, punctuating each sentence with the quiet, cold clang of a drawer closing, "everyone is equal. In death, we're all the same."

Before each drawer closed, Sienna hesitated a moment, her face reflecting a forlorn sadness as she gently ran a finger down the girls' cheeks, as if giving them a proper goodbye. A hint of care in the otherwise sterile environment.

When all drawers were closed, save for the one in question, Sienna looked up. "So, you'll have to excuse me if I expected you to ignore the Goblin Girl. There are many more who have never had visitors.

It's frustrating that this woman's death is only important because of someone else's."

"That's not true," Dani said harshly. "She might be the key to this whole thing. She might be—"

"Listen to yourself talk. She's the key to *someone else's* murder. What about her *own* murder?" Sienna raised her voice, shook her head. "She's the key to her own damn murder."

Silence followed. The term *deadly silent* had an all new meaning.

"Sienna," Matthew began, but one sharp look from her silenced him.

"She died first," Sienna said simply. Her face was impassive, but anger simmered below the surface. "I can't say exactly why, but either she was the intended victim, or she was giving the most trouble. Or perhaps, the killer just wanted the mayor to watch. Though I am leaning away from the last suggestion because there was nothing sexual about the nature of their relationship. I don't suppose the mayor cared about her in any visceral way, so I also doubt the killer would have used her for bait."

"How certain are you about that?" Dani asked, looking as if she instantly regretted asking. The ME's returning glare was fierce.

"I'm positive," Sienna said. "My thorough examination showed that this poor woman—girl, rather—was a virgin. I can't tell that *absolutely* for certain, but she hasn't had sex in quite some time. Judging by the shade of her skin, the ink on her Goblin Girl license was still wet when she met with the mayor. The two had not been intimate in any physical way."

Dani nodded, biting her lip.

"You're not as surprised as you should be," Sienna said, watching the detective's face. "Why?"

"It didn't feel right." Dani's focused intently on the Goblin Girl's face. "It felt like the killer had staged it that way as a distraction."

Matthew watched as both females—the two alive—looked toward the dead in thought. They set down their battle axes and found a unique sort of harmony in working together to bring justice to those who could no longer seek it for themselves.

"They were both fully clothed," Dani continued. "I didn't see anything sexual in nature from the Residuals. What I can't figure out is why the two were together at all. They must have had a meeting of some sort, or..."

"Or she's a completely random victim," Sienna said. "Killed only to provide a distraction."

Dani looked up at her, curious.

"I mean, look at you. You're looking into her death as a key to his. What if she's merely a tool in this mess?" Sienna shrugged. "To those who commit murder at this level, usually it's a disposable thing and morality isn't a pressing issue. What's one more body—especially that of a Goblin Girl—if it'll distract the police from the real issue?"

"Then what *is* the real issue?" Dani wondered aloud. "What was the mayor onto that he couldn't tell anyone but felt strongly enough to pursue on his own—and eventually end up killed?"

The room returned back to the quiet lull that came with spending time around the dead. Eventually, Sienna ran her finger down the girl's cheek, her eyes bright with a wash of emotion, which still surprised Matthew. He'd known Sienna for years, worked with her many times, but had never seen the necromancer so affected. He wondered why, but would never ask, and certainly not in public. It was too personal a question.

"Like I said," Sienna stiffened once more as she faced the cops. "I think the killer expected the bodies to defrost so there'd be less evidence. He didn't bother to take the clothes off them because I'd be able to tell there'd been no sexual interactions. I believe he counted on the two bodies being found together as a distraction. I can't tell you much more than that, though the rest of the write up can be found in my report. If you'd like access, have Ursula pull it for you."

Dani thanked Sienna. When it was Matthew's turn, he hesitated, lingering in the cool room even as Dani waited at the door. "I'm very sorry," he said, "about the other girls. They deserve closure too. As much as anyone else."

Sienna gave a short nod. An acknowledgment of his good intention, but nothing more. "Words don't mean much. But I'm not here to argue with you. I just deal with the dead. Have a nice day, Captain, Detective."

The door clanked shut behind Sienna as she sealed herself inside the morgue and returned to her work. Dani strode quickly, firmly toward the front desk where she requested the report from Ursula with impatience.

As they left the building, a copy of the files in hand, Matthew rested a hand on her wrist. "It's not your fault. We have officers assigned to each of their cases. It's hard for Sienna to see the girls resting there, day after day, their bodies unclaimed even by family or friends."

"I should be helping more," Dani said, her lip trembling with frustration as she spun to face him. "I retired. That was selfish and stupid of me, and I should be in there, looking at the girls' faces with Sienna. Studying the causes of death. Putting killers behind bars, and yet—"

"And yet you're doing exactly that." Matthew refused to reach out and touch her because that would only lead in one direction, and he'd promised not to go there. To simply step closer to her, to breathe in her scent, would push him to the point of no return. "You came back when we needed help."

"Because the mayor died! What about all the girls in there?"

"Danielle," Matthew spoke sharply, catching her attention with the full use of her name, yet the jarring lack of professionalism to it. "You were a detective. You retired. While you will always have a streak of cop in you, there's no possible way you can blame yourself for others' senseless murders."

"I let him..." She shook her head, took a shuddering breath. "I let him control my life. It's because of him that I resigned, because *he* played me a fool."

"It's not foolish to fall in love."

"It was foolish to fall in love with Trenton."

"You're forgetting one thing," Matthew said. "It's partially my fault."

"How is it your fault?" Dani's eyes shot up to meet his. "Oh, Matthew, no. You can't blame us. The breakup—us separating—wasn't your fault."

"I broke things off with you."

"And what?" Dani raised her arms, a wry smile on her face. "You broke me? No. My choice to date Trenton was all my own."

"If we'd still been together, you wouldn't have—"

"Stop." Dani rested a hand on his wrist, the gesture surprising to both. "It's neither of our faults. But I'm allowed to feel remorse for throwing away time on him. And for letting him affect the thing I loved most: my job."

Matthew flinched, as if he'd hoped she'd say something else. Unrequited love never ceased to sting.

"I still wonder if I made the right choice." Dani regrouped, her emotions leveling as she strode toward the station. "I still don't know."

Matthew had his own opinion, but he'd given it to her before she'd left the force. She'd left anyway, despite his pleas to keep her in the Sixth Precinct.

"Anyway, sorry," she said. "Didn't mean to burden you with my choices, but—"

"If you ever want to come back," he said softly. "We'll take you in a heartbeat."

To Dani's credit, she appeared to consider it. Then she gave one last shake of her head, and the conversation was over.

"I think we go to the mayor's office next," she said firmly. "We'll talk to his assistant, confirm his schedule, and find out where he had dinner last night. Residuals are ticking down next to nothing, and we *need* to find that crime scene."

Chapter 15

City Hall wasn't far from the mayor's mansion.

Also located in Sorcerer's Square, the building sat low to the ground, sprawling longer than it was tall. The space was everything the marketplace located just south of it *wasn't*. While the markets steepled a mile high and teemed with activity and bustle at all hours of the day and night, City Hall was a gleaming white building with stone columns across the front placed in precise, even lines, and a quiet calm to the yard around it that came with the subdued nature of day-to-day bureaucratic business.

Matthew and I pressed quickly through the carefully manicured front lawn and past the columns standing guard outside the building. We signed in quickly at the front desk, secured visitor badges, and waited while a demure woman in a plum colored business skirt and matching jacket showed us to a small waiting room outside a cluster of offices. On the door to the largest office was a sign that read Mayor Lapel.

I averted my eyes, feeling almost voyeuristic when a young woman popped her head out of Mayor Lapel's office, sniffed, and pulled down the nameplate. She glanced up at the last second, surprised to find visitors, and fumbled the plastic sign. It dropped to the floor as she burst into a new round of tears.

Matthew was across the room by the time the signage hit the floor. He picked it up and handed it back, then returned across the room to stand next to me. I could feel the awkwardness radiating off of him.

"Smooth," I told him. "Very human of you to move like that."

The woman looked up at us. Her hair was dark blond and pulled back into a low bun at the nape of her neck. Her eyes were a light shade of brown, her face pretty, her posture stiff.

"Thank you," she said, though there was a hint of mystified surprise in her voice. "Um, you must be—sorry, you must be the detectives? I just got a Comm. Sorry, I'm distracted. I was the mayor's assistant, and this is all—it's just so chaotic."

I could tell she meant *tragic*, as there wasn't much chaos happening around us. One or two other worker bees moved quietly, boxing up the mayor's things to send to Mrs. Lapel, I assumed, since the crime scene techs had already combed the place earlier in the day. There'd been nothing significant in the report, at least, nothing that might lend a clue to uncovering the mayor's murderer.

"We're so sorry for your loss," I said. "And I hate to be here today in the midst of all that's happened, but—"

"But he was k-killed." Her lips trembled, and big, fat tears appeared in the assistant's eyes. "I know. It's horrible. Who would ever do such a thing? Mayor Lapel was just the nicest man."

I nodded, sensing a trend. Everyone seemed to think the mayor was a great guy, including his staff and his wife, and nobody could find a bad word to say about him. While impressive for a man in the public eye, it certainly didn't help us pick up on his enemies.

Matthew was across the room in another blink of an eye, offering the woman a tissue. "Here," he said. "Sorry for your loss."

"You're going to give both of us a heart attack if you keep doing that," I murmured when he again returned to my side. I gave the assistant a moment to mop her tears. "I'm truly sorry, Miss—"

"You can call me Verity," she said. "Verity Small. I assume you'd like to come in and ask a few questions?"

"That would be wonderful," I said. "We're sorry to impose."

"Not a problem. Do you want any coffee? Harry, can you bring some coffee, please?"

"Oh, it's fine—" I waved a hand, but she seemed to need the perk more than I did, so when a young man brought in a tray of three coffees with a somber expression, I smiled, nodded, and accepted the beverage. "Thank you."

Matthew declined the coffee, as per usual, but Verity gestured for her colleague to leave both coffees. She pulled the tray toward her as we waited for Harry to leave the room. When he did, Matthew closed the door and took a seat.

The three of us sat around a small table in the corner of the spacious office. None of us looked toward the mayor's desk. It felt odd enough to have a meeting in the office without Mayor Lapel present, and none of us were confident enough to sit around his desk.

"Again, I apologize—" I started, but Verity shook her head.

"Don't apologize. I know you're just doing your job," she said charitably. "However, I don't think I can be of much help. Like I said, he was so nice to me—to all of his employees."

"Let's start with the *why*. If you don't have any ideas about *who* wanted him dead, can you think of why someone might want him out of the picture?"

"N-no, I don't know that either," she said with a stutter. "He was the best mayor Wicked has ever had, in my opinion. I was honored to be his assistant."

"It's an election year," I persisted, jumping around with my questions—hoping to scramble her just enough so that she'd reveal whatever secrets she kept for the mayor. "Elections breed enemies."

"Not for Mayor Lapel." She shook her head resolutely.

"What do you think about Blott's chances of winning the election?"

"Stronger than I'd like to admit." She whispered this, as if it were sacrilege in the office of the former mayor. "Then again, I suppose I'm right because now he'll have no competition."

"Exactly," I said. "Which is a pretty strong motive for murder."

"Well, he wasn't exactly *desperate*. What did you say your name was?"

"Detective DeMarco," I said. "And my partner is—"

"Captain King, I know who *he* is," she said with a breathy smile. "I'm a huge fan. The mayor was, too, as a matter of fact."

I let that statement hang in the air for a long moment. It made Matthew uncomfortable, as I knew it would, and I relished in the way he shifted uneasily under her gaze. "Looks like you have a fan club," I mumbled to him. "The King Club."

I had meant for only Matthew to hear, but apparently Verity's talents lay with strong hearing because she blushed. "I only meant we thought you did very good work for the Sixth Precinct."

Her words sounded rehearsed, as if she'd spent the last term perfecting a blandness, a certain flattery, to the way she spoke. I could see why the mayor had chosen Verity as his assistant. She was pretty, intelligent, and diplomatic. One who could be trusted to manage his business affairs and personal business with a certain discretion.

I cleared my throat, startling Verity, who had been studying Matthew carefully under her thick, gorgeous lashes. "Anyway, sorry to bring the subject back to murder, but I'd like to hear who you think might've killed your former boss."

Matthew blinked in surprise at the quick change in subject—he didn't exactly appear *offended* by Verity's obvious adoration of him. He glanced at me with curiosity, his lips quirked into a smug smile which I promptly ignored.

"Take a guess," I prompted Verity. "We need help. You worked with him closely. You had to know if someone rubbed him the wrong way."

"I don't understand," she said with a frown. "I already told you—"

"I hate to break it to you," I interrupted, "but the mayor's body was found dead in a hotel room with a Goblin Girl. Let me tell you—neither of them experienced death from natural causes." I paused, wondering if I was pushing her too far. I hated to scar Miss Innocent, but time was running incredibly low on Residuals, and I had the nagging sensation that Verity wasn't as honest as her name implied. "Ever seen a dead body, Verity?"

"Er—um, no, ma'am."

"Detective," I corrected. "It's not pretty. The smell is horrible. The circumstances are generally awful. It's unpleasant to think of someone wanting a loved one dead, but the worst part? The look on their faces. Did the victim know it was coming? Did he *know* his attacker? And really, which is worse? Murder by a stranger's sword, or death by the knife of someone we love?"

By the time I finished, tears were streaming down her face. "I don't know, I swear."

Matthew stared at me, and I could tell I was testing his patience. I truly disliked being so tough on an interviewee, but if the woman would just tell the damn truth things would be so much easier.

"She's said she doesn't know," Captain King said softly, and we reverted into a good cop, bad cop routine we'd played out several times before. "That's good enough for now, Detective. Verity, can I get you a glass of water? Maybe we can chat a bit more about your work for the mayor—nothing that should cause you stress."

"Wouldn't want to cause *stress* to the King fan club," I muttered.

Verity didn't hear me. Her eyes were focused on Matthew as she nodded gratefully. Matthew ignored me and retrieved the water, returned, and launched into the tedious business of background information gathering.

Throughout his inquiry, we learned that Verity had worked for the mayor officially since day one of his term—and even before. She'd helped him campaign for office in a volunteer position. She lived alone, was twenty-seven years old, and had one cat.

Verity had never held another job, and if the mayor hadn't been elected for the next term, she had no idea where she might go or what she might do. She'd been confident in Mayor Lapel's reelection so thoroughly that she hadn't looked for work elsewhere, despite Homer Blott's strong chance at making a run for office.

"Now what will you do for work?" I asked, easing back in with a gentler tone. Verity still looked at me like a skittish cat, and I raised a hand. "I'm sorry to ask, and you don't have to answer."

"No, no, that's fine," she said, accepting my olive branch of a truce. "The answer is really that...I don't know. I might look elsewhere within City Hall—I enjoy working here, and I live close by. I excel at my job, but I just can't imagine working for anyone other than Mayor Lapel."

"If Blott asked you on as his assistant, would you take the job?"

She looked at me, pained. "I don't know, Detective. Honest answer. I suppose it'd be smart to consider it, but...he's not like Mayor Lapel."

"What do you mean by that?"

Verity cringed, as if she'd said too much. "I don't know him well enough to say. But he seems...rough around the edges."

"Rough in what way?" I asked. "Rough in a murderous sort of way?"

"No!" She recoiled. "That's why I didn't say anything earlier. I don't think anyone would kill over the mayoral office, including Homer. It's really a thankless job. I'm just not certain he has the best interests at heart for the borough."

"Fair enough," I said, sensing that I wouldn't get more out of her on the subject. "Last questions and then we'll leave you to things here. Could you please go over the mayor's schedule for yesterday? Don't leave anything out."

She took a shuddering breath, then nodded. "It was a fairly typical day. At least, recently."

I took in her words, matching them up with the testimonies from the rest of his staff. It was a nearly universal truth that Mayor Lapel's schedule had changed six months ago, but it appeared nobody could quite put their finger on *why*.

"He had breakfast at home, or so I assume, because he didn't have me order bagels like he does sometimes. He was in meetings all morning—I have a copy of his schedule somewhere that you can have."

She fished around on the shelves behind her for a notepad and pulled it toward her. Cracking it open, she found the page labeled with yesterday's date and studied it for a long moment. His schedule was neatly handwritten with notes up and down each side in careful, precise script.

With a sudden burst of frustration, she tore the page out and thrust it across the table. "Guess I won't be needing this anymore."

Matthew's eyes focused on the sheet of paper and studied the schedule. My gaze lingered longer on Verity as she raised a hand to wipe across her eyes. The woman appeared truly distraught. I wondered why. Mayor Lapel might have been a fair, good head for Wicked, but really, was it only the loss of a leader that had Verity upset?

"It looks like you have lunch blocked off here, but no details to accompany it?" I raised my eyes to study Verity. "Is that typical?"

"The last few months—I think six or seven months—he started blocking off lunch hour," she said uneasily. "I don't know where he went."

"You didn't find that odd?"

"I did at first." She puzzled on it. "But I assumed he was meeting his wife somewhere."

I gave a shrug. "Seems to me he would've just told you, like he did on the other days." I pointed to a notation the week before. **DIN-**

NER WITH MRS. LAPEL. "It looks like he had you schedule all of his other dates with his wife."

"I-I really don't know where he went. I figured he had private business to take care of, but it wasn't my duty to ask him about it. Lunch was his personal time."

"I'm just finding it hard to believe that you cared so much," I said, giving a pointed look to the pile of tissues in the trash can next to the desk, "yet you didn't look into your boss's odd change of behavior even a little. Did you suspect he was meeting Goblin Girls?"

I was goading her on, and it worked.

"It wasn't an affair or anything of the sort, okay?" she said, defensive. "He was an honest man. Mayor Lapel and his wife were the perfect couple."

"Then what was it, Verity? He's dead now. The only way you can help him is to be honest with us."

Her lip trembled. "But—"

"What is it?" I asked, softer. "Please, you have to trust us. Someone killed him. Think of Mrs. Lapel, of everyone who loved him. Think of the office, of Wicked—we all want to see his killer brought to justice."

"I-I think he was involved in The Void."

That announcement was a shock to both myself and Matthew. Matthew rarely flinched, rarely showed any emotion at all unless it was something carefully construed, but this time he couldn't seem to help it. The slight widening of his eyes and straightening of his shoulders was a dead giveaway.

"What do you mean?" Matthew recovered first, inching up the underlying, calming drawl to his voice in order to coax the truth from Mayor Lapel's assistant. "What would the mayor have been doing with The Void?"

"He—well, he stopped spending so much time with his wife," Verity said, reluctance scrawled on her face. "I only know that from the appointments. And the number of times she called here asking where he was...when I thought he was with her. I covered for him most of the time, but it got tiresome."

"Did you ever confront him?"

"Yes, twice," she said. "The first, he brushed me off with an explanation about his campaign. I believed him, actually—thought maybe he was meeting with a marketing team or the elves or something, or at the worst, maybe adding a hint of magic to the advertising campaign."

She blushed, as that was considered illegal when running for public office. But it was also a rule that candidates rarely followed and were even more rarely punished for—it was the mayoral equivalent of littering. Frowned upon, technically illegal, but not often punished by law.

"That wasn't it?" I asked. "What about the second time?"

"It was a few weeks ago," she said on a sigh. "He missed his anniversary with his wife. I didn't cover for him; I trusted him, I still do to this day. But he was so wrapped up in whatever it was that he was allowing it to devour him. I told him if he didn't let up, it would..."

"It would what, Verity?"

Her lip quivered. "It would kill him."

I gave Matthew a look that said we might have finally caught our first break in the case. It wasn't much, but Verity was the first person we'd had outwardly admit the mayor had a secret.

"Did you ever hear, or see, or find anything that tipped you off to what he might be doing?" I asked. "It says here he had dinner plans on the night he died, but there's no location."

"No," she said. "He didn't give me any location. He made his own reservations—normally that would be unusual for him, but over the last few months..."

"He'd started making his own private reservations," I said with a nod. "I see. I sense there's still something you're not telling us, Verity."

"Trust us," Matthew added, "we don't want to smear Mayor Lapel's name through mud any more than you do. But he deserves justice, as well as his wife—and to some degree, even the public. We need your help."

She tilted her chin upward. "I'm only telling you this because I know he was innocent. Whatever he was doing—it was important."

"How are you so convinced?" I asked. "He kept secrets from you."

"But he didn't want to," she argued. "I could see it was killing him to be hiding things. He wouldn't have done so if there was another way. Haven't you ever had anyone you trust—implicitly—no matter what?"

"Yes," I said, my jaw set. "And I was wrong about him."

"Then you don't know what I mean," she shot back, "because you trusted the wrong person. The mayor was one of the good guys—I swear it."

"Where'd he go last night, Verity? I think you know."

Her eyes flashed in anger, but fueling it was the deep pain of loss. I knew the combination well.

"I wasn't supposed to know," she said softly, "but the restaurant called to confirm his reservation, and I answered. I never got the chance to tell him before he..."

"Where?"

"The Hollow Haven," she said. "Early dinner for two."

We spent the next few minutes wrapping things up with Verity, but it appeared we'd drained her—mentally, physically, emotionally. She was wiped out, and the second her colleague reappeared to ask if we needed more coffee, she quietly excused herself and said that we could look around, but she needed a break.

We poked around, quickly checked in with her colleagues who hadn't a thing to add, and then said our goodbyes and thank-yous to Verity. We returned our passes and retreated to the sunlight, heaving a huge sigh of relief as we stepped outside onto the front lawn of City Hall.

"So, Detective," Matthew mused as we strolled between the neat rows of hedges. "I have to say, I saw a new side of you today. It was nice, in a way."

"Which side was that?" I asked. "You've seen the front and the back sides of me, and though they're nice, they're nothing new."

He laughed, the sound foreign enough that it made me smile. The genuine grin shared between us was so pleasant that for a moment, it felt like old times. "Sure, but that's not what I meant."

"Oh?"

"Jealousy, Detective—it's not a good color on you."

"What are you talking about, Captain? I don't understand."

"I think someone's offended by their lack of fan club."

I rolled my eyes. "You think Verity's little King Club had me turning green? Think again. While you're signing autographs, I'll be doing my job: locking up killers and bringing justice to the world, one homicide at a time."

"Sure." He leaned in, gave me a little elbow that was hard as stone against my ribs. It was a struggle not to wince in pain. "If you want an autograph, I can spare one for you."

"With all due respect, Captain," I said, "shove it."

He laughed again, and we continued toward the center of Sorcerer's Square, stopping along the way when I spotted a nearby food truck.

"We have two options," Matthew said as we hopped in line. "We need to visit Blott, and we have to check out the Hollow Haven."

I ordered a Hex Dog with extra ketchup. Matthew wrinkled his nose in distaste. After I received my food, we made our way to a nearby bench and sat next to one another.

"Best case scenario, we have six hours left on the Residuals," I said, checking the time and noting the late afternoon hour. "Worst case, we'll have under two at the real crime scene. If we want any chance of finding it, we have to split up."

"I don't like that plan."

"Because I'm a *special consultant*?" I raised an eyebrow and polished off the Hex Dog. "You're going to have to trust me. Let me tackle Blott—I want to check out his hands for any lingering Residuals of Moving Magic."

"But the Hollow Haven—"

"It's a bar in the middle of the marketplace," I told him with an eyeroll. "Any Residuals will be so swamped and diluted by the flow of people in and out that I won't do any good there. You can work your pretty little voice magic and get some poor, unsuspecting lady bartender to spill her guts to you. Then we'll meet up."

"You wax poetry, Detective."

I stood. "Time's ticking. I'll meet you at the bar after?"

Matthew stood. "Don't push Blott too far, DeMarco. He's likely the next mayor of the borough now that Lapel's out of the way. If you screw this up, and he makes my job hell..."

"Understood," I said, wrinkling my nose. "Though I appreciate the confidence."

"Good luck, Detective."

"Aye, aye, Captain."

Chapter 16

Councilman Blott had set up shop on the cusp of the Golden District and the Goblin Grid—close enough to the glitzy high-end shopping to appear successful, just far enough across the border into the goblin territory to be affordable.

I knocked on the front door of a sweeping Victorian mansion that had been repurposed from an old wedding dress shop into campaign headquarters for Homer Blott. The shop had closed a few years back due to the fact that no bride in her right mind ventured into the Goblin Grid for such purchases. Since then, the building had gone on and off the market as office space, a hair salon, and a shipping facility in no particular order. For the last year, it'd been back in business as campaign headquarters for the new mayoral candidate.

I greeted the front desk goblin with a smile and asked for Blott.

"Yeah," she said, frowning. "He won't want to talk to a cop. He's busy with his campaign."

"Yeah," I drawled right back. "He doesn't have much of a choice."

"Maybe a different time?"

I flashed my badge. "I'm not a cop, and I'm not here to chit chat. If Blott doesn't want to talk to me, he might not have much of a campaign left."

The goblin stared at me with a dead expression in her eyes. Unlike so many goblins, there wasn't the craftiness there, or the cleverness to try and fool me. She mostly just looked bored.

"Yeah," she finally said again. "I'll get him and see what he says, but he won't be happy."

"Well, I'm not happy either, so that makes two of us," I said, taking a small step back from the desk. "Don't worry, I'll wait right here."

The goblin rolled her eyes and stood, muttering under her breath. I pretended not to hear.

She returned a second later, joined by an eye roll that might've put a crick in her neck. "You can head upstairs to his office."

I wrinkled my nose in an attempt at fake cuteness. "Thought you might say that."

There were a few comments that had nothing to do with my being a cop and much to do with my being a witch—plus a few substitute letters thrown in for good measure—as I proceeded up the stairs.

It was common in most areas of Wicked to see old houses transformed into office spaces. As the borough had grown, it'd gone up in height instead of outward. The most in-demand properties were condos above Floor 375, which left the ground houses reserved for those large families who needed more space. Or, of course, for groups of young paranormals living in packs of five or six to a house because they couldn't afford loftier spaces.

However, most houses were on some sort of historical registry, making it so the city couldn't tear them down to build more highrises. That left us with abandoned buildings scattered throughout Wicked, and it only made sense to fill them with businesses.

The smell of dust and paper greeted me as I climbed, my hand lightly skimming the wooden old railings along the staircase. Plastered between photos of the last family that'd lived here were banners proclaiming BLOTT FOR MAYOR! I skimmed past a variety of awards the candidate had won for charity and other fine acts of service, and I wondered if the man waiting upstairs had wanted this position enough to kill for it. Power was a strong motive. Add on prestige, wealth, and seven years of living in the mayoral mansion—I could just about see it.

"Councilman Blott will be right with you." A perky woman, probably a spellslinger, greeted me from behind a rickety old desk. As she leaned forward on her chair, the uneven legs wobbled, and she looked down to balance herself. "You're the detective, right?"

"Uh, yes," I said, watching as she cursed a blue streak at the chair. "That's me."

The woman squinted her eyes closed, then pointed her finger at the wooden seat beneath the desk: "Rotten wood, I hate you so. Never ever let me go. Steady, steady, on your legs, or I'll turn you into stupid pegs!"

My face must have betrayed my concern for her spell—or lack thereof—because Little Miss Shirley Temple's wide eyes met mine for one quick second before the magic took hold.

"Oh, crap," she said, and then at once, the chair vanished and she went down with a clatter. To her credit, she bounced right back up, giving a hard kick to the splintered pile of tinder on the floor. "My stupid cousin!"

I couldn't decide if laughing or offering sympathy would be the best option, so I remained silent. The spellslinger's curly hair bounced around her pink cheeks, her strawberry-colored lips curving into an 'O' as she looked toward me.

"That wasn't a real spell, was it?" she asked, cringing. "I'm so gullible."

"No, it wasn't. But it sounded good," I said, surprised to find myself so taken by the girl at first glance. If I had a younger sister, I imagined she'd be like her—except, if she were part of my family, she'd have dark hair, a loud voice, and half the charm. "You have an older male cousin, I take it?"

She nodded sullenly. "He's only older by a day."

"I have a twin, so I know the feeling," I said, grinning. "Along with three other brothers. It was a mess growing up with them."

She gave a shy smile. "Yeah, but I bet for someone like you, it's not so bad."

"Someone like me?"

"You know..." She stuck her hand out and did a sassy sort of wave. "You're all badass and smart."

"Oh, boy, you can't be more wrong."

"I'm just..." She pouted. "I'm *peppy*. That's about all my mother can say for me. I'm not even truly magical. Any hint of a spell is one I've saved up for and got off the shelves! Stupid peg leg bullshit."

I couldn't help it. I cracked up, doubling over in laughter at her honesty. There was something so innately likeable about this woman, regardless of the fact I didn't even know her name. As soon as I calmed enough to speak, I asked for it.

"I'm Willa. Willa Bloomer," she said in a faint British accent, wincing as she glanced my way. "I know, I could never be as badass as you with a name like that."

"Out of curiosity, what is it that makes you think I'm badass?" I gave her a skeptical glance. "My brothers would, uh, heartily disagree with you."

"Yeah, because they're *boys*," she said, a cute wrinkle appearing on her nose. "They speak a different language than us. Anyway, you are totally cool. You have that sweet leather jacket and those boots...plus, I bet you have a gun and a badge. And I heard you talking to Greta downstairs. She's a real, well..."

"Greta the goblin?"

Willa grinned. "Yeah. Anyway, I got distracted. Sorry about the, ah, mess."

"Oh, it's no problem. In fact, if you want me to show you how to—"

My offer of assistance to Willa was interrupted by the opening of a creaky door and the appearance of Homer Blott behind it. He was a tall man who wore a suit, and though he was quite wide all around, he wore the extra weight well. If anything, it added to his intimidation factor, which was already high with the scowl on his face.

"Dammit, Willa!" Blott took one look at the crumbled chair. "What'd I tell you about slinging spells in here? You want to work for me, throw the grocery store garbage away."

"Sorry," she cringed, "it was just—"

"Maybe," I interrupted smoothly, "if you supplied your employees with better chairs, she might not have to worry about using magic on the job in the first place."

Willa gave me a grateful look, though there was an air of fear on her face. "I'm sorry, Mr. Blott. I just—"

"Councilman Blott," he said, frowning at his assistant. "Pick up the chair. I want it gone by the time our meeting is over—and trust me, this won't take long."

"We'll see about that," I said tersely. "Where would you like to chat?"

"Come into my office," he said. "Don't bother taking your coat off."

As Blott walked into the room, I hung back. I gave Willa a quick apologetic glance, and then muttered a Chair Repair spell—one that had come in useful many times when I had a crappy office at the precinct—and restored the wooden shambles to a sparkling new mahogany seat.

Willa gushed silently, blowing kisses in my direction as she slumped into it with relief. It lifted my mood, something I desperately needed as I brought myself into the dimly lit office of the probable future mayor of Wicked.

"Councilman Blott," I said, extending a hand in hopes for a chance at a civil conversation. When he didn't return the gesture, I sighed. "I see how this is going to go."

"What're you here for, Detective?" Blott pressed a pipe to his lips and lit it. He neither opened a window nor asked if it bothered me. "Is this about Lapel?"

"More specifically, it's about Mayor Lapel's murder." I stood up, moved to the window, and threw it open. My patience waned. "Where were you on the night he died?"

He didn't seem surprised by my question. "None of your business."

I faced him, leaning against the windowsill as I inhaled a breath of mostly fresh air. "What do you mean, it's none of my business? You must've known that we were going to come around asking questions. With Mayor Lapel out of the way, you're almost a shoe-in for the spot."

"Eh," he said. "Things happen. Doesn't mean I had anything to do with it."

"*Did* you have something to do with it? You're not exactly convincing me of your innocence."

"Why do I have to? You don't have any evidence on me. I don't have to talk to you."

"It'll go a long way in helping your case if you do," I said. "Lawyering up looks guilty."

"I don't care what it looks like," he said with a shrug. "I've got a campaign to run, and I'm not going to let the death of my opponent stop me now. Rest in peace, Lapel."

I frowned. "Mister Blott—Homer, may I?"

"Councilman Blott, I prefer."

"Thanks, Homer. I appreciate that." Two could play his little games. "Did you kill him?"

"Look, lady—"

"Detective DeMarco."

"Sure." He leaned forward. "You obviously aren't seriously considering me as a suspect."

"What makes you think that?"

"They didn't send the vamp." Blott sat back, satisfied, in his seat. "They pulled you in—some special consultant or whatever—to take my statement as a formality. We all know they send the vampire when shit really hits the fan."

I leaned forward. "Did you do it?"

"No." He heaved his big shoulders forward, leaned on the desk. "I don't have the time for murder, nor the interest in it. I would've won the election fair and square. Now get out of my office. I want a lawyer next time, or else send the vampire."

"The vampire's name is Captain King," I said, "and he sent me here today."

"Because I wasn't important enough for him to come himself."

"That's not—"

Blott raised an arm, silencing me. He was a sorcerer through and through, albeit a dark one, an anomaly to those who were fair in spirit and absorbed in the craft of magic. He muttered a spell that sent the door flying open so hard it cracked.

I stormed through. There was another *slam* as it shut behind me.

Closing my eyes, I willed my frustration under control. Matthew would kill me if I opened my mouth and ruined things between him and the possible-future-mayor before he'd even stepped through the door.

"Deep breathing works really well when he's upset," Willa said in her sweet, musical voice. "So does picturing the councilman in your grandma's panties. Can you imagine?"

She giggled at the image, and while it didn't do much for me, I opened my eyes and smiled with her. It was impossible not to feel just a breath lighter around her.

"How do you work for that sexist, masochistic—" I stopped and bit back the worst of it. "How do you work for *him*?"

"I needed a job. He hired me," she said. "I don't have all that many talents, so I can't be picky about where I work."

"Well, Willa, I happen to disagree." I reached into my pocket and slipped out one of the new DeMarco's Pizza cards I'd had printed that listed the store's location. "I'm hiring for my pizzeria. Swing by sometime if you're interested. Even if you're not, maybe I can show you how to properly cast a spell."

"You mean it?" She grabbed the card and held it to her chest like a life raft. "You're not just saying that because you think I'm pathetic?"

I found myself smiling when I answered. "No, I swear."

"Pizza," she said in a dreamy voice. "I'm going to take you up on this, Detective. Thank you."

Blott opened the door, his eyes livid. "Did you just steal my employee, Detective?"

I turned to him, my anger so fierce at the sight of him that I didn't bother to lie. "No, of course not," I said. "I just offered to show her some spells."

"Well, then *have* her. I don't share." Blott looked at Willa. "You're fired."

"But—" Willa's mouth opened and closed. "Oh, no. I can't be fired. I have—no, please—Councilman Blott, I need this job. I have bills to pay. My mother's sick, and my cousin lives with us sometimes—oh, please no."

"She didn't do anything!" I argued, though I already knew it was hopeless. "That's against the law, Blott—you can't just fire her for no reason."

"She's showed up late to work three days this week and busted my chair. She filed two reports wrong yesterday," he said, "and do you want me to start on the amount of personal Comms she takes on the job?"

Judging by Willa's bitten lip, the councilman wasn't entirely wrong.

"F-fine," she said, gathering her piteously few things from the desk drawers. "Although, I will have you know, Mr. Blott, that your cologne does not smell nice, as I told you. It makes me want to vomit in my mouth."

Then Willa turned and stomped out of the room, and I had no real choice but to follow along after her. We moved quickly past Greta the goblin, and by the time we hit the street, Willa had completely lost her cool.

Tears streamed down her pink cheeks, and her lips curled into a pout. "What am I going to do?!" she wailed. "I can't believe I got fired again!"

"Again?"

"I really am horrible at my job," Willa admitted, toning down the wails as a group of goblins looked over at us. "It's not that I don't try, it's just...my lack of skills."

"I'm sure you don't have a lack of skills." I glanced at the business card she still clasped to her chest. "Come on, for now you can work at the pizzeria! It's not a glamorous job, but it pays okay. Better yet, I don't wear cologne, and nobody's going to yell at you."

Willa blinked dewy eyelashes at me. "Do you mean that? It sounds like a dream come true!"

I debated if that were actually true, but she seemed to mean it. And, I'd gotten the poor thing fired, so really, it was the least I could do. I smiled and nodded. "If you don't have anywhere to be tomorrow, you can swing by."

"I'm free now," she said. "I'll walk with you. Wherever you're headed. Doesn't matter to me."

"Oh, um," I said, hesitating as I struggled to find a way to tell her I preferred to work alone. Then her eyes watered again, and my resolve crashed. "Sure, that'd be nice."

"Thank you, Detective. I appreciate it," she said as we strolled toward the marketplace. "I can't wait to tell my mum about you. She'll be so happy for me."

"I'm sure my family will be excited to meet you," I said, only slightly worried about Jack falling instantly in love with her. He tended to do that with women. "And for the record, I thought you were pretty badass back there."

"Really? You mean when I told the councilman off?" She gasped. "I hated for you to see me like that. Rare form, for sure. I was just so mad, you know?"

I considered her cologne insult to be quite mild, but I nodded anyway. "Like I said, badass."

We marched to the marketplace, Willa chattering pleasantly the entire way. She only stopped talking when we reached the Hollow Haven and entered, and she caught the look of murder on Matthew's face.

Nash stood next to him, and he didn't look happy, either.

"So," Matthew said. "I hear you pissed off the councilman, got this poor woman fired, and learned nothing about the case? Do sit down, Detective. I'm all ears."

Chapter 17

Matthew enjoyed watching Dani squirm as she tried to explain. Matthew knew Blott, and he knew the man could be all sorts of unagreeable. But Dani had insisted on going alone, and she refused to learn lessons from others. Or heed advice. Or follow rules. Which was why Matthew had assigned Nash to trail after Dani in case she needed assistance. She hadn't—clearly.

Dani's fists clenched and unclenched as she studied Matthew and Nash. "Did you send him—" she pointed a finger at Nash—"to babysit me? You had me *followed* to the councilman's office?"

"I sent backup," Matthew said carefully. "Nash wasn't to interfere, and if I understand the story correctly, he didn't."

"Oh, not at all," the blond, curly-haired woman next to Dani said. The girl couldn't be over twenty-one, pink-cheeked and bright-eyed, and Matthew wondered how she'd gotten wrapped up with a seasoned, sarcastic detective like Dani. "We didn't even know he was there. He totally stayed out of the way. Good job," she added toward Nash. "A-plus work, er, sir."

"Thanks, Willa," Dani said through tight lips. "Glad you're on my side."

"I thought—" Willa's eyes widened. "Aren't these your friends?"

"It can be difficult to tell with her," Matthew said. "I'm Captain King. You've obviously met Detective DeMarco, and this is her brother, Lieutenant Nash DeMarco."

At the word brother, Willa looked knowingly at Dani and nodded. "Oh," she said with new understanding. "I get it."

"And you are?" Nash asked, looking with interest toward the newcomer. He extended a hand. "You can call me Nash."

"We're here on business," Dani snapped. "Let's be professional, eh?"

Nash blinked at her, retracted his hand. Willa leaned forward, offered a sympathetic wave, and chirped that it was nice to meet him.

"Where were you?" Dani asked Nash, then directed her second question to Matthew. "And what made you think it was a good idea to send a babysitter after me?"

"Nash is not your babysitter, nor was he sent because he's your brother." Matthew felt a bit uncomfortable navigating an argument between family members—family had never been his strong suit—but he didn't let it show. "I sent Nash because I knew you were meeting with a mayoral candidate who would not be pleased to see you. I couldn't go myself, or I would have. Nash was on duty and nearby, so I told him to swing past the offices. He did, and he saw—or rather, heard—that you handled yourself just fine. Then he left as per his instructions."

"Coward," Dani murmured, but Nash let it roll off him with practiced ease. "Sorry—this is Willa Bloomer," Dani said, turning to Matthew and gesturing to her new friend. "She's the woman who I accidentally got, uh, let go from her job. She's tagging along with me to the pizza parlor."

"For a job?" Nash asked sounding hopeful.

"No, for a slice," Dani said, still peeved at him. "Of course a job."

"But that means you'll introduce her to Jack." Nash visibly cringed. "Jack is..."

"Who's Jack?" Willa asked. "Another brother?"

Dani nodded, her jaw set. "Jack won't even look at her the wrong way, or he'll have to deal with me."

"I would believe her, if I were you," Willa whispered, pointing at Nash and Matthew. "The detective was a total badass to Homer, by the way. So was I."

Dani gestured for the guys to be seated, then slid onto a bar stool around the table and motioned for Willa to do the same. "Did you find anything here, Captain?"

Matthew's lips pursed. "It appears Mayor Lapel was never here."

"What are you talking about?" Dani perked up, an air of professionalism settling over the table. "That's impossible; if he wasn't here, where would he have gone?"

Matthew shrugged. "I looked through the reservation lists—nothing that would indicate he stepped foot in here. Obviously, he could have used a fake name."

"Did you ask around?" Dani pressed. "The servers would..."

She trailed off at Matthew's dark stare. "Yes, I asked around," he said. "Either everyone's too afraid to say something, or the mayor wasn't here."

"Well, I didn't see a hint of Moving Magic on Blott's hands, though I wouldn't mind putting some there just to keep him out of office." Dani shook her head, lamenting the very notion. "I can't believe we're going to be stuck with him as the face of Wicked. We'll finally live up to our name."

"Unless someone else runs for office..." Nash said. "The election is still a few months away."

"Yeah, who?" Dani asked. "It would have to be someone really well liked with a huge platform—I mean, campaigning began months ago. It'd be impossible for someone low profile to catch up."

Matthew stayed perfectly still, only realizing that everyone's gaze had flipped to him in expectation. He raised one dark eyebrow. "Hell no."

"You could do it," Dani said, though she sounded unsure of herself—as if she didn't want to suggest it. "You've got an excellent history, people know your name, and you'd be the first vampire mayor in all of Wicked's history. It could help in your favor."

"I said no." Matthew rested his hands firmly on the table. "End of discussion. What else did you learn about Blott?"

"That he's a mean old pig," Willa muttered. "And doesn't appreciate good employees—er, well, bad ones. I really wasn't very good at my job." She glanced around, the gazes having switched from Matthew to her. "Oh, you meant about the case. Sorry—I have to learn to keep my mouth shut."

Dani heaved a sigh. "Unfortunately, Willa's right. I was not impressed with his cooperation. He seemed offended you'd sent someone in your place, Captain."

"Offended?"

"Apparently my being a woman, sir, means I'm not good enough. I didn't, ah, stroke his ego." Dani's voice was layered with bits of emotion and flecks of frustration. "He said he wasn't actually a suspect if they didn't send the vampire."

Matthew's jaw set and his fists clenched tight. One thing he didn't tolerate was the mistreatment of his employees—by anyone—especially not for a reason as stupid as rank or gender. "Then I'll have to pay him a visit myself and set the record straight about Detective DeMarco's capabilities."

"Don't," Dani warned. "Don't make this personal, Matthew. If you go over there, you'll be giving him what he wants."

"Did he offer an alibi?"

Dani cringed. "He said he didn't need to because he didn't do it. And yes, he refused to cooperate and threatened to lawyer up. I didn't push him too hard."

"Well, you pushed him hard enough to break the door," Willa offered, her eyes scanning over the menu and not paying attention. When she looked up, she saw Dani's hard eyes on her. "Shut up, Willa," she told herself, and dove back into the menu.

"You have a thing for causing doors to break," Matthew said, a light smile breaking out. "You'll have to begin listing that on your resume."

Dani's eyes darkened. "It was his own fault he broke it. Anyway, I have to say that despite everything, Blott doesn't seem like our guy. He's cocky and arrogant, but I think he's so sure of himself that he assumed the mayoral position was already his."

"Willa," Matthew said gently, "you worked for him. Would you agree with Dani's assessment?"

Willa's head snapped up. "Me? You're asking *my* professional opinion on a case? That's *awesome*."

Matthew blinked. "Yes. Is there anything you can offer us on Blott that might help clear his name or point us in his direction?"

"I don't think he killed anyone." She wrinkled her nose. "He says he's going to all the time. I think I have a count of four death threats against me, personally."

"Jesus, Willa—that's not normal," Dani said. "You should have quit weeks, or months, ago. You should never have stepped into the place."

"I'm really not that good at my job," she said again, now sounding like a broken record. "And I needed the money."

"There are plenty of places to work that don't require you to deal with..." Dani took a deep breath. "People like him."

She shrugged. "Wasn't so bad most days. Anyway, I was saying I don't think he killed anyone because the man is just too lazy. If he ever killed anyone, I think it'd be from a fit of rage."

"I should have been there," Matthew said, frustrated. "I'm sorry I sent you alone, Detective."

"I wouldn't have let you come," she said quietly, looking to Matthew as if reading his mind. "I told you I wanted independence if I was coming back to the force, and I appreciate you giving it to me."

Matthew swallowed, wondering what it'd be like to have Dani's perception of others. She had a way of reading people—him, especially—that could feel almost invasive with its thoroughness. He had to think that was one of the reasons they'd made such a magnificent pair—he had never been comfortable discussing, feeling, or dealing with emotions, and Dani had never pushed him. She just understood.

"I agree with Willa," Dani said, moving the conversation forward before it veered too personal. "Blott wouldn't have had the patience to kill his victims with runes. That sort of death is long and slow and arduous. If it'd been Blott, they'd have been conked over the head with the nearest heavy object. It just peeves me he wouldn't cooperate and give us an alibi. It would've left things on better terms."

"What night was the murder again?" Willa asked, frowning. "Late last night?"

"That's when the bodies were found," Matthew said. "The murder happened before."

"Do you know where he was, Willa?" Dani asked her. "Did you have access to his schedule?"

To everyone's surprise, the dainty woman giggled. "Well, it's embarrassing for him, so that's probably why he didn't want to give you an alibi. I'm sure he thinks it's better for people to think he murdered someone than it is for him to admit to dating an ogre."

"What?!" Nash reacted with wild surprise, then struggled to recover. "An ogre?"

"Um, hello," Dani gestured between herself and the vampire. "Dating cross-species has been legalized for years."

"*Ooh*," Willa looked between Dani and Matthew, her face all swoony and excited. "I so hoped the stories were true about the two of you dating. You are so perfect together, and you'd have the cutest babies. Can you imagine? The little fangs."

Dani choked on the sip of water she'd taken and Nash thumped her on the back. Matthew handled things more gracefully, though Willa had rattled his cage, as well. "Unfortunately, we're no longer dating," Matthew said. "That's old history by now."

"Oh." Willa sat back. "Well, sorry to make things awkward."

"It's not uncomfortable—we work together," Dani said with a smile. "We're used to uncomfortable. But anyway, about this ogre—"

"She," Willa said, frowning briefly at Dani. "She is a very nice...creature. I met her once, on accident, and that's the only reason I know about their little rendezvous."

Dani nodded for her to go on.

"She swung by the office once, and I could tell it was unexpected. Really, you guys, she was the sweetest. She brought flowers and chocolates on the day of a preliminary vote to celebrate Blott's win."

"How could anyone like him enough to do that?" Dani asked. "Poor woman."

"You have to understand that Councilman Blott can turn his ego on and off like a faucet," she said. "When he speaks to crowds at fundraisers or the like, he really has these people believing that he's a good man. It's a skill."

"Apparently," Dani muttered. "Because he's not winning on raw personality alone."

Willa shrugged. "True. But he *can* captivate people; you have to admit that much."

"Grudgingly," Dani said. "So, what happened with his girl-friend?"

"Well, obviously I got to chatting with her. You know how I am." Willa waved a hand that insinuated them talking. "Blott was on a Comm meeting. When he came out, he was furious. And I mean an-gry. He had veins popping everywhere and his nose started to bleed. It does that sometimes when he's really upset—it's like he just ex-plodes a little."

Dani looked concerned for Willa. "What did he do when he found the two of you chatting?"

"Well, that was the first time he threatened to kill me," she said nonchalantly. "Because I let in someone who didn't have an appointment. Like I said...sorta bad at my job."

"Willa—"

"The weird thing was." She raised a finger and looked around the table, nonplussed. "He was really gentle with her. Blott just shooed her into his office. I felt bad for Olga, of course, because it was clear he was embarrassed at having her show up in public. But he really did—*does*—like her because I didn't hear a single raised word in his office."

The server arrived just then, and Willa ordered an Appletini, despite the fact that the rest of us stuck with water. The drinks arrived a minute later, and Willa took a sip and grinned.

"Anyway, when she left, Blott was in a rage. But he was also scared, I think. He didn't threaten to kill me for a few more weeks. Then he started getting all angry again, and I asked him once about Olga. I thought maybe they broke up which was why he was cranky. Right away, he got all scared and nice to me again."

"He thought you were blackmailing him," Dani said with a laugh. "And you were just curious."

"I was! She hadn't come by, and I was worried she broke things off." Willa sipped her drink, practically bouncing on her chair with the flavor of each gulp. "Finally, he told me if I asked about her again, or told anyone about the two of them, he'd fire me. I mean, he already fired me, so I guess it's safe to tell y'all now."

"What does this have to do with the murder?" Nash asked, careful not to lead her onto any answers. "His dating an ogre doesn't convict him of anything."

"No, it frees him," she said blandly. "He was with Olga all day yesterday."

"How do you know that?" I asked. "Are you sure?"

"I arranged transportation for him. I mean, he could have left Olga's and gone and done the murders or whatever, but all you'd have to do is ask Olga. She'll tell you." Willa leaned in. "It's a shame he thinks she's an embarrassment because she's not. She's way nicer than he is." Willa sucked her Appletini dry. "Olga's a great woman. She deserves better. But they have that weird sort of relationship where they just fell so hard and fast, like it consumed them. They can't stay away from one another."

"How do you know?"

"Because if Blott could stay away, he would!" Willa blinked. "He's muttered about breaking up with her every week, but he can't seem to do it. No, I think he's in love."

"But if Blott didn't do it," Nash said, "and the mayor's trail stops at his office, then we're back to square zero."

"Not so fast." Dani stood, her eyes focused on the back wall as her chair screeched against the floor. "I think we've got a pack of liars on our hands."

Willa's eyes glowed as she sensed the ramp up in energy. "Who's lying?"

"The mayor was here last night." Dani gestured toward the wall in the far corner. "That's his Spell Splash all over the wall. He sat right..."

Dani moved across the room, her eyes focused on one spot along the wall. Matthew loved to watch her work, loved the way she tuned out the rest of the world, the way she couldn't be deterred when she caught the scent of something. It was like watching her hunt.

Dani kicked two shady-looking goblins out of the booth in the corner, apologizing as they scurried away. Once they were gone, she climbed onto the booth, sat on the table with her feet on the seat, and studied the wall with curiosity. After some time she leaned forward, her hand propped against her chin in thought.

"This is weird," Willa muttered. "It looks like she's staring at the wall."

The Hollow Haven was filled with enough strange folks that Dani's actions only warranted lightning fast glimpses in her direction. Once the bartenders realized she wasn't disturbing the peace, and the other patrons noted her interest was only in an empty wall, conversation resumed and Dani was left to puzzle in peace.

"What's she doing?" Willa asked. "Are there Residuals there?"

"That'd be my guess," Nash said with a wry smile. "When we were kids, everyone thought she was a huge freak."

Matthew smiled at the thought. "And now?"

Nash laughed. "She's still a freak, but at least we know why."

At that moment, Dani slid from the booth and returned to the group. "He was here," she said firmly. "So was the Goblin Girl. And they weren't alone."

Chapter 18

"They weren't alone?" Matthew asked, his brow furrowing. "How do you know?"

"There's been a contract sealed in that booth," Dani said. "The Residuals are just barely holding on—and they'd have disappeared if they'd sat in any other seat."

Nash frowned. "What do you mean?"

"The corner booth has less turnover. The mayor sat in the middle with his head tilted back." She gestured with her hand, revealing a display invisible to everyone else. "His Spell Splash is all over the wall." At their confusion, she explained. "Residuals have a quality that's a little like dust. If left alone to settle, they might linger in a corner for some time. Even longer than the average twenty-four hours. But if left to their own devices in the middle of the room, they'll drift through the air, swirl around people as they move, cling to the clothes of passersby."

Willa frowned. "Then they disappear? I wish the dust in my apartment disappeared after twenty-four hours."

"The contract?" Matthew asked. "Can you tell the type?"

"Of course," she said. "It's nothing telling, though, or even that interesting. It's a simple Silencing Spell—a legal bind that'll prevent the persons at that table from sharing anything that was discussed."

"That could be one of the reasons nobody's speaking up," Nash mused. "Maybe they can't. They could be physically and magically bound to silence."

"Maybe," Dani said. "More likely, whoever was with the mayor was discussing something incriminating. That would also keep them silent."

"Well, I think we can rule out a romantic evening," Nash said. "On the basis there were three of them. That wouldn't need a contract."

"We rule nothing out," Matthew said, gently chiding, "until it's proven."

"Exactly," Willa said with a firm nod. "I can think of ten romantic reasons there might be three people and a Silencing Spell for their romantic evening. And that's just off the top of my head."

All three law enforcement officers shifted their gaze to Willa. Nobody wanted to admit they were curious.

"What?" Willa shrugged. "I have an active imagination, and I like romance novels."

Dani burst out laughing. Some shared female bond between them, Matthew thought. He let it go on for a moment, enjoying the sight of a true smile on Dani's face as he wondered if this burgeoning, odd new friendship might be good for her.

"Barring romance," Nash said, "I think we need to consider other reasons they might've been together."

"Or," Willa said, raising her hand to flag down a waiter. "We just ask."

"No, Willa—" Dani tried to stop her, but the server had already seen the call and approached the table.

"What can I get for you?" The server was male, a possible member of the shifter family, though not an active werewolf. The assumption was based solely on the amount of hair that covered his neck and arms. "Another Appletini? Drinks for anyone else?"

"Actually, can I get a Hex on the Beach?" Willa purred, resting her hand gently on the waiter's arm. "My friends here, they're still looking at the menu. I had to bring them by to try the flavors—they're *ah*-mazing."

The waiter seemed stunned into silence by Willa's touch on his arm. He nodded.

"In fact, I was here last night," she mused, pulling her fingers slowly back so they brushed across his skin. "We had a server who told us to say hi—the one who worked that booth. Do you know who it might be?"

Willa pointed toward the booth in the corner, and Matthew watched as Dani's eyes lit up with pride. Somehow, the lone wolf had found a friend. In a manner of speaking.

"Oh, right. That'll be Dillon," he said. "Want me to send him on over?"

"That'd be lovely. Just want to thank him for bringing us back here. But I'd still love that drink from you...?"

"Wallace," he filled in. "Wallace Prinkle."

"Thank you, Wallace." Willa waited until the very hairy server disappeared from view before turning to the group with a grin. "And that's how it's done! Sometimes when you want something, you just gotta ask."

"If this works, Willa," Dani said, "I'm hiring you on as my assistant."

"You mean that?!"

Dani's face colored. "I mean, I don't have an assistant, but if I did..."

Willa tossed her a playful elbow. "I'm joking. Though I'm not kidding about taking that job at the pizzeria if you're offering."

Dani didn't get the chance to confirm or deny the offer because at that moment, a smaller, hunched man who couldn't have been more than thirty approached the table. His eyes were dark and hooded, and purplish bruises underneath signaled a severe lack of sleep. His hands folded before his body twitching nervously, and when he addressed the group, he stared at the ground.

"Someone ordered a drink?" he said, hardly able to draw his head upward—from nerves or exhaustion, Matthew couldn't tell. "I have a Hex on The Beach."

"That'd be me," Willa said. "Sorry, don't go anywhere just yet, though."

Dillon looked up, his eyes latching first on the vampire, then the other two officers, before landing on Willa. "Aw, man! You guys are cops. I didn't do anything—I swear."

"It's him," Dani said, so softly nobody heard save for Matthew. "Residuals are a match. Ready?"

Matthew understood her at once. He gave a quick nod, watching as she stood, biding her time.

"Now," she said, and Matthew moved.

Together, they worked seamlessly: Dani brought the man down hard against the table, startling Willa into spilling her new drink straight down her blouse.

While Dani handled the physical force, Matthew snapped a pair of handcuffs to the man's wrists with startling speed and finesse. This entire process took under ten seconds and was near silent, save for the yelp from Willa as her shirt turned colorful.

"You're not going to say anything," Matthew warned Dillon softly, "because you don't want to draw attention to yourself. I'll take the cuffs off for a civil conversation if you promise you're not going to attempt a getaway."

Dillon looked dryly around the table. "Doesn't seem like I have a choice."

"Not much of one," Dani agreed. "In fact, let's head over to the booth in the corner."

At the mention of the booth, the man shifted uncomfortably against the table. "What do you want from me? You didn't see nothing because I didn't do a thing wrong. I'm just here working, attacked by the cops, and—"

"Dude," Nash said, giving a calm shake of his head. "She's a Reserve. He's a vampire. You really want to argue that you're innocent?"

Dillon hissed at the word vampire, but it was Dani to whom he looked first. "I knew something was weird about you. Staring at the wall like a lunatic."

"Unfortunately for you," Dani said, "I'm a lunatic who can see a Silencing Spell all over you. Fortunately for you, the man who made it is dead—which leaves you free to talk to us all about it."

"D-dead?"

"The mayor," Dani said. "You've obviously heard the news by now."

"But the mayor didn't slap a Shusher on me," he said, using the slang term for a Silencing Spell. "It was the chick."

"The chick?" Dani glanced toward Matthew. "I think we need to sit. Come on, you get the seat of honor. Scoot into the middle, buddy."

Chapter 19

I shoved myself on one side of the server while Matthew situated himself on the other. Dillon's slim figure was dwarfed by that of Matthew, though he seemed more frightened of me than of him.

Nash rounded out my side of the table while Willa disappeared to the bathroom to clean up her shirt and, I believed, to give us some privacy. She was already better at her job than she knew.

"He's going to remove the cuffs," I said. "And you're not going to budge, got it?"

Dillon gave a shrug.

"Thanks for your cooperation," I said dryly. I quickly introduced the rest of the table to Dillon before getting started. "We're investigating the murders of Mayor Lapel and the Goblin Girl with whom he was found dead."

"No name for her yet?" Dillon said with a smile. "She called herself Crystal. Obviously, a fake name."

"Crystal," I said, as Nash pulled out a notepad and began jotting notes down. "Last name?"

"Lady, does the Hollow Haven look like a place where last names are given freely?" He shook his head, the shadows under his eyes giving him a haunted look. "Nah. I didn't even recognize the mayor until I sat down and started talking to them. I don't think he used a Cloaker, but he'd altered the way he looked a bit. You know, a human-style disguise. A hat and all that junk."

"Start from the beginning," I said. "Did you know you were meeting them here?"

"I didn't know in advance because the chick roped me into it. I thought we had ourselves a little something romantic going because she'd been in here last week. I was her server, and we got to talking. She asked when I worked again, and I told her."

"What was she asking around about?" I continued. "This is important. Please try to remember everything."

"She was just shooting the breeze at first," he said, thinking back. "In fact, she kind of reminded me of the other chick with you."

"The other one?"

"The chick with the see-through shirt." He nodded toward the bathroom. "You know the type. Young, hopeful, all bubbly and innocent and shit. The Goblin Girl was a bit like that—she was just barely green."

I remembered the light shade of the woman's skin. "So, you two hit it off. What specifically did you talk about?"

"She asked what I liked to do for fun, you know, small talk. I told her about this new—" He stopped abruptly. "I don't think I can talk about it."

"Yes, you can—the contract is null and void. Crystal is dead, Dillon. We think whatever happened at this table helped to get her that way."

"No, I don't think so. I can't tell you." Dillon shook his head, his lips tightening. "You guys are cops. You wouldn't understand."

"Believe me, I'll understand more than you give me credit for. In fact, I'm so understanding," I said with a drawl, "that I bet I can get the vampire to go easy on you for whatever hole you've dug for yourself. You aren't getting out without a shovel, buddy, and we happen to have one we might let you use. Talk, or we'll work to get you put away for accessory to murder."

"I didn't do nothing! I'd never kill anyone! I wouldn't—couldn't, come on, lady," he said. "Don't play me like that."

I sighed. "Matthew—"

He moved so quickly even Nash jumped in surprise. Matthew had Dillon outside of the booth and marching toward the front door before I could take a breath.

"I'll talk," he muttered. "Let me go—I work here. I don't want to cause a scene."

"That's what I figured," I said, once he returned. "Thank you, Captain. Now, let's keep this friendly—and honest. I catch you lying, and we'll parade you out the front door in front of all your coworkers and your boss."

"Fine," he said, his voice lowering. "I was trying to impress this chick—"

"Crystal?"

"Of course Crystal," he snarled. "Last week. She kept asking about what I liked to do for fun, if I liked to go out, if I—whatever. I told her sure, and that if she wanted me to show her a good time, I had this new...*thing.*"

"What sort of thing?"

"I don't know the official name. It's some sort of stimulant, and I've heard a few people call it PowerPax."

I leaned toward him and caught a whiff of fried food lingering on his clothes. "A stimulant? That must be a new narcotic—I haven't heard anything about it. Nash?"

My brother shook his head, which was a big surprise. As a former narcotics officer, he kept his nose close to the ground and often heard about new drugs the second they were developed.

"PowerPax," I said. "Where'd you get it from?"

"Well, I found it."

"Excuse me?"

He shifted uneasily in his chair. "I found it."

"What did I say about lying?" I frowned, glancing over his shoulder to Matthew. "What kind of idiot picks up an unidentified drug and uses it? And how'd you find the name?"

"Fine, I didn't exactly pick it up off the street, but I'm the idiot who used it anyway." His eyebrows furrowed with concern. "There's this guy I buy SpellHash from—don't crack me on the Hash, alright?"

"The Hash is the least of your concerns," I assured him.

Oddly enough, he seemed relieved. "Don't ask me the guy's name. He was referred from a friend—he's anonymous to my friend also. These guys, they're good. They don't want any connections."

Nash gave a single nod, confirming Dillon's statement.

"Anyway, once in a while my guy will send a sample along."

"Fishing," Nash said under his breath. "Trying to hook them onto the harder, more expensive stuff."

"Fishing," Dillon said, though he seemed to dislike the term. "Sure. Well, normally I don't try it because I don't got the money to buy more, and that shit is addictive."

"Yep," I said. "Go figure. Drugs."

"Well, this time, I tried it. I ain't never seen anything like it before, and I figured it was free, and it'd be a one-time deal. Special treat, you know what I mean?"

"But you liked it," I said. "And you needed more."

"Yeah. I put in a request to my guy—don't try to find him; I'm sure he'll already know I've been talking to cops. These guys spook easily."

Nash again looked pained, signaling that Dillon was likely right.

"Sorry to inconvenience you into having to find a 'new guy,'" I said. "Keep talking."

"Lady, I'm trying to help," Dillon said. "Yeah—I needed more of it. I got my request filled the day before Crystal showed up here. I swear, it was only the second time I ever used it. I don't have any left."

"You could only afford one serving?" I asked. "Guess customers need to tip better around here. The good stuff doesn't come cheap."

"I could afford two servings, alright? But when the first one ended, the second one, man, I needed it. It was like...ugh, like I couldn't breathe without it."

"Wait a minute," I said, holding my breath as I studied him. The twitchiness, the dark eyes, the odd behaviors. "Are you still on it right now?"

"I have no clue how long they last. I took the second dose a few days after I met Crystal, so maybe I'm weaning off it. The first one lasted half a damn week."

"At its strongest, what does it do?" Nash's curiosity got the better of him, and he leaned forward, interested. Nash had a complicated history with narcotics. "How do you feel on it?"

"Dude, the name," he said. "PowerPax. You feel like you're on top of the world. Freaking invincible. I ran a mile in five minutes the other day. Why? No idea. I just could. I haven't run since...well, since my ma chased me around with a ladle as a kid to smack my behind. It's incredible."

Nash was transfixed by Dillon. "How much does it run?"

"Cost me a month of pay for two doses."

"Ouch," Nash said, sitting back in his seat.

I pinned Nash there with my gaze. "Now that the fun's out of the way, tell me what the talk was about yesterday."

"Crystal came in here, as you know, and she took a seat in the booth. I came over here to say hi to her, you know—I liked the chick."

"Where'd you sit?"

"I sat right where I am. She sat sort of where you are. The mayor joined later and took up most of the space on that side." He gestured toward the wall, directly under the place where Mayor Lapel's Spell Splash Residuals faded from view even as we spoke. "Yo, lady, is that what you were looking at? Where he sat?"

"Sure," I said, not wanting to explain again. "Where was the mayor when you sat down?"

"No clue. I only had eyes for the girl. If I had to guess, he was either hiding out in the restroom or he hadn't come into the bar yet."

"After you sat, what happened?"

"Started with basic small talk again." Dillon sat back, bit his bottom lip as he contemplated. "She seemed eager again, and excited, but a little too energetic. Like, she was zooming off the walls. I wondered if she hadn't had a PowerPax herself—in fact, I think I joked about it."

"She knew the name of the drug?"

"Yeah, well, I called it that. Didn't know it was a secret."

"How'd she react when you made the joke?"

"I guess she just brushed that part off. She did ask..." Dillon shrugged. "Actually, she asked if I had any left. Mentioned she might be interested in going out, maybe to a party together, like I'd suggested."

"Romance is in the air," I said. "But unfortunately, you didn't have any more."

He gritted his teeth.

"But you didn't tell her that," I said. "You told her sure, you'd pick some up and meet her—when?"

"This weekend," he said. "My friend's having this thing Saturday night, but, obviously that's not gonna happen. That's when she asked if she could tell me a secret."

"And?"

"I said yes, *duh*. I liked her." He stared at me like I was the idiot. "I let her put a Shusher on me—I thought she was just doing it to be cutesy. You know, like the human pinky swears or whatever. Then the mayor walked up, and the mood was broken."

"Tragic," I said. "What'd he say?"

"That's when shit got weird. I think the two of them were working together. They definitely didn't seem romantic. He was all nervous and sweaty, and she was like I said—zooming with energy. Real nervous or whatnot."

"Why the binding?"

"They wanted something from me—I guess you could call it a favor." He shifted uncomfortably in his seat. "It was about the Power-Pax. They wanted to know if I had any left, and if I knew where to get more."

"Did you have the answers?"

"No. The only thing I could tell them was that I have a pickup and drop off location in The Depth." He took a deep breath. "There's a little nook, a cave of sorts, where we trade gold for goods. I get a rock on my doorstep when there's a package for me. I pick it up, leave money behind."

"What happens if you don't leave the money?" I asked. "Ever tried?"

Nash's face turned white, as did Dillon's.

"You don't *not* leave money," Dillon said. "That's not an option. If I didn't have the money, I wouldn't pick up the goods."

"Do all your friends go into The Depth for drug exchanges?"

He shook his head. "I almost got the feeling my guy's part of the pack. He's in and out of the woods—never seems to miss a beat. I mean, nobody goes into The Depth willingly unless they're blooded, right?"

"Um, you've gone in multiple times," I pointed out. "You're no wolf."

"No, but I don't go deep into The Depth. I just pick up my stuff and get out of there. This guy—he knows the place. Plus, I've seen paw prints around the site. I think that's how he can watch me so well."

"Have you ever had a drop off or pick up around the full moon?"

He thought. "As a matter of fact, I haven't. I have to bring lights because it's always the darkest nights, it seems."

"Could be a wolf," I said in Nash's direction. "We'll have to loop in Narcotics."

"On it." Nash shifted. "But what'd the mayor need from you?"

Dillon sighed. "You know it's re-election year, right?"

"Vaguely aware of it," I said sarcastically, thinking of my interaction with Blott. "Unfortunate timing about Mayor Lapel's death."

"Exactly my point. The mayor was a cool enough dude around the borough, but the rumblings were going around. People were starting to think Blott might have something up his sleeve that'd allow him to win the election," Dillon said. "Mayor Lapel told me all that. Lapel thought that if he had something up his own sleeve, it might secure a win."

"Something such as—a huge drug bust?"

"You catch on quick. He wanted PowerPax," Dillon said. "Even the cops weren't aware of its existence. No offense, dude," Dillon said in the direction of Nash.

"How'd the mayor and Crystal link up?" I asked. "Did they say?"

"Crystal was a volunteer for Mayor Lapel's campaign," Dillon said. "But she had to drop out because she had bills. Volunteering doesn't pay."

"Right."

"So, she became a Goblin Girl. She needed the money, but she still supported the mayor's campaign in her free time."

"I'm assuming she ran across PowerPax in her line of work?"

Dillon nodded. "Some highfalutin guy was boasting about it in the casinos. I guess he said something about how the government is all corrupt, so the big dogs could hide the drugs real well from the cops. When Crystal heard that, she brought it back to Mayor Lapel. The dude started looking into things and discovered a huge web of drug trade in the borough."

"That's what the narcotics unit is for," Nash said. "He should've brought Crystal to us and let the professionals handle it."

"Yeah, but no offense, sometimes cops muck things up. Crystal only *got* that information because she was a Goblin Girl. If she'd been a cop, she'd have scared him away."

"Mayor Lapel thought if he and Crystal could work together to find some of the larger dealers," I mused, "then they could expose them just before the election. The borough would be awash with excitement over the news, and the mayor would be a shoe-in for reelection."

"That," Dillon said, "and the fact that the dude cared."

"Which dude are we talking about?" I asked. "Be specific."

"Mayor Lapel actually cared. You could tell," Dillon said. "He gave this huge long speech about wanting to clean up the city and make it a safe place for all of us who live here. Crystal totally agreed. I mean, it was hard not to agree when you heard him talk—the dude, er, Mayor Lapel was convincing."

"They were working their way up the ladder by coming to you," Nash said. "Crystal heard the gossip, heard you talking about it, put things together. They figured if you could get them some more, and they followed you—found your guy—they'd be close to the source."

"Wait a second." Dillon put a long finger on the table and tapped it. "You're telling me Crystal didn't *like* me? She just wanted to use me to get at my stash?"

"She might have liked you just fine," I said. "But yes, I do think you were a tool in the scheme of things. You were going to help get them where they needed to go. Speaking of, what was the outcome of the Shusher? Did you agree to lend a hand to the mayor and Crystal?"

"Sort of. I said I'd put in a request for two more servings from my guy." Dillon saw my searching gaze and rolled his eyes. "Yes, I did it—last night. I haven't seen a rock on my doorstep, so he hasn't delivered yet."

"Where'd you get the money for it?" Nash asked. "You're using SpellHash on the regular, which isn't cheap. I'm going to venture your waiter's salary doesn't give you a ton of extra cash to blow on a new drug that you might not even get to use."

"The mayor," he grumbled. "I got a wad of cash."

"You still have that wad of cash?" I asked. "Or did you spend it?"

"I have it."

"Well, we might just look the other way about that money since it's not in anyone's books."

"What's the catch?"

"You draw us a picture to your little drop off and pick up place, and you let us make the next pickup."

Dillon shook his head. "He'll know I ratted him out. He'll smell cops from a mile away. That's a big fat *nope*. Ain't worth a few grand to me. I can't use it dead."

Willa finally wandered back, her shirt free of liquid, but her eyebrows furrowed in concern. "I got the stain out, but I somehow turned the blouse permanently inside out."

"Bad spell?" I winced, pointed my finger at her, and murmured a Straightener Spell. "There you go."

"Ah!" She giggled, looking down at her fixed shirt. "Look at that. Thank you, Detective!"

"*She* can go," Dillon said, flicking his chin toward Willa. "That's the only way I'm taking the deal."

"No, absolutely not." I responded first, before Matthew or Nash caught on. Willa stared blankly at us. "She's a civilian. It's too dangerous."

"Exactly; she's a civilian. She'll be fine—my guy will think I got a new girlfriend or something. We'll go together."

"No, absolutely not," I said again. "Never gonna happen."

"I want to help," Willa said with a wide, earnest smile. "Please, let me help. If you can use me, please do."

"Think about it," Dillon said. "That's my last offer."

I looked around the table, sizing up Nash and Matthew. Neither of them appeared to have a solution.

"When will the pickup happen?" I asked. "We need to talk this over."

"I can't predict that." Dillon looked both ways. "I've told you everything I know. Now, if you want any chance for the pickup to happen at all, you'll let me go and we'll pretend this didn't happen."

"Comm me, the second there's a rock on your doorstep," I said, sliding over a card. "And I'm going to want a map drawn up before you leave as backup. Non-negotiable."

"Fine," he said. "But if you try to send anyone but Willa, the deal's off, and it's your head on the line. I'll deliver the map when it's time to move. I don't trust you not to blow it."

I glanced at Matthew, but before he could chime in, the emergency Comm around his wrist went off. He stood, moved swiftly into the back hall and out of sight. Dillon took advantage of his absence by squeezing out of the booth and returning to work. I let him go, watching until the kitchen door closed behind him.

"Whatever you need, I'll do it," Willa said in earnest. "I told you I've never been good at my job, but I'll try my best. I want to do good, too, Detective. Please, trust me."

I covered her hand with mine, gave a squeeze. Nash looked interested in the gesture, probably because I rarely showed affection and especially not on the job. But Willa was a special circumstance.

I debated the best way to let her down gently, but Matthew returned first. His face was gargoyle still; something was wrong.

"What is it?" I stood and moved around the table. "Who was that?"

"Lorraine," he murmured. "She's gone."

Chapter 20

"What do you mean Lorraine is gone?" I finally asked. "Where did she go? Skip town?"

"Seems she didn't show up for work today," Matthew said grimly. "Grey called her brother to ask if he'd seen her, and her brother got worried. Went to her apartment and said she wasn't there."

"So, she got spooked." I stood, threw enough coins on the table to cover Willa's drinks and our time spent taking up a paying booth, and headed toward the door. "She took off. Do you want to put out a search for her?"

Matthew's cool skin brushed against mine as he grabbed my wrist, pulled me to a stop. "What if she didn't get spooked?"

I whirled in a circle, nearly slamming into Willa as I faced Matthew. "What's the alternative you're suggesting?"

His jaw set. We both knew the answer, I just didn't want to hear it, and he didn't want to say it.

Matthew recovered first. "We have to consider the fact that someone thought Lorraine was a weak link."

"Not to mention," Nash added, walking up behind us, "that's two women gone missing in the last few weeks."

"Women missing?" Willa's face went white. "What did they do?"

Nash put his hand on Willa's shoulder in a rare display of outward softness. "Don't worry; it won't happen to you. We won't let it."

Willa's face furrowed into a frown, and she smacked his hand away. "I wasn't worried about that, you jerk, I was worried about the poor girls! I want to help get them back!"

Nash stared at his hand, speechless.

I hid a smile as I faced Matthew. "What would you like us to do, Captain?"

"If we go after Lorraine—both of us—we might lose the opportunity to study Residuals at the real crime scene," Matthew said. "We're getting close to the crime scene, but if we delay by even a few more hours..."

"They'll all be gone." I allowed myself the luxury of imagining a perfectly intact crime scene brimming with Residuals, pointing a glittering finger at the guilty party. Then I thought of Lorraine, and whether or not she'd go on the run voluntarily. She *might* have, but it didn't feel right.

"Lorraine," I said quietly. "We need to go after her."

Matthew leaned in, though he'd heard me quite clearly. "We can split up—I'll take Lorraine while you hunt for the crime scene."

"She's alive," I said. "The mayor and Crystal are dead. We have to go after the living first."

"Very well."

"Where'd the call come from?" I asked. "Any information on the last place she was seen?"

"Her brother called the station, and they directed his call to me. He seemed to think that Grey walked her home around lunch—possibly stayed to spend time with her, though that's not been confirmed," Matthew said icily. "Lorraine was supposed to return to the Howler for her closing shift and still hasn't shown—she's a few hours late and no sign of her."

"Has this happened before?"

"I don't know. I say we head back to the Howler."

"Willa, I'm so sorry," I said, turning to my new sidekick. "I'm going to have to leave you here. Are you okay to get home alone? What's wrong?"

"I want to help, too!" she said. "I've come along this far and been useful, haven't I?"

"Yes, but you're a civilian," I told her. "We barely know one another. I can't involve you in police matters."

She crossed her arms and pouted. "I gave you all that information about the councilman and helped at the bar. If I hadn't been helping, you'd be ten steps back."

"That's true, and it was fortunate you were here," I said. "But this is incredibly dangerous. And Nash is right. We have two unexplained disappearances in the last few weeks, and I'd just feel better if you left the case alone for now."

"I'll take her home," Nash suggested. "Three's a crowd, and you two have Lorraine covered. I'll walk her back."

"I'm right here!" Willa said. "And I can handle myself. No need to walk me back—I've been doing it every day of my life since I could stand, and I'm still here, aren't I?"

"Nash, why don't you take Willa to the pizzeria if she has time?" I suggested. "Jack's been running the show all day. He'd love some help."

"That'd be cool," Willa agreed. "By the way, when's my first shift?"

"Tomorrow?" I asked uneasily. "I would owe you big time!"

"Oh, perfect!" Willa returned to her natural bouncy state. Retrieving lip balm from her purse, she slathered something that smelled like strawberry across her mouth that seemed to interest both men. When she finished, she made a popping sound with her lips and smiled at Nash. "Ready?"

I had to elbow Nash to get his attention. As he did, he offered his arm to Willa like either an idiot or a gentleman—I couldn't be sure which. She looped her arm through his as they disappeared from the Hollow Haven.

"My brothers better leave her alone," I said with a groan. "What did I get that poor woman into?"

Matthew smiled, extended his arm to me. "She seems like she can handle herself. Shall we?"

I glared at his extended arm, left it hanging, and stomped out ahead of him. "Come on, King—death doesn't wait for anyone. If we're stopping Lorraine's, we have to move fast."

MATTHEW AND I HOPPED a trolley that shot us across the city. We leaped off a few feet from the Howler, just outside the shadows of The Depth.

On the way over, we'd discussed possible solutions to the Lorraine issue, but everything ended in a big, fat question. Had she left of her own free will, or had she been taken? And who had secrets to share?

The looming, unspoken suspect was Grey. He had seemed genuinely surprised about Lorraine's lack of cooperation in the back room of the Howler—but had that been an act on his part?

We marched straight into the bar and found Liesel behind it. Liesel seemed to be a permanent fixture there. He was older than me and shorter, though he had the sort of look that grew more handsome with age. Salt and pepper gray hair, a dry, wrinkled smile and a well-maintained body that complemented his calm demeanor. Even our approach didn't seem to faze him.

"Captain King," Matthew said, introducing himself as he kicked off the informal interview. "We're looking for Lorraine—can we ask you a few questions?"

"Off the record?" Liesel's eyes landed on me as he polished a glass. "You were both here the other day."

"I'm Detective DeMarco," I offered. "We're worried about Lorraine. We apologize for barging in on you, but we don't have much time."

He frowned. "You think she's in trouble?"

"I don't know," I said, since Liesel seemed more responsive to me than Matthew. I slid onto a bar stool and made eye contact with him. "She didn't show up for work this afternoon, did she?"

Liesel gave a brief flick of his head that signaled 'no'. "Then again, you guys rattled her cage pretty well the last time you were here. Have you checked her apartment?"

"Not yet," I admitted. "But her brother called the police after trying to find her. It's likely nothing has happened to her except a good spooking. I hope she just disappeared for a few days to gather herself, but..."

"Just in case, you have to act," he said. "Or it wouldn't look good on the department."

"Or it wouldn't help Lorraine," I shot back. "Most missing persons who aren't found within forty-eight hours aren't found alive. I'd rather look like an idiot and find Lorraine back to work in the morning than find her lying dead in some alley because I didn't do my damn job. Now, do you know where she is?"

Liesel's face went slack at the mention of death. "No. And I did think it was weird she didn't show up for work today. She's not the type to do that, at least not without a good excuse. If she can't make it in, she Comms. We all trade shifts on the fly, so it's not unusual to get a last minute Comm from another employee asking someone to clock in on the hour. But we never leave each other hanging—except for today."

"Did she say anything to you after we talked to her last?" I asked. "Even frustrated mumblings or things that didn't make sense?"

His eyes flicked to Matthew for a quick moment, then back to me. "She had some colorful words to describe y'all, but I suppose you don't want me laying them out."

"What'd she say about Matthew?"

Liesel visibly paled. "Nothing. Just—girl talk."

"Lucky thing I'm a *girl*," I snapped. "What'd she say?"

Liesel blew out an annoyed breath. "I don't see how it'll affect the investigation at all, but—"

"Do you want to see your friend back alive?" I pressed. "What did she say?"

Liesel's eyes glanced to Matthew again, then moved away, the glass in his hand shaking from the tremble in his fingers. He set it on the counter and gripped the ledge hard for balance. "Fine. Lorraine was mouthing off about how she wouldn't have minded if he took a bite out of her. Then she wondered why *you*, Detective, had let him go."

Matthew went perfectly still—a nearly imperceptible movement to most people, but not me. I was so dialed into him that I could tell when he was mimicking human behaviors—which was almost all the time—and when he forgot and slipped back into his natural state. This was one of those rare occasions where he'd gone all vampire.

It was difficult to break the awkward silence, but saying *something* was better than sitting dumbly with my mouth hanging open. "By chance, was Grey around when she said that?"

Liesel's gaze turned to me, real worry showing. "Look, Detective, no—that's not what I meant. Grey is a good guy. He would never have done a thing to hurt Lorraine. I see what you're trying to do here, and no—I won't let you. Grey loved her."

"You didn't answer my question."

"I don't need to! It's irrelevant." The wind deflated from Liesel's sails, and finally, he gave in and sighed. "Grey was here. I don't even know that Lorraine tried to hide her commentary—she's one of those women who looks at a Wolverine Weekly magazine and comments on the ass of every one of them. It's not my type of woman, but Grey didn't seem to mind. He's secure, you know? And Lorraine would never do anything about it. She's just flighty like that."

"But that's a magazine," I said, "not a real, live human."

Liesel coughed as I described Matthew as a real, live human, but I held his gaze until he relented.

"Sorry," Liesel coughed and lied badly. "Wrong pipe."

"You know what I'm getting at," I prompted. "Do you think Grey was jealous of Matthew? How did Grey react when Lorraine said all that?"

"Grey doesn't get jealous," Liesel said. "You have to understand. He's secure, and powerful, and young, and...well, you've seen him." He nodded toward me. "You're a woman. You understand probably better than me, right?"

I froze him with a stare—pinning him to the wall with the icicles in my gaze. The problem was that I knew exactly what he meant: I'd stood next to Grey, watched him through my own eyes. Hadn't I envied the sort of attention he gave to Lorraine, wanting something similar for myself? Hadn't I found him attractive in that distant, mechanical sort of way?

"If you had to guess," Matthew interrupted, "where would you suggest we start looking for Lorraine? Assuming she left voluntarily."

I shifted my weight in the bar stool, annoyed I'd let Liesel's words past my armor. I listened as Liesel stalled for a few more seconds, wondering what Matthew thought of it all.

"I know sometimes she walks with Grey in The Depth," Liesel said. "But they don't go in very far, and she'd only go if Grey was with her—otherwise it's not safe in there."

"When would they walk?" I asked. "During her breaks?"

He shrugged. "I don't know her schedule outside of the bar. I just remember once or twice over the course of the last few months, she'd come back with this huge smile on her face and talk about them going into The Depth together. Probably during the day, but maybe it would be evening, not sure."

"The Depth is a big place," Matthew said. "Hard to find anyone in there. Is there any chance—"

"Don't say it," Liesel said, surveying the bar even as he cut off Matthew. "Don't you dare ask if a wolf can track her. They're not dogs, though they'll tear you apart if you treat them like one."

"I was going to ask you for something of Lorraine's," Matthew said with a dry smile. "Turns out the wolves and I have something in common: excellent sensory abilities. Though it would probably be best to get something from her apartment."

Liesel breathed a sigh of relief. "I'm sorry—I wish I could help you more, but really—we were coworkers at the end of the day. Friendly, but not friends, if you know what I mean."

"What about Grey?" I asked as Matthew prepared to leave. "Have you seen him since all of this happened?"

Liesel opened his hands in question, then shifted with discomfort. "I don't know what you mean—*since all this happened*. All I know is that Lorraine didn't show up for work."

"Have you seen Grey after lunch today?" I asked pointedly. "Answer the question."

"No, I haven't." His gaze was downcast. "I think you should be going now."

We said a tense goodbye to Liesel and made our way out of the stuffy, dark bar. The tension in there had been simmering, frothing at the surface. It didn't take an astronomer to tell that a full moon was headed our way, and fast. The amount of tension, even between friends in there, had been oppressive. I was glad to be free of the stink.

"What do you make of it?" I asked Matthew once we were outside. "Do you believe Liesel?"

"I do. Now, to the apartment. We'll check it out for Residuals or signs of foul play. While we're there, I'll retrieve an article of clothing Lorraine has recently worn or touched, and I just might be able to catch her scent." We strode in silence as Matthew Commed with the station for Lorraine's most recent address. When he got off the line, he turned to me. "And Grey?"

"What about him?"

"You seemed interested in his involvement."

My eyes flashed to Matthew. "He's dating Lorraine—the first place we look is the significant other. That's Investigation 101."

"Do you think he might have..." Matthew trailed off before rephrasing. "Do you think Grey might be involved with her disappearance?"

"I don't think he hurt her, if that's what you're asking." The afternoon sun had begun to sink beyond the edges of the world. Soon enough, the shimmer of dusk would arrive, and with it, a whole host of other problems. "Now, if she ran away, do I think he might have helped her?" I shrugged. "Love makes people blind."

"Danielle—"

"Isn't this Lorraine's address?" I interrupted. "I think we have cause to go inside unauthorized, don't you?"

Matthew's eyebrows pinched together, as if he was unhappy with how our conversation had ended. But duty called, and he was nothing if not loyal to the job. "We have authorized access." He raised the Comm. "Just came through. There's an official missing persons report filed on her. We'll have about ten minutes before tech gets here to go through her things, so let's make this quick."

Chapter 21

Ten minutes spent in Lorraine's gaudy apartment was more than enough for Matthew. His senses were overwhelmed in every way: The pink walls hurt his eyes, the scent of perfumes and oils and lotions rested heavily in the air, and the sight of jewelry and picture frames and makeup on every spare surface bothered his very being.

It was a cluttered, feminine apartment, and Matthew wondered how every werewolf in the borough hadn't been alerted to Lorraine's trail by now—her scent was distinct, and it carried. Unfortunately, Matthew hadn't picked it up anywhere between the Howler and her apartment. It was as if she'd never made the journey to and from the place, and Matthew wondered if his sense of smell was failing him, or if she'd never set out to return to the bar.

He'd expected to find some indication of where Lorraine had gone from her apartment, but everything appeared to be very much in place. Despite the chaotic nature of the apartment, Matthew had the feeling that in an odd way, everything *was* exactly where it should be: it just wasn't the place it belonged in theory. Dishes were stacked on the counter instead of the sink, makeup sat on her bed instead of in the bathroom, and clothes had been thrown on the chair instead of in the hamper.

"I don't think she packed anything." Detective DeMarco lightly perused over a *vanity*—Matthew had just learned the word for the little desk, thanks to Dani—and studied the contents there. "This face cream is worth a *lot* of money. Is it sick that I want to take it?"

Matthew flicked a smile at her. "Lorraine would have your head."

"You sound so old sometimes," Dani said, looking up at him. "I really wish you'd just tell me your age."

Matthew had never told Dani his age for two reasons. One, he really was old. Ancient, compared to her, and when they'd been dating, he had worried it would bother her. So, he'd kept it to himself. Now that they weren't dating, it wasn't her business, so he still didn't tell her.

That didn't stop her from latching onto each of his phrases and trying to pin his year of transformation and birth down. She had figured one of his phrases to be from the early eighteen hundreds, but so far, she hadn't uncovered anything beyond that. If only she knew.

"She didn't pack anything," Dani continued. "I hate to say it, but I am starting to lean toward the second option."

"That someone took her?"

"Yes. If Lorraine ran and left all this stuff behind, well, that would be really smart. She didn't pack a single item of clothing or face cream or whatever. I just don't see Lorraine as being that smart. Or having that level of self-control," Dani said, and wistfully looked at the face cream. "Hell, I'd take the face cream with me, and I'm a detective."

Matthew smiled. He enjoyed working with Dani—even on the toughest cases, she could bring a smile to his face. That was important in this industry, or one began to lose their soul. If, of course, they had one to begin with—and Matthew knew all too well that many people debated the very existence of his.

"Unless she's working with Grey," Dani said. "If she's working with Grey, he would've pried the face cream from her sticky little fingers and made her leave it behind."

"You're painting such a picture," he said dryly.

He thumbed through Lorraine's explosion of things, carefully selecting a gauzy white scarf that smelled strongly of her. She must have worn it yesterday. He would hold onto it in case he needed to track Lorraine.

"Would Grey go through all that to help Lorraine?"

Dani seemed offended at the question. "Of course! He loves her. I don't know what to think about Grey, and I don't even like Lorraine much, but I believe more than anything else in this case that they love each other."

"Grey might not have wanted to get involved."

"I don't know that him helping her disappear constitutes *getting involved*. He might just want to keep her safe until this case wraps up. Do I believe he'd do that for someone he loved?" She leveled her gaze on Matthew. "I believe most people would."

"We don't know if Grey is involved with the rest of the case. What if he knows about the new drug?" Matthew pressed. "What if Lorraine's refusal to talk was her protecting him, and he realized she wasn't good enough, wasn't worth the hassle. What if he killed her—"

"No." She was shaking her head, adamant. "I don't see it. I think—"

"Detective." Matthew's voice snaked through the room, calm, secure, dangerous. "You said yourself that love blinds a person. Isn't it possible that the two loved each other despite one of their past times being illegal?"

Dani's eyes landed on Matthew's, a gentle brokenness in them. At once, Matthew regretted his words, though he knew it to be imperative to the case. Dani had suffered enough—he should have left it alone, but he hadn't.

"I think we're done here," Dani said quietly. "We need to look in The Depth. Do you think you can pick up her scent?"

"DeMarco, I'm sorry—" Matthew reached for her, but she yanked her arm away quickly. "Danielle, please."

She turned smoothly at the door, her gaze hollow. "You're right. I was allowing myself to get distracted by an emotional response."

"You have a point about them being in love; I was just playing devil's advocate. I didn't mean your situation was anything like theirs."

"Didn't you?" she asked flatly. "Regardless, I think we need to pursue all options. You're right. The most likely scenario is that Grey is involved somehow."

"Danielle, please. Don't close down."

"I'm not closing down, Captain, I'm doing my job." She cocked her head, listening. It was a sure sign of Matthew's distraction that Dani heard the techs arriving downstairs before him. "I have revised my opinion, and I believe it's likely that Grey played one of two roles in the matter: Either he helped Lorraine to vanish, or he took her himself and is holding her captive or worse."

"It's not the same," Matthew warned. "Stop it, Dani. It's not the same at all—you can't keep comparing your own situation on the job. It's not healthy."

"I know, dammit." She leaned forward, hissing in a low voice as the techs climbed the stairs. "Why the hell do you think I quit? Now come on before we have a dead body on our hands. We've got to find Grey."

Chapter 22

While Dani and Matthew launched their hunt for Grey, Matthew assigned officers to interview Lorraine's brother, other tenants of her apartment building, and girlfriends she might have called in a pinch.

The officers reported they'd found nothing. It seemed Lorraine had gone home from work in a bubbly mood—excited to see Grey during her break—and then she'd simply vanished. No Comms, no visitors, no exit from her apartment...nothing. It was as if she'd gone into her room, stepped into the closet, and disappeared from the face of the earth.

Meanwhile, Dani and Matthew returned to the Howler and repeated their questioning there, but the tension of an oncoming full moon made the air feel like gelatin—thick, sticky, heavy—and they left without any new leads.

"So, the guy has no friends, no home, no patterns," Dani said, frustrated, "except that he came to the Howler to collect Lorraine. He spent time with her, and then disappeared."

"He must dwell in The Depth," Matthew said. "Assuming he's attuned to the pack, it would be the safest, most logical place for him to go."

"We don't know if he's part of the Sixth Pack—nobody has confirmed that. All we have to go on are his tattoos."

"Fair enough," Matthew said. "Unless you have a better idea?"

"We can't—" Dani hesitated. "There's no hope of finding a werewolf in The Depth."

Matthew raised an eyebrow.

"I'm sorry, you might be fast and have a ridiculous sense of smell, but he knows The Depth much better than you," Dani pointed out. "He'll know how to hide, how to mask his trail and cover his scent."

"You forget…" Matthew stopped walking and reached for Dani's face. A strand of hair had fallen from her ponytail into her eyes, and he gently brushed it away, hating that she flinched as he did so. "You forget how long I've been alive. I might just know The Depth better than you think."

"If you'd tell me how long you've been alive, maybe I wouldn't have to guess," she growled, and he laughed. "It's not safe to go in there tonight with it being the full moon. But I don't see any other way. We have to go if we want any chance of finding Lorraine."

"The Depth never used to be dangerous for all," Matthew said. "Years ago, it was an enchanted marvel. Fairy hollows and gnome colonies intermixed. Pixies had their own set of branches and even the goblins toiled in the caves. It was all one magic forest, as it should be."

"Why did it turn south?"

Matthew gave her a sad smile. "We can't have nice things because someone will always find a way to ruin it. Now, The Depth is ruined—unless one is willing to kill or be killed. That is the last standing rule. I'm afraid it's too dangerous for you, and I'll have to ask you to stay back."

"Not a chance," Dani said. "If you're going in, I'm going in."

"Then consider this an order, Detective: Go back to the station and follow up on Lorraine's contacts. Hopefully, something will turn up and the journey into The Depth will be for naught."

"It's not for *naught*," Dani spit the word as if it tasted foul. "Dillon's drop site is in The Depth. Something is going on in the forest, and it has to do with PowerPax. Take me with you, or I'll follow you anyway."

"I gave you a command."

"And I don't report to you. I'll give you my badge back and go in as a civilian," Dani said. "Either let me stay by your side so I have a chance of making it out alive, or send me to my death."

Matthew gave the longest of sighs. "You are most dramatic."

Dani smiled. "Great. That's what I thought. Which way, Captain?"

The Howler bar was located near the forest—easy, Matthew supposed, for the bouncers to toss unruly wolves back where they belonged. Matthew idly wondered how many shifters would be tossed out before midnight. By the wee hours of the morning, surely the bar would be emptied save for the few dangerous souls who dared stray near The Depth on a night the moon appeared in full: Usually, these were the souls who didn't much care if they made it home alive.

A howl sounded in the distance, and Matthew tensed.

It had begun.

Yet here he stood, leading the precinct's most valuable resource into the jaws of the forest on its most dangerous night in the cycle. He must be going crazy to have agreed to it. Then again, he didn't have a choice. The alternative was worse, and Dani was right. She didn't work for him, and he couldn't give her an order.

She never had, hence the reason their relationship had been acceptable. Unlike many of the women Matthew had dated over the last few centuries, Dani stood up to him. She argued her points, and she didn't give in when she believed herself correct.

Also, unlike most women, she hadn't wanted to be 'his', to be a thing that Matthew loved and cherished like a childhood teddy bear or a piece of fine jewelry. She had wanted to be partners—equal in all ways, together as one entity—and that is what had grabbed Matthew and held him by his unbeating heart.

Though he wanted to reach for her hand, he knew she'd slap it away the second their skin brushed together. Instead he cleared his thoughts of her and focused on the scarf he carried in his hand.

Where Dani's scent was fierce and feminine, potent and lethal—to Matthew, at least—Lorraine's smell was like a carefully crafted bouquet of fake flowers: sickly sweet, pretty for a moment, and then too overwhelming. Dani was more like the rose that bloomed once per year—a visceral, rare beauty.

"I haven't picked up anything," Matthew said when Dani looked at him questioningly. "I think we should walk a bit. She didn't come from the bar, so we might not have crossed her trail yet."

"Wait—" Dani stopped. "We should get Dillon to make good on the map to his drop spot."

"We don't have time for that now," Matthew said. "I'll send Nash over to get the map, and we'll follow up on it tomorrow."

"What if we start there? If everything is interconnected, that's as good a place as any. We're not going to get anywhere wandering the forest blindly. It's a death wish with the full moon happening in a few hours."

Matthew raised his wrist to his mouth, turned slightly away as he Commed the station and requested the information. The officer at dispatch promised to get in touch with Dillon and transmit the results to the captain at once.

While Matthew waited, his eyes scanning the darkness around them, he noted Dani's tense posture. The tremor of concern in her voice when she'd mentioned the moon. The quickening beat of her heart. He realized that despite her bravado, she was worried.

Good, Matthew thought with the slightest of smiles—at least she wasn't stupid.

Finally, the department buzzed him back and passed along the information. "Dillon's drawing up a map at the station now," Nash said, "but I can give you a quick rundown to get started."

"Ask about Willa," Dani murmured. "Did she make it home okay?"

Matthew relayed the question, and Nash barked with laughter. "No, she didn't go home. She's still at the pizzeria! Already claimed a chef hat and is firing away at the oven. If you guys get back before closing, you'll find her there. Jack's drooling over her like a wolf pup."

Dani snarled at the mention of her brother, but Matthew pulled the Comm higher to listen, and smiled.

"Nash said that Willa can handle herself," Matthew relayed the Comm to Dani. "Apparently Jack tried to flirt with her and is missing part of his eyebrow. Not sure how that happened, and I don't have time to find out. Come on, we're heading this way."

Matthew brushed past Dani. The instructions from Nash had been clear enough: Enter The Depth and follow the jagged rock trail until it stops. Veer to the right under the weeping willow. Pass a log that looks like the jaws of an alligator. Climb over that to find a small cave.

The exchange supposedly happened in a small crevice on the right wall inside of the cave. Dillon had, as per his agreement with the mayor, put in the request for more of the PowerPax, but he'd not yet received a sign it was ready. Dillon had warned Nash it was likely his supplier was aware the NYPD were onto him.

Matthew wasn't worried for himself. The moon might be full and The Depth overrun with werewolves, but the vampire was as good as created from stone. Matthew was fast and strong, and he knew the forest well. Good luck to any werewolf trying to kill him.

The only fear he had was for the warm body next to him, her heart beating, breath coming in near silent drags as she walked. Dani had too much confidence to be considered safe in the forest at night—and he was only one man. A vampire, but a single one. However, revealing the fear he kept for her would only frustrate Dani, so he remained silent and brushed on ahead, leaving her to keep up the pace.

The mouth of The Depth opened like a gaping hole. Trees lifted high to either side while mosses and branches swung down at all angles, leaving dramatic shadows on every surface. The canopy above them knitted solidly together, and glimpses of moonlight between the heavy green leaves were slim.

The forest floor had been washed by pine needles and bramble, and at times, the underbrush was so thick it was impossible to move forward. Following the stone path was the easiest part, and as they walked, their footsteps crunched against the uneven path. By the time they reached the turnoff for the weeping willow, Dani was slightly out of breath.

"Shall I slow?" Matthew asked.

"Don't even think about it."

He continued as promised, stopping only once to help Dani over a particularly gnarly bunch of ThornThistle. They were painful when implanted in human skin, though Matthew was immune. He reached for her, put his hands on her waist, and ignored the flinch and sigh of frustration from Dani as he lifted her gently, then put her down on the other side of the thistle.

They didn't speak. That would only make her mood worse. She was already frustrated at needing assistance, and Matthew knew her well enough to keep his mouth shut. If anything, he resumed his march faster, making Dani jog to keep up with him. That way, she didn't have enough breath to argue.

They brushed underneath the weeping willow and continued until they found the log that looked uncannily like the jaws of an alligator. Maybe an hour had passed, though they hadn't been going deep into the forest—much of it had been a lateral movement along the edge. Matthew kept an escape route to civilization within view at all times. Just in case.

"Not long now," he muttered. "Should be just—"

He stopped abruptly. Dani was moving at such a clip she couldn't stop, and she bowled straight into him. It didn't hurt Matthew, but for Dani, it felt like running head first into a brick wall.

Dani bounced off Matthew, scowling, and rubbed her collarbone where it had collided with his arm. If she'd been going any faster, she just might have cracked it. "What was—"

Matthew's hand came up, pressed over her mouth. Dani knew enough not to argue. She waited, patiently straining to hear the same things he did. Since there was no chance of that, she concentrated on ignoring the electric tingles Matthew's finger created on her lips.

When Matthew was satisfied, he lowered his fingers, positioned himself into a semi crouch, and drew her near. "Are you armed?"

"Of course I'm armed," she said. "We went into The Depth on a full moon. I've got my Stunner, and—what is it?"

He frowned. "You'll need a lot more than a Stunner to take down a fully transformed wolf."

Matthew noted the mild look of surprise on Dani's face, but she recovered quickly. "I'm a witch. You're a vamp. I think we're good."

Normally, Matthew would agree, but Dani couldn't hear the light pitter patter of paws, the harder thuds when the beasts landed on stone instead of grass. They were out—many of them. Most of them had turned into animals. They no longer had the ability to differentiate between human and animal, friend or foe, hunter or hunted.

Standing, Matthew forced himself to keep an impassive expression. His ears strained on high alert. If Dillon's map was correct, they needed to go just a few more paces to arrive at the cave.

"We do a quick scope of the cave," Matthew murmured. "If the Residuals and scents come up free of Lorraine, we're out of here. We can cover the rest of The Depth in the morning."

Dani agreed with a nod.

At this point, Lorraine was either hiding somewhere safe, or she was already dead. Either option didn't call for the losing of another life—especially when that life belonged to Matthew's one true love.

Matthew had known he and Dani were fated mates from the day they'd met: It'd been a visceral, gut reaction, something in the flair of her scent and the sound of her laugh. He'd known it like a fact—like the sky was blue and grass was green. It'd exhilarated and terrified him all at once, so thoroughly that he'd pushed her far away—so far that she'd thought he'd disliked her. But the reality couldn't have been further from the truth.

Then they'd dated and, while there were normal ebbs and flows within their relationship, Matthew had been whole. Content. Matthew had been the one to break things off, but not by choice. The circumstances had called for it the moment his fang had pierced her neck—if he couldn't control himself around her, he needed to step back. At least she'd be alive.

Months had passed, and Matthew had made it his life's goal to keep away from her. It was futile. He was drawn to her, and found himself circling, protective even when she dated another. The least he could do for someone he loved so dearly was keep her safe. Allow her to be happy, and through that, he'd derive at least some joy.

Until he'd failed her.

He'd known that Dani had never truly loved Trenton. He'd seen her pain, her suffering, and her attempt to fill a void. Matthew should have stepped in sooner. He should have warned her. He should have taken care of Trenton himself when he had the chance, but he hadn't. Matthew had been so busy trying to stay away that he'd missed what was right in front of him, and Danielle had suffered.

He watched her now, crouched in the bushes as they moved together through the thick, twisted weeds. *Yes*, he thought. He could spend a lifetime with her—*and his lifetime lasted forever*.

She was all he'd need... but he couldn't have her.

Not just yet, at least.

"There it is," Dani said. "Matthew, are you paying attention?"

He'd been torn between listening to the rhythmic beat of paws in the distance and the tune of his own reveries. And just like that, he'd missed it. That was the problem with his being around Dani—he got distracted. And that was a dangerous thing.

Holding back a hiss of disapproval at himself, he stepped in front of Dani and, keeping their bodies close, edged toward the black yawn.

The cave was in an interesting location—one Matthew had never seen before, despite his extensive study of the area. For an entire quarter century from 1802-1827, he'd decided to attempt living completely off the land and away from human or paranormal civilization. During those twenty-five years, he'd explored many miles of this forest and knew it as well as the wolves.

"I can see why this would be a good spot for a drop-off," Dani said. "Distinctive."

Matthew nodded, surveyed the landscape. A stream wound through the area, and on either side sat white sandy shores, as if hundreds of plain seashells had been trampled and pounded for years to make such fine dust. A few frogs sung into the night, hidden in grasses that reached as tall as Dani's shoulder. The moon shone bright and unobstructed over it all, which concerned Matthew. Wolves drank the moonlight; they'd be drawn here.

"We cannot linger," he said. "Anything in the way of Residuals?"

Dani's eyes squinted as she studied the mouth of the cave, the edging around it, the ground before it. "Not really, but I think I see..."

She inched forward. Matthew reached out to stop her but retracted his hand at her scathing glare. He moved alongside her, crouched, listening to the rapidly increasing rate of her heartbeat.

"I'm going to need to step inside," she said. "I feel like there's a shimmer just beyond my realm of vision."

"No," Matthew said. "Let me."

"But—"

He brought himself up to his full height, towering almost a foot over Dani. His suit gleamed under the moonlight and his skin turned the softest of pales. Like werewolves, Matthew was strongest at night.

The sun didn't burn him, but the moon fed him—he was a lunar being, like his four-footed natural enemies. It had taken Matthew years of civilization and training before he could tolerate the smell, the nature, the very nearness of their kind, and years more before he'd been ready to embark on a career as an officer. Every species was equal in the eyes of the law—wolves included.

Dani studied him, her eyes flashing to a shade of violet that stunned Matthew for a moment. The violet combined with the moonlight—it was an ethereal, erotic combination that just about sent his fangs descending, his hands reaching for her. His desire to uphold his promise slipped like silvery drops of mercury from his grasp.

That's when he heard it. The faintest of sounds. Dani didn't notice, so Matthew feigned disinterest. A creature prowled behind him through the forest, hiding, waiting, predatory. Still, Matthew was unsure of the species—it didn't smell like a wolf, but he couldn't think of another creature who'd brave the forest tonight of all nights, aside from a vampire.

As Matthew inclined his head to listen, keeping his eyes focused on the cave before him, Dani turned to face him. She clearly wanted to ask what he'd heard, when suddenly, her hand snaked out and gripped his arm.

"Oh, God, Matthew—" Dani's voice cracked. "*Look.*"

Matthew followed her gaze slightly away from the cave, over to the stream they'd seen upon arrival to the drop location. He saw the body at the same moment the creature attacked. Pale skin, red stains on the white sandy shore, trails of blood picked up and carried away by the stream.

Lorraine, he thought—just as he spun and sent a fist into his attacker's face.

Chapter 23

"Matthew!" I yelled, but I was too late.

He'd heard the noise lightyears before me, which was why he'd prepared for the attack. All in one go, Matthew had sized up the sight of Lorraine's still corpse, processed it, and turned to face the creature from the forest. Matthew shifted to fight the wolf, and I used the distraction to hurry to Lorraine's side.

While Matthew launched his counterattack on the growling blur of fur, I rested a hand against Lorraine's pale white wrist, feeling for a pulse.

There was never a hope for one.

She had claw marks slashed across her face, her chest, and most of her body. The life had gone out of her hours ago, and her blood had drained into the stream, soaked into the sugar-white sand beneath her. I felt a wave of sympathy for her, but it'd been years since I'd seen my first dead body, and I'd come a long, long way with processing my emotions in a high-pressure situation.

These days, taking in the sight of the dead was mechanical—a short, essential human wave of sympathy, and then back to business. The rest of the emotions were locked away in a closet labeled *WORK*, and that was the end of it. It had to be, or I would've broken long before I finally did.

"She's gone," I said softly.

I knew Matthew heard me, but he didn't stop to acknowledge it as I stood to join the fight. His training had combined with his very nature to give him laser focus on the task at hand: survival.

I felt fear for the first time in a long while as my gaze landed on the scene. Matthew stood with his back to the mouth of the cave, retreating, while a wolf the size of a tank moved toward him.

This werewolf was huge—the largest I'd ever seen, even in training videos and simulations during my early years on the force. Those videos were supposed to have trained us for the worst, but obviously they'd failed. Unless somehow this was a new species of wolf we were dealing with—a new breed, something never seen before.

The wolf snarled as I pulled my Stunner and shot it from behind. The electrical blue strike of lightening hit just above his back haunches, and he reared up with an ear-splitting cry. The wolf landed on all fours and spun to face me. His eyes were bloodshot and wide, feral in their thirst for death.

My mind registered blood on his front claws—it stood out bright in the light of the moon and against the white sand beneath him. There was a good chance the wolf had taken Lorraine here, killed her, and then waited to finish us off. But who could *he* be? And how had he known we'd come?

As the wolf leapt toward me, I fired again, my Stunner hitting him between the eyes. At the same time, I rolled to the right and up the hill, closer to Matthew. When my shoulder hit dirt, my Stunner broke contact at the impact and stopped firing. The creature stopped, gave a dazed shake of his head, and then faced us.

"Nothing in the cave at the drop spot," Matthew said as we stood shoulder to shoulder. "We must get out of here. Someone leaked our location. I'm going to go for him, and I need you to run. Show the others where to find us."

"I'm staying," I mumbled. "Use your freaking Comm."

"Already did. They won't get here in time."

I glanced at Matthew, saw worry in his gaze. He knew, too, that this was no ordinary werewolf. "What is it?"

Matthew didn't get the chance to answer because the creature lunged toward us. Matthew and I split, spiraling in opposite directions with the practiced movements of a synchronized swim crew or a well-trained team of gymnasts. The wolf crashed into the edge of the cave. The force of it rocked the ground. It should have broken the wolf some, but a mere cry and yelp of discomfort, and he was back on his feet—this time, headed for me.

While the wolf had recovered, I'd taken a moment to study his Residuals. Oddly enough, there were some. Wolves didn't have magic, save for that of their transformation, which meant someone had put a spell on the wolf. That was the only explanation for the unfamiliar dance of dust around the gray fur. It reflected under the starlight in bright, psychedelic shades of greens and pinks and yellows and blues. I'd never seen anything like it.

"Residuals on him," I called to Matthew. "Who the hell enchanted the wolf? Wolves burn through spells in a second when they're transformed."

"Look out!" Matthew was by my side in a flash, having left all remnants of humanity elsewhere as he crouched before me.

I had half a mind to tell him I could do this myself, but the fact was—I couldn't. I had no clue what I was dealing with, and my Stunner had proved twice ineffective with its pre-programmed Stunning Spell. It was *supposed* to work briefly on a fully transformed wolf. For some reason, the charm had held no impact on him whatsoever.

If the wolf slammed me with half the force of which he'd crashed into the wall, I'd be dead before I hit the ground. At least Matthew stood a chance with his stone-like build and the lethal nature of his fangs. One good bite, a solid hit to the wolf's belly, and the nature of the fight would change in a heartbeat.

I raised my Stunner again, shot and fired. I hit him and held the button down on maximum force, but even the max setting wasn't enough to faze the beast. He leapt, dodged Matthew's outstretched arm, and landed at my feet. Its jaws opened, and he came down toward my arm. I continued Stunning him with the gun, flinching only when Matthew let out a roar that echoed for miles.

Matthew lowered his shoulder and rushed the wolf, hitting him square in the midsection. The two somersaulted together, locked in a supernatural wrestle that flashed far too quickly before my eyes. I'd barely turned to the sound of a splash by the time the two had leapt to their feet.

They'd crashed into the river and now both stood there, dripping wet—Matthew in his expensive as hell suit, and the wolf in his shaggy fur that reflected streaks of starlight in the water clinging to his coat. Beneath them, the river ran red, and I realized Matthew had taken a chunk out of the wolf's shoulder.

Another crash, a tangle that rattled The Depth.

It would be useless for me to get between them, a mere witch—I'd tear like a sheet of paper. I closed my eyes, murmured the incantation for a Security Sphere, and waited impatiently while the bubble grew to the size of a beach ball.

I lobbed the spell toward Matthew, securing it to him with a final evocation, and watched, satisfied, as the translucent bubble expanded to cover the vampire's extremities. I didn't hold out much hope that it would work long against an attack of this magnitude though.

The spell held for the first few hits of the wolf—long enough for Matthew to look over and wink—before the creature cracked it on his third launch. The bubble popped, disintegrated, and the war was back seconds later.

I reached around my waist, searching for something—anything I might use as a weapon. The Stunner had run out of juice during my last zap, and I hadn't come stocked with an arsenal of weapons. All I had was a large vial of Aloe Ale on my travel belt.

It'd been purchased from the Mixologist herself, a spell meant to heal small aches and pains, cuts and burns. The equivalent of a light dose of pain killers. I uncorked the cap, waded closer to where the vampire and the werewolf swayed in their deadly dance.

Matthew struck first, slashing the shoulder he'd already injured. The werewolf yelped in pain, toppled backward, and fell. Matthew stepped closer, hovering over him.

"Give it up," Matthew snarled. "Show yourself, or I'll kill you."

"Matthew, look out—"

The wolf had recovered faster than Matthew anticipated and lashed out, his teeth gnawing for Matthew's leg. The wolf snarled as his teeth hit skin as tough as stone around Matthew's knee, but there was a crack, and Matthew's face lost its moonlit shimmer. His expression went pale, slack, and he stumbled. The wolf had pierced Matthew's skin, broken through bone.

"Matthew!" I yelled but couldn't reach him. I was too far, and the wolf was too close. So, I did the only thing I could think of and launched the Aloe Ale directly into the wolf's eyes.

He blinked, cried out in an earth-shattering yowl that had wolves across The Depth responding in turn. Writhing around, he tried to free himself of the blindness, but it was impossible.

The wolf splashed in the stream, turning in circles, while I crumbled to Matthew's side. "Matthew," I murmured. "Matthew, we have to get out of here—it's only a matter of time before—"

"Dani?" The voice belonged to Nash. "Matthew? What the hell is *that*?"

Nash arrived on the scene flanked by at least six other officers. They stopped short at the sight of us, the sight of the bodies, the wolf howling and scampering into the forest.

"Go," Nash quietly ordered to those around him, and they took off into the woods. Then my brother knelt, felt for Lorraine's pulse, and acknowledged its absence. A light went out in his eyes, and I wondered if mine did the same when I saw yet another senseless death. "What happened here?"

"We need to get Matthew help," I said to Nash. "That's not just any werewolf."

"I see that." Nash's teeth were gritted. "Never seen a wolf's teeth penetrate vampire bone. Come on, Captain, let's get you fixed up."

"You're going to be okay." I pushed Matthew's hair back, leaned in to kiss his cheek. "I swear it. You'll be fine."

Matthew managed to open his eyes, and he smiled. "Deal's off."

"What?" I stared at him. "What deal?"

"You kissed me," he murmured, his hand seeking mine, finding it and squeezing. "Which means the deal is *off*."

Chapter 24

Nash and I hauled Matthew out of The Depth. When we neared the Howler, we roped in a flying broomstick from an old woman who lived along the way and promised to pay her back in the morning. We threw Matthew on top and, though the vampire hated anytime his feet weren't on the ground, it gave us an easier way to travel.

I lifted the front end of the broomstick and Nash held the back, though it hovered on its own. We only guided it along. The entire way Matthew cursed at the craziness of the witches and wizards who'd ever dreamed of enchanting broomsticks.

"With all due respect, King," Nash said. "Stuff it—or you can walk."

The captain shut it.

We made it to the hospital. I checked Matthew into the emergency room while Nash took care of a boatload of paperwork. My brother also sent out an alert to the chief and anyone else who needed to know Matthew was injured.

"Will you shut your brother up?" Matthew growled to me. "I'll be out of here before the alert even goes out."

"A werewolf bit through the bone in your knee," I said. "Lay down for an hour, will you?"

By the time we got Matthew in bed, he was arguing that he was ready to go. Judging by the hole in his leg, he was probably wrong. I stood guard next to Nurse Anita—a red-haired, feisty pixie whose specialty was treating cops—and gave her full permission to use whatever means necessary to treat the vampire.

"This is completely unnecessary, and—" Matthew stopped talking. "What is Felix doing here?"

I turned, unsurprised to see that Matthew's hearing had been correct. He could pick out the footsteps of any cop from what felt like miles away. "Hey Felix," I greeted the tech. "Did you bring flowers?"

"A balloon." He gave a broad grin and handed over a bright pink, heart-shaped balloon that read GET WELL SOON on it. "Whaddya think, Captain?"

Matthew's face went slack. Calmly, he picked the pen straight out of the nurse's hand and sent it whizzing past my ear with such force that a few degrees in one direction, and the pen would've taken my eye out and gone straight through my skull.

As it was, the writing utensil pierced the balloon with a resounding pop and hurtled straight into the wall beyond. It stuck there, halfway into the cement, with the limp pink plastic hanging from it.

"I liked that pen," Nurse Anita said. "I don't like you as a patient, Captain."

"Glad to see that cheered you up," Felix said as the nurse stormed good-naturedly out of the room. "How you feeling?"

Matthew barely managed a quirk of his lips upward. "How do you think? I've got Anita pissed at me, Dani saved my life, and a bum knee. I'm annoyed."

"That's not an accurate depiction," I said to Felix. "He saved my life, and this is what he has to show for it."

Felix shrugged. "I don't care who saved who, all I care is that y'all are both alive enough to see this."

Matthew and I looked curiously toward Felix as he stretched his hands before his body. His palms faced each other then spread, one of them leveling with his head, the other his waist. He held a HoloDisc on one palm, and from it, bright streaks of light snaked upward to his other palm. The hex painted a portrait.

"This guy look familiar to you?" Felix asked. "It's what the Holo-Hex artist came up with for you based on the info Donny gave."

Matthew pursed his lips, gave a slight shake of his head. "I can't place anyone who looks like that. I don't think it's anyone I've ever seen before."

"It's nobody I know," I said, staring at the face between Felix's palms. The image was just as Donny had described: reddish hair, average features, a male probably a few years younger than me. "But I can't say I haven't seen him before. I swear he looks familiar, and I hate that it's not coming to me."

"Well, think about it." Felix clapped his hands together and closed his fist over the HoloDisc, and then handed it over to me. "We'll need the HoloDisc back when you're done with it. Damn budget cuts."

I looked down at the disc on which swirling, twirling specs of light had been carefully constructed with a hex and formulated to show us the mystery man. We could flash it around the casinos, the hotel, wherever we needed—in hopes someone could place his face with a name.

"We're still working on the HoloHex for the Goblin Girl. I have the artist at the morgue," Felix said. "We'll have it to you first thing in the morning."

"Thanks," I said. "Hopefully something will trigger someone's memory, and we'll be able to get an ID."

"What happened with the, ah, woman who disappeared?" Felix asked the question with unusual sensitivity. "Is she in the hospital, too?"

Felix was an awkward sort of man—half goblin, half nymph. Nobody asked how that one had happened, but apparently it had. He was taller than me but shorter than Nash, with a little potbelly and a flop of brown hair that never quite looked fixed. He tended to wear ill-fitting jeans that were pulled up a little too high and button up shirts that always had a small stain from lunch on his pocket. In the pocket, of course, was an array of pens and potions.

"She..." I cleared my throat. "Lorraine is dead."

Felix blinked. The news wasn't a surprise to him, seeing as Matthew—a nearly indestructible vampire—had been brought to the hospital. It was a miracle I made it out alive.

"Cause of death?" he asked.

"I don't know," I said. "Nash left one of his guys behind with her body and sent a tech team out there. We'll know more later, but it looks like a werewolf, or a wolf of some sort, got to her."

He winced. "Ouch."

I gave a nod of finality because really, there wasn't anything else to say.

"Any idea which wolf?" He looked between the two of us, then gave a grim smile at Matthew's knee. "Must've been one big-ass wolf to put a dent in the captain."

"Ha-ha," Matthew groaned as Nurse Anita returned and bent over his leg, slathering a wicked purple potion that had a nasty odor onto the wound.

"This might sting," she said, and then grinned. "I'd pretend to be sympathetic, but it serves you right for stealing my pen."

Felix wrinkled his nose. "I best get back to the station. I can already hear the tech team tapping on my door and asking for overtime hours. See ya, Captain. Detective—it's good to have you back."

"Speaking of the big-ass wolf," I said, turning back to Matthew. "Do you think it was..."

"Grey?" Matthew raised an eyebrow. "It'd make a lot of sense, wouldn't it? Especially if he were involved in the new PowerPax drug distribution. Let's say they used it on Joey—a test run, maybe?—and Lorraine helped Grey deliver the dose. Or watched him do it. Either way, she knew. We came sniffing around, and he realized she was too much of a liability."

"But he loved—"

"If you give me the love argument one more time..."

"It's true! It just doesn't seem like him."

"Danielle." Matthew leveled his gaze at me, so deadly serious that Nurse Anita started a false whistling tune and disappeared from the room, closing the door behind her. "You must understand something."

I stepped closer to his bedside, keeping my eyes averted from the festering wound on his leg. Now that the purple goop was all over it, the injury was healing at an impressive rate. It was sickening to watch.

"Beings like me, we have only one mate. One love. One true other half." Matthew reached over, took my hands in his, and looked me in the eyes. His gaze was as soft as I'd ever seen it. Velvet, kind, loving—and it drew an ache from my heart that I didn't know still existed.

"Lorraine is not Grey's mate," he said simply. "And that means we can't discount the fact that he might have killed her. Before you argue—I don't doubt that he loved her. I don't doubt that they were happy together. I don't doubt any of that, but I know for a fact it wasn't..." He sighed. "She wasn't *his*."

I swallowed. "How do you know?"

"These things aren't subjective," Matthew said, his gaze all too serious. "It's like knowing how roses smell, or what the sunrise looks like. To a werewolf it's the urge to drink the moon, or for a vampire, the taste of blood. When we meet our other half, we know."

He stopped, abruptly. My heart—I wasn't sure if it still beat.

"What are you saying?" I asked. "What does this mean for us, Matthew?"

He looked over my shoulder as the door opened. Nurse Anita stood there with Nash at her shoulder.

"Those claws belonged to some sort of werewolf," Nash said, striding into the room, oblivious for the moment he'd interrupted. "But they don't belong to any legally registered shifter in the system."

I looked up at him, lifted a chin. "There's a shifter who goes by the name Grey—is he registered?"

Nash pursed his lips. "I'd heard the two of you discussing him, so I specifically checked. He's not in the system. Nor has anyone seen him since Lorraine disappeared."

I turned, met Matthew's gaze. "Fine, we'll look for him."

"It could be him," Matthew said. "But the scent wasn't quite right. Of course, he could have been wearing a Cloaking Spell, or perhaps he was on the drugs himself and it made him an entirely new creature."

The thought of a new creature, a new breed of werewolf enhanced by a drug as strong as PowerPax, was terrifying. "We need to find him," I whispered. "Before he kills another."

Nash gave a quiet nod. "First, you both need to rest. Matthew, you're staying here for the night—Chief Newton's orders. I'm going to take Dani home."

Matthew didn't argue, which surprised me.

"Fine," I said, "but give us a minute first."

The nurse and Nash disappeared, along with a tall, broad ogre that would be the security guard from the precinct placed outside Matthew's room for the night.

I turned to Matthew and looked deep into his gaze. There, I saw something that scared me, terrified me—frightened the very core of me. I saw the rawness of Matthew's soul, the way he'd fought for my life, even after I'd turned him away.

"About mates," I said, then trailed off. "Are you and I..."

Conflict rose in Matthew's face and he raised a hand, pressed it sweetly against my cheek. "No, Dani. Not unless you want us to be."

"What does that mean?"

He put his hand behind my head, pulled me toward him with gentle force. I reached for him, my lips on his as we connected over his hospital bed, my arms wrapping around his neck as his hand slid around my back and pulled me close.

When we finally parted, he sighed. "If you must know, I love you. I still do."

"You already said that a vampire can love someone," I said, "without it being his one true love."

"Yes."

"So that means..." I blinked back tears. Surely, he would have just told me if we were meant to be together and saved both of us the heartache. If I was his mate, his love, his other half—it wouldn't be so hard to be together, would it?

"Goodnight, Danielle." He kissed me once more, and this time, it tasted like goodbye.

Chapter 25

"Brother and sister out for a midnight stroll, huh?" Nash glanced over toward me. "Cute."

"I suppose." I wasn't in a chatty mood.

My mind was lingering back at the hospital on how I'd left things with Matthew. Or if we'd left things at all. A part of me felt broken inside, as if an open door had been permanently closed, locked, key cast aside into the water.

Some part of me had always assumed that my breakup with Matthew wasn't the end. It was just a temporary pause on moving forward—a break from everything happening so fast. From having to decide how to be in a relationship with someone so different than everything I was used to, but so important to me nonetheless.

"Why's this one worse than the others?" Nash asked as we walked. "You've seen plenty of dead bodies. Was Lorraine someone special to you?"

I blinked, looked up, and realized my brother thought it was the case getting to me. In a way, maybe it was, but not how he'd expected. "No, sorry—just thinking."

"Is it about Matthew?"

I looked down. "Do you think he could have done it?"

"Hell no! Plus, wasn't he with you all day? And yesterday?"

"Not Matthew—Grey. The new werewolf who's been around town. He and Lorraine were dating and nobody has seen him since she disappeared."

"Yeah, I guess he could have. I mean, why take off if he wasn't involved somehow?"

"True. It just—it doesn't feel right to me."

"Why not? You know something we don't?"

Nash smiled, but I couldn't force it. "No, that's the problem. Gut feeling, but those don't work out well for me."

"Danielle." Nash gave a knowing sigh. "You have to let him go. None of that was your fault."

"I dated a murderer, Nash!" I stopped, faced my brother. "Tell me how that's not my fault."

Nash had many similar traits as me, but so many different ones, too. Where I was plain and practical, he had swaths of dark hair and a gleam in his eyes that drew women to him from across the borough. He was handsome in an objective sort of way—not the I'm-his-sister-and-forced-to-say-it way. Even as I spoke, his perceptive eyes turned bleak, and I knew he was imagining things from my lens.

"How could you have known?" Nash asked. "He came over for dinner how many times? None of us saw it coming. Ma wanted you to marry him!"

"You were all just so blinded by me," I said. "Poor, heartbroken Dani—*we told you things wouldn't work out with the vampire.*" I mimicked my mother. "*We're just so glad to see you happy again.*"

"Dani—"

"I suppose in a way I was happy. Not that really carefree, true happy you see when a couple is absolutely, totally in love, but happier than when I'd been wallowing in the months after Matthew and I broke up."

"You didn't wallow. You went through a grieving process. You and Matthew dated for two years. It's fair for you to have a few months to grieve."

"We both know that I was desperate," I said. "By the time I met *him*, I just wanted anyone to love me."

"You're the least desperate person I know," Nash said. "You opened yourself to love, and you fell for the wrong person. It could've happened to anyone. That's on *him*—not you. Risking your heart for love is one of the greatest things you can ever do—one of the bravest. And when it works, it pays off for you."

"How do you know?" I snapped. "I don't see a ring on your finger."

Nash straightened. "Just because I haven't found the right person doesn't mean I've never been in love. I've been burned, and I'm sure I've burned others. Yes, it sucks. But I never thought you should have let it affect your job. You are the best Reserve the borough has ever seen."

"I'm not the best if the murderer is sharing my bed at night and I didn't even know it!" I snarled the last words, but it sounded like a roar in the silence of night.

We both stopped moving, and luckily, the world seemed to be empty. A full moon could do that. Save for the distant howls from The Depth and the creaky sounds of late night life shifting and settling, the world was quiet.

"I don't know what more to tell you." Nash said slowly. "Nobody believed you to be at fault—of anything. Trenton Brimstone killed two people of his own accord. Most of the force agrees that he targeted you *before* the murders so that when they happened, nobody would look twice at him. It was a cold, pre-meditated strategy of the worst kind."

"Great. He preyed on the weakling. How does that make me feel better?"

"So what you have a weakness? We all do. It's the part that makes us human. That gives us a soul. That separates us from animals."

On cue, werewolves sounded in the distance, and I was reminded of the bloodthirsty look in the wolf's eyes earlier tonight. That was all animal, I thought. Humanity burned off into instincts.

"Nobody is faulting you for opening yourself up and falling for him," Nash continued. "He was a charmer, a con man, a psychopath."

"How could I not have seen the psychopath?" I felt my legs beginning to crumble. Nash must have realized this because he gathered me up and led me to the nearest bench beside the dusty dirt road that led toward the pizzeria. "That's my job—my life, Nash. I studied killers. Learned their ways, their movements, their habits. If I'd just looked closer at him, I could've seen..."

"You did see. In time to stop him from killing again."

"That's not good enough."

I sank my head into my hands and let the moonlight wash over the back of my neck. I didn't cry—crying was for sadness, for sympathy, for pity, and I wanted none of that. The guilt sometimes felt like too much to bear alone.

Nash was right. It wasn't my fault, but it sure as hell felt like it.

And the day I'd realized it...the day I'd looked over at his face and the truth had snapped into place—the day I confronted the man to whom I'd just said 'I love you' hours before—that day had ended my career. Because if my instincts weren't good enough to recognize the man I had thought I loved as nothing more than a monster, how could I trust myself to do my job?

I stood. "Let's go."

The conversation was over, and we moved more quickly toward the pizza parlor. Nash watched me, but there was nothing more interesting than the kick of dust at our feet for him to study, so eventually, he turned his gaze forward.

"The HoloDisc," he said. "You have it?"

"Planning to take another look when we get home. Hey, have you put out an alert on Grey yet?"

"Yes. I initiated one at the hospital. Not a single ping has come in yet," he said. "Then again, I can't say I'm terribly surprised. If he's one of the pack, he'll be running around The Depth tonight and good riddance to him. We'll nab him in the morning. It's too much of a hassle to take down a fully transformed wolf."

"Speaking of..." I licked my lips and asked the question that'd been hovering on the horizon. "What happened to the one tonight? The wolf your men chased away from Lorraine?"

"He got away—had too much of a head start by the time we arrived," Nash said with a grimace. "We followed the blood trail as far as we could—Matthew really nailed him with that injury—but it's like he vanished. Just disappeared at one point, and we lost all scent. It's bizarre, Dani. I don't know what to make of it."

"He wasn't like any werewolf I've ever seen," I said. "I still wonder if that's truly what he—or she—was."

"It has to be. The strength, the build, the look." Nash contemplated. "It must be."

"But the Residuals."

"Don't underestimate the horrors and wonders of drugs," Nash said, his own past flickering behind his eyes. "Over the years, I've seen things I thought impossible happen when someone has been using—gnomes casting spells, humans defeating vampires, the strongest of wolves dying from a cut in their paw...there's no predicting whether it'll make the user the strongest creature in the world or kill them. And there's rarely an in-between."

"I'm just saying that we can't know whether it was a true werewolf or some variation," I said. "We have to keep our mind open to the possibility of a new breed."

"I've never seen a werewolf affected by drugs while they're transformed," Nash admitted. "Usually, if one of the shifters is on Spell-Hash before the full moon, the drugs burn through their system by the time they change, like most spells. It's a defense mechanism. I've never seen one last, and that's the part that scares me to death."

I nodded as we came around to the pizzeria. "You coming inside?"

He gave a shake of his head. "Jack's probably already asleep, so he can be your bodyguard for tonight." Nash winked, knowing how much I hated to be babysat. "Enjoy."

"Are you going back to the hospital?" I knew my brother well enough to know he wouldn't be going to an empty house to sleep. If there was work to be done, he'd take a quick nap and get back to it. Like I used to do.

"Might as well."

"I need you to do me a favor." I faced him, looking straight into his eyes as I spoke. "There won't be any Residuals left from the original crime scene at this point. None on the murderer's hands, either. I would like to turn my badge over. I'll still help on the case, but...I can't be considered a Special Consultant any longer. My skills are rendered useless."

Nash watched me, his eyes flicking between mine for a long moment as he waited for a punch line. When none came, he threw his head back and laughed.

I crossed my arms. "What's funny about that?"

"You weren't brought back only because of your Residuals ability. I mean sure, that's part of your talent—like Matthew is ridiculously fast and can hear a ghost fart from three towns over, but that's not why we have him on staff, either."

"But—"

"If I accepted your badge and presented it to Matthew, I'd have fangs in my neck before I could explain." Nash gave me a smile that wasn't meant to be patronizing but came off that way. "I'm sorry, I can't accept."

"Special Consultant means that I have some sort of *special consulting* skill I'm offering to the department."

"Get some rest. You're talking crazy."

"Nash! Don't pretend this is cute with me. They're paying me."

"Yes, and what a generous salary us cops make," he said with a roll of his eyes. "It's why we all do it, don't you know? For the money."

"That's not what I meant and you know it." I pulled the badge out of my pocket. "Just give it to him, will you? I'm still going to work the case."

Nash kept his hands in his pocket and the amusement drained in his voice. "No offense, but shut up, Dani. Matthew came to you because you're smart, talented, and perceptive. We didn't only need your ability to spot Residuals on the case—yes, it's an amazing talent—but that's not why he asked you. You are a good cop. I know it, Matthew knows it, and deep down, I think you know it too, and you're disguising it with this."

He threw his hand up at the pizza parlor that I'd spent eight months working to perfect. To hone the level of cozy meets family, to secure the right depth of pizza crust and the widest array of toppings. To create a business plan that would lead to affordable meals for people in the borough and still turn a profit that'd allow me to survive. At the time, it'd felt like a passion project. Now that it was done and running...I couldn't help but wonder if that's all it had been. A distraction.

"Goodnight," I said to Nash. "Tell Matthew I'll hand it in tomorrow—or don't. I can tell him myself."

"I'm sorry—I shouldn't have said that." Nash reached for me, pulled my arm back. "Come on, it was supposed to be a pep talk. It shouldn't come as a surprise that I never wanted you to leave the force. The only person who fought harder than me to keep you there was Matthew."

"I know. But that wasn't your choice to make." I gave a quick smile. "Goodnight, Nash."

I let myself into the pizzeria and shut the door behind me. I leaned against it, my heart still pounding as I waited several minutes for Nash to leave. I never did hear the retreat of his footsteps, but I glimpsed the shine of moonlight against his hair as he strode away from the shop.

He'd meant well, but it still hurt too much to hear the truth. Whether or not Trenton had been my fault, whether or not I should have quit the force—I'd made those choices, and they were done. I was the owner of DeMarco's Pizza and a former cop. That was all.

I'd turn over my badge in the morning and assist on the case as needed—just like all the other hard-working detectives. I locked the door with a huff. Life was unfair.

I hadn't asked to be born a Reserve, and I hated that the skill was wasted on someone as ordinary as me. I was the almost-youngest of five kids. A daughter. A sister. A friend. A woman. A cop. But that was it—everyone could be those things. Why the gods had hit me with the Residuals stick as a baby was a mystery to me, and sometimes I thought life would be just a little bit easier if I'd been born normal.

Once Nash had disappeared from sight, I allowed the thoughts to slip from my mind—a skill I'd perfected over the last year. I stood in the silence, thinking nothing—absolutely nothing—for one blissful moment.

At this hour, the pizza shop had gone dark. Most nights, we stayed open until the late hours of the morning. On full moons, everything closed early. No shop wanted to be the only one with their doors open—serving the bedraggled werewolves as the moon's spell lapsed and they wandered back to town, exhausted and irritable and still on edge. Though probably, I mused as I headed to the kitchen and studied the sheen of cleanliness there, it would be an excellent business model. The wolves had to be starved after a night spent traipsing the woods.

Or, I thought as a sickening sensation hit my gut, they might not be hungry at all. I'd never asked a wolf how he fed when transformed, but simple evolution and biology was probably a good enough indicator as to how they took care of that basic need.

"I'm sorry, but I heard everything." The voice came from the darkness, a pale whisper of apology. "I'm really sorry, Detective—I didn't mean to eavesdrop, but the window was open, and there was all this howling, and I couldn't sleep."

"Willa?" I pressed a hand to my chest and flicked on the light. "You scared me! What are you doing here?"

"I hope you don't mind, but your brother is a real macho man and insisted I not walk home tonight alone," Willa said. "I Commed my mother—she's fine without me, so I took the bench."

With the light on, I took a few deep breaths to calm my racing nerves and studied the room in better detail. As expected, Jack was there sleeping, dead to the world. Willa's head poked up from a nearby bench where she'd apparently set herself up with a makeshift bed.

Once the shock and annoyance had faded, another round of frustration set in as I caught sight of Willa wearing the same clothes she'd worn during the day, minus the outer layers. She had on a thin tank top that showed off the soft curve of her shoulders, and she'd piled her blond hair high on her head in the cutest of messy buns. On me, it'd all look ridiculous. On her, it looked both in vogue and adorable.

Jack had so graciously—*insert eye roll*—offered her a skimpy bedsheet he must've pulled from the closet in the upstairs hall and a pillow from my couch.

"I'm so sorry, Willa," I said. "Jack is a huge idiot. He's a fullgrown man, but I swear, he's still a child inside."

"I knew this was a horrible idea." Her eyes widened as she scrambled to her feet, revealing she wore nothing but boy shorts. "I shouldn't have stayed. I told Jack it was dumb, but he insisted, and you know me—Dumbelina over here just listened to what he said. I'll get going now."

"Put some clothes on or you'll freeze!" I averted my eyes, but apparently, it wasn't needed as she began dressing while still holding my eye contact. I knew most women were more open with nudity than I was, but I hadn't prepared for this. I liked Willa, but I wasn't sure I liked her *that* much. "I didn't mean he was an idiot for letting you stay; I meant he was an idiot for thinking it was acceptable to give you the bench. Come on upstairs—I'll get you some real pajamas and you can stay on the couch."

"Oh, don't be ridiculous. I have a bed of my own at home. I'll just be going now," she gushed. "But thank you so much for the opportunity to work here. I loved it. I hope Jack thinks I did a good job; I think we sold a bunch of pizza, and we were busy all evening until closing, so that's good, right?"

"Look at this place—it sparkles!" I gave her a broad smile. "Willa, relax. Come upstairs. You're welcome to stay with me, but I refuse to let you sleep on a bench."

Willa's eyes shifted to the corner of the room to where a sleeping bag shifted in the booth. "What about—"

"Eh. My brother deserves the bench. Let him stay." I waved at Jack, who must've been too lazy to walk home again after closing. I really should look at putting an extra futon somewhere so that he had a relatively decent place to curl up, since I didn't see his laziness going away anytime soon.

"He's really nice," Willa said, gathering the sheet around her body and tiptoeing across the room. I grabbed her purse and a few other things and led her to the stairs. "He showed me what to do, and he was so generous—except, you should know I did tell him off."

"I heard." I laughed. "I like you more for it. I'm sorry I didn't warn him to keep his hands and eyes off you beforehand."

"Oh, it was totally innocent, and I didn't mind at all. I just—I don't want to sabotage this job, Detective. I really think I'm going to like working for you."

"Call me Dani and consider your job permanently un-sabo-taged." I couldn't help but grin at her. "I'm just glad I didn't have to arrest my brother for bothering you."

Willa blushed and muttered something about Jack being cute. I pretended not to hear it because my brothers were never cute, in my opinion. I fluctuated between feeling annoyance toward them and a genuine fondness. That was about as big of an emotional spectrum as I could muster for the DeMarco boys.

I showed Willa the bathroom, the towels, the workings of the shower, and told her to make herself at home.

"Oh, thank you," she said, taking a towel and holding it to her cheeks. "I love the smell of pizza—just not on my face, you know? Also, is it totally rude of me to say I'm hungry? I mean, Jack gave me pizza, but I guess the adrenaline of the day just wore on me. Shall we order takeout?"

While she showered, I yanked open my fridge to look for food. Most takeout wouldn't be available due to the full moon. So, we were stuck with a smorgasbord of whatever I could find between the fridge and the cupboards.

"Gentle, gentle," Fred warned as I grasped him by the handle and yanked. "What the heck are you thinking, woman? You just about tipped me over."

"Why aren't you more interesting?" I snapped at the fridge. "Why can't you be filled with dainty little pastries and delicious things?"

"Because you didn't put them in me, asshole," Fred said. "And it's not like you need them, anyway. I've seen the way you plow through a box of donuts when left on the counter. It's better not to have that stuff lying around."

"I just wanted a fridge, not a counselor."

"How'd your night go, dahlin'?" asked Marla. "Did you see that fabulous vampire?"

"Yep, and a dead body," I said. "Romantic."

If a coat rack could scowl, she would have scowled. "What happened to etiquette? To ladies being home in the kitchen and raising cherub-faced babies, and letting the men do the dirty work? I loved those days. They really loved me too, you know. All these dinner parties—I had the most handsome of coats thrown on me in those days. Now, all I ever get is a spare set of keys and your ugly leather thing."

"It's not ugly!" I couldn't believe I was defending my clothing choices to a coat rack. Then again, my life wasn't exactly normal. "It's in style these days."

"Sure," she said, and I could hear the impossible eye roll. "Whatever you say, darling. Now, do tell us who the delightful young woman is who just trounced through here? She does seem like a party to me. Quite sunny, don't you think?"

Willa could absolutely be described as sunny. Bouncy, perky—nice. Willa was nice. Pleasant. Wonderful, really. It was amazing she hadn't gotten sick of me yet, what with my crass attitude and underwhelming personality. I had no problems with my personality, I just wouldn't qualify as...*delightful.*

"She's a friend of mine," I said. "Can you please all agree to keep quiet and treat her respectfully? I don't want any of this attitude directed her way. Understood?"

"Are you gonna set her up on me?" Carl sounded a bit too eager for a couch. "It's been too long since I've had some nice imprints on my cushions."

"I was going to, but apparently my couch is a pervert," I said. "She gets the bed. You get my ass."

Carl groaned.

"Yeah, and I'm going to eat dairy tonight," I told him. "So, just enjoy, my friend."

I pulled out a hunk of cheese, some saltines that probably weren't expired, and cereal that definitely was expired. Did cereal really expire though? I wondered. To me, it just tasted vaguely more like cardboard.

"Don't feed that poor girl your expired junk," Fred said. "She's a friend, not an enemy. Take some time to buy me groceries, and this embarrassment won't happen."

I shoved the cereal back in the cupboard. I'd still eat it, but he was right—it wasn't exactly food for bright and sunny Willa. I heard the shower flick off and ran downstairs to the kitchen.

I'd made a pact with myself that I wouldn't steal food from my own kitchen, but it looked like that wouldn't be happening. I whipped up a quick salad from the prepared ingredients, grabbed some pizza and mozzarella sticks, and headed upstairs. Willa was just emerging from the bathroom looking clear-eyed and smiley.

"I have food!" I held up my offerings and kicked the door shut behind me. "I'm sorry you're probably sick of the food here, but I didn't have a ton left in the fridge."

Her eyes widened. "Oh, that's perfect. Sit down, sit down. Let me fix you some tea."

"Um—"

"Yes, I know you're the host, but you had a long day at work, didn't you? My mum always fixes me some tea when I come home from a horrible day at Blott's office. She feels so awful that she can't work and help bring in money, but it's not her fault. She's so ill."

"I'm sorry, Willa. I didn't know. What does she have?"

"Sorry," she mumbled, scrounging below the cabinet, "but do you not have a tea kettle?"

I couldn't tell if Willa was dodging the question or just scattered, but I understood wanting to not talk about a subject, so I let it go. "I think I have an old one in that cupboard."

"*Voila.* You do. My mum's from England. She was born human, but went through Orientation when she met my father in order to move with him into the borough. Gave her a right bloody shock when she realized he was a wizard!"

"Does your dad...is he—" I stopped. I didn't know how to word the question.

"I don't know whether he's alive or dead," Willa said. "He left when I was four. That's about the time my mom started to get sick, and she's been going downhill since."

"I'm really sorry, Willa. I would never have guessed." I sat at the table as she popped the kettle onto the burner, already surprised by how comforting the simple image of her leaned with a hip against the stove, a finger pressed to her lip in thought, was to me. "You always seem so optimistic, and—what am I saying? I've only just met you. I guess I'll just shut up now before I get myself in trouble."

She bubbled with laughter. "No, no, it's a fair question. I guess I just think about it and figure—what do I have to be sad about? I don't want to be a grumpy old gus because my dad left when I was a kid. So what? I had a nice time with my mum. We made the best of things. Now, I am just making the best of whatever time I have left with her. When she's gone, I suppose I'll be alone, and maybe that will be harder."

My heart hurt for Willa. "No siblings?"

"Sorta hard when there's no man in the equation, isn't it?" She gave me a rather grim smile. "I'm sorry, I joke about it because that's how my mum says I deal with conflict. No, I'm an only child. I would've loved to have a barn load of brothers though, I think. Never a dull moment. My cousin—the one with the bum spells—is around quite a bit, though."

"Never a dull moment," I agreed. "Not sure that's always a good thing, but we'll go with it."

She laughed again as the kettle boiled. "Now, those teacups?"

"Um, teacups?"

"Surely you have a teacup?" Willa spun around and looked as if I'd just admitted to murder. "Well, I guess if you don't, we'll make do with this thing."

She pulled a huge mug-style soup bowl from the cupboard, and then a second plain white one with a chip in the side. From the scrunch in Willa's nose, I could tell she didn't approve, but she didn't say anything aloud.

"Sorry," I apologized. "I didn't realize teacups were supposed to be a staple."

Willa waved her hand, scrounged up two teabags from an old box I hadn't realized I had, and dunked them in. "Here," she said. "It'll do. Tell me about your day, hon."

"No, it's a drag. I don't want to bore you with it."

"Detective, you've got blood on your sleeve and you wandered in at one a.m. on the night of a full moon. No offense, but your night was probably more interesting than mine."

I gave her a wry smile. "Are you sure you want to hear about it?"

She nodded at the pizza. "We've got tea and food. The only thing that's missing is gossip. Now, spill."

I never would have considered policework gossip, but it did have that feel as I sat back in my seat and cupped the large mug in my hands. Oddly enough, once I started talking through the case, the words just kept coming and coming as if I couldn't stop. She *oohed* and *ahhed* at all the right places and looked downright exhilarated when I described the battle with the werewolf. She asked me to tell it twice and giggled with delight the second time around, cheering on Matthew in the virtual scene.

I told Willa all but the more confidential bits of the case, ending with a list of my doubts. My doubts about Grey's ability to have murdered his girlfriend, about whether or not the creature we'd fought had actually been a werewolf, and why the HoloHex portrait had looked familiar to me, but I hadn't been able to place it.

"That'd be downright cold of him, I think," Willa said with a frown. "Grey, I mean. Even if he wasn't mated for life with Lorraine—love is love, you know? I suppose it could have been a crime of passion, or maybe a wrong place, wrong time sort of thing. Say, if she was around when he transformed and it was an accident, but I agree with you, Detective. I don't think he did it."

"It's Dani," I told her for the zillionth time. "You don't have to call me detective."

"It's either detective or boss, and I feel like detective makes me sound more badass," Willa said with a grin. "But if you really don't like that, I can call you Dani."

"I prefer Dani. I'm retired from the force, and plus—you're..." I almost said she was a friend, but that was ridiculous. We'd only just met. I must be more desperate than I thought! After all, the only thing we'd done was spend some of the day together and talk over tea. But that was my brain speaking, not my heart. I knew, deep down somewhere, that Willa was the kind of friend who came around once in a blue moon. "You're a friend," I finished. "Let's stick with Dani."

"Oh, Dani." She stood up so quickly her chair flopped over, and I could hear Fred groaning at the abuse of his buddy. "You're such a great friend."

She threw herself onto me with such wild abandon that it was overwhelming. As she squeezed me to her chest, I realized it had been months, maybe years since I'd gotten a hug like this one.

Sure, when I'd gone through breakups I'd gotten the sympathetic pat on the back from acquaintances. My mom hugged me, but in a motherly way which was great, but different. When Matthew had hugged me, it'd been a firm, strong, protective stance—he'd never have thrown himself so freely at me for fear of breaking my bones.

I hugged her back.

When we parted, I cleared my throat to ensure no emotion leaked through when I began to speak, but Willa beat me to it.

"God, you're a great hugger, you know that?" Willa exclaimed, beaming. "I've never made much in the way of girlfriends before. I mean, there are plenty of women I like, whose company I enjoy, but never that real deep friendship it seems others magically have. Maybe that will be us! What do you think, Dani?"

I laughed. "I think I'd like that."

"Let me top off your tea. Any chance it's illegal to show me that HoloHex thingy you were saying?" She teetered over to the stove dressed in the spare pajamas I'd given her—red flannel pants and a loose fitting black t-shirt—and put more water to boil. "I've always wanted to see one. Never been privy to the workings of a secret agent."

"I'm hardly a secret agent, but sure—I can't imagine there'd be any harm in showing you." I reached into my pocket and retrieved the small HoloDisc Felix had given me. I laid it flat on my palm, then brought my other hand above it, like I was holding an imaginary beach ball before my chest. I waited for the image to appear as it had for Felix.

As the beams of light blinked and glimmered, working their way into the proper lines and curves that represented the face of Charlie Bone—our mystery man—Willa laughed and clapped and watched like I was performing a magic trick or a fireworks display.

When it settled in and displayed the man's face, I was again tugged by the threads of recognition, though I still couldn't put my finger on where I'd seen him before. Or if I had seen him. It was possible that he simply looked like someone I knew, and my brain was playing tricks on me.

"Oh, brilliant, you!" She clapped again. "How do you know Harry?"

"Harry?"

She pointed to the face and frowned. "Isn't that Harry LeFloyd? I guess I could be wrong, but I just saw him the other day. He came in for...are you alright, Dani? You look a bit peaked. Let me pour you that tea. Do you have honey? Oh, who am I kidding. You don't even have a stick of butter in the house, poor thing. I'll have to grocery shop and show you how to fill a fridge."

I barely processed Fred's audible sigh at Willa's mention of pampering the insides of his shelves, nor did I notice Willa's delighted exclamation at the sight of a talking fridge. I was too busy staring slack jawed at my brand-new friend.

"Rewind," I said. "How do you know Harry?"

Willa turned around slowly. Something in my voice had tipped her off that my question was more important than a sassy refrigerator.

"Um, he came into Blott's office a few times. He was in just last week, actually."

"Why was he in Blott's office?"

"Well, I probably shouldn't be saying this..." Her eyes shifted to the floor then back up. "You know, it's understood that a receptionist keeps things confidential, but—"

"Willa! Not only is this a murder investigation, but that pig fired you! Yes, because of me, but still—he treated you horribly. Who is Harry LeFloyd?"

"He worked for Mayor Lapel," Willa said, and at the mention of the name, her face went white. "Oh, bloody hell. This is horrible, isn't it? I just realized how this must look."

"But he was talking with Blott?"

"He wasn't just talking with him," Willa said. "He worked for him. Blott stole Harry from the mayor."

My brain went blank. When it kicked back into gear, I studied her for a long second and let my mind work overtime. As it caught up, it clicked for me—where I'd seen him.

"Harry," I said, "he was an assistant or something, right? He's the guy who brought coffee for me and Matthew when we went to talk to Mayor Lapel's assistant!"

"Oh, you met Verity, too? She's really nice. I even wondered about asking her if Mayor Lapel had an opening they'd consider hiring me for. You know, what with how awful Councilman Blott was, I liked to keep an ear to the ground. I figured he'd fire me sooner or later, and as for political parties, well, I don't give a damn." She winced. "I mean, that's horrible of me to say seeing as I worked for Blott, but I'd really rather just have the nicest man win. I can say for a fact that the nicer man wasn't Mr. Blott, and I'd only met Mayor Lapel a few times!"

"Tell me everything you know about Harry."

"Let me grab this kettle first. It's about to boil."

I gritted my teeth, working through my impatience and forcing myself to not demand that Willa sit down and spill her guts at that very moment. I waited patiently while she poured the tea, dunked the bag a few times, and then looked in the fridge for unspoiled milk. She gave Fred a frown, then returned empty handed to her seat.

"I'd really love a few biscuits to go with tea," she mused. "I need to introduce you to the ones my mum buys for us. They're freaking delicious!"

"Willa—"

"Right, right. Sorry. Murder." She grinned. "Well, all I know is that Harry was some lowly assistant at Mayor Lapel's office. I mean, he hadn't worked there that long, so how could he possibly have gotten a raise and a promotion yet? Seriously, some people—the nerve. Anyway, where was I?"

"How'd he come to work for Blott?"

"I couldn't tell if the councilman recruited Harry or if it was the other way around, but somehow, they connected. I think Harry first came into the office—oh, a month ago? I didn't recognize him then.

He was just a name in the appointment book and not a very chatty person at all. So, I let him into the office and they talked for a while. I only remember that so clearly because the councilman was whistling after. The councilman never whistles unless he's got something truly horrible planned for someone else."

"Something like murder," I finished. "Dammit, I knew that man couldn't be innocent. Carry on—sorry. I'm just so furious."

"I didn't say murder!" Willa's face went white. "Don't take any of this as an accusation, Dani—I am just telling you what I saw, okay? If I'd watched someone plan murder, for fucks sake I would've gone to the police!" She looked a pinch angry for the first time. "Sorry for the French. Or English, rather. My mum is a bad influence on me."

"I'm sorry, I just think aloud. I wouldn't dream of jumping to conclusions without evidence, and we're far from having proof on either Harry or Blott."

She exhaled a breath, a strand of hair fluttering before her face. "Good. I just wanted to be sure. Anyhow, they talked, he whistled—nothing came of it, and I forgot about it. Then he returned a few more times, and I heard even less of their conversations."

"Was there more whistling?"

She shook her head. "Not after that first time. Harry barely spoke to me when he came into the office. I hardly bothered to look up when I knew he had an appointment. It felt rude to me, but who am I to judge? Then, the whistle returned last week."

The way she said it felt like a sense of foreboding. "Did you hear what happened during their meeting?"

"Enough of it," she said. "But it was the meeting Blott called with me *after* that turned really weird."

"Well?" Willa was making me drag the story out of her by the ear. She really had a flair for the dramatic, I realized, and this was her moment in the spotlight. "What did he want with you?"

"He told me he was planning to hire Harry LeFloyd. Which wasn't all that weird, you know, since he hires and fires people quite often. There's a lot of turnover in the office. This time, though, he said it was different—had to be kept quiet. We were to not file any paperwork for him...yet."

"Did he say for what? Or why?"

"Oh, sure." Willa paused for a sip of tea. "He said that Harry was amazing at campaign advertising and the councilman wanted him on our team. He then explained that the subject was a touchy one because stealing employees from the opponent's team is sort of frowned upon. You know, malicious and all of that."

"Yeah, I'd say so."

"The councilman told me that Harry was planning to quit his job in the next week. We'd be hiring him right away, but if we put him on official payroll and all of that jazz, the mayor would know and would be livid."

"Probably."

"So, for the next few months we were going to pay him under the table. When a long enough time had passed, Blott would hire him and things wouldn't look suspicious. Harry could always pass off the change in party as being desperate for money and taking any job that paid." Willa shrugged. "You know, like me."

"He's nothing like you," I said, but Willa was uninterested in my commentary. It was her spotlight, and she wasn't looking for sympathy. "Carry on."

She sighed. "There's not much more to it, actually. After that meeting, I didn't see Harry again. He had probably already started on ideas for the councilman's campaign, but I hadn't paid him yet."

"Why did Blott tell you all this? Wouldn't it make more sense for him to meet privately with Harry?"

"I was in charge of making withdrawals and payments. You have to understand the councilman was very busy." She leaned forward and whispered: "By busy, I mean lazy. He probably figured that even if I'm somewhat horrible at my job, I'm not so dull I wouldn't recognize the same man returning to the office over and over again. And the way he explained it, the whole thing was like no big deal, you know? I didn't really think much about it until—well, until tonight. It didn't even cross my mind that it might have something to do with the mayor's murder."

"We're not sure it does," I assured her, though I couldn't possibly see how it wasn't related in some way.

Donny had described seeing someone who looked like Harry at the location the bodies had been found—he must be our Charlie Bone, the man who'd rented the room at the Motel Sixth where the bodies had been dropped. Harry had a connection to the dead mayor—*and* to Lapel's opponent. In my mind, the biggest question was who suggested murder: Harry or Blott?

"I need to—I need to talk to someone about this," I said, standing. "I'm going to have you take the bed. I might have to run out tonight, and—"

"Dani, take the night to think about it." Willa glanced at Hector for the time. "It's almost two in the morning. Seriously—get a few hours of sleep. You look like you haven't slept in days."

"I'm fine."

"Did you sleep last night?"

"A few hours."

"Matthew can't walk. You're drooping. Harry doesn't know you have the HoloHex or that you're onto him yet, right? So why would he run?" Willa made an excellent point. "Go to the hospital in the morning, tell Matthew, and then the two of you can go together."

"But—"

"If you tell Matthew tonight," she said with a crisp, motherly tone to her voice, "you know he won't rest. He has a freaking hole in his knee, Dani. Let the poor vampire recover."

I laughed—I couldn't help it. Nobody had ever called Matthew a 'poor vampire' before. Yet it sounded fitting coming from Willa.

"It's just a few hours of sleep," she said. "And no offense, but you need a shower. I've been trying not to look at the blood on your arm because it makes me queasy if I do, and I lose my appetite."

"You just finished half a pizza and several cups of tea."

"Well, then I probably needed to eat a full pizza and drink an entire pot of tea," she said, though a grin tugged at her lips. "You know I have a point. Now go—get in the shower. I'll clean up."

I followed her pointed finger like a trained dog. I knew I needed rest, just like I knew I needed a shower. And Willa was correct. Telling Matthew tonight would only slow his recovery by forcing him into action. If Willa hadn't been here tonight, I wouldn't have figured out Harry's connections to the mayor and councilman, and I'd be going to bed anyway.

I flicked on the water, resigned to sleep as per Willa's instructions. I took a quick, hot shower and scrubbed all signs of death and destruction off my body. I had a quick thought about Lorraine, felt a wash of sadness for her, and wondered how Grey played into all of this.

Was I wrong in thinking Harry and Blott had anything to do with the case more than a little shady marketing campaign? Or was I wrong about Grey, and his devotion to Lorraine was just an appearance?

I climbed from the shower and toweled off, somberly listening as my gut told me that love could be faked. Even the nicest of men, the sweetest of gestures, could all be for show. A ruse. A trick to hide the monster inside.

I should know—I told one I'd loved him too.

In retrospect, I knew I hadn't loved Trenton—I'd loved the idea of him, and the way he'd made me feel cherished and important and special for just being me. Not for being a Reserve, or a cop, or anything of the sort. For being plain old Dani DeMarco.

And, of course, it hadn't hurt that I'd still been reeling from a shattered heart.

A woman didn't date Captain Matthew King and walk away unscathed.

I slid pajama shorts and a T-shirt over my body and left the steamy haven of the shower behind. I meandered into the living room and stopped short. Willa had somehow cleaned and tidied the entire place. All lights were off except for the dim glow of Hector's face. He winked at me when he saw me checking the time, cheeky little bastard. Willa, however, was nowhere to be seen.

"You need to keep that one, you know," Marla drawled. "She's a delightful little thing. A good friend, too."

"And she knows how to feed the soul," said Fred. "I might finally be full for once if she sticks around!"

Carl heaved a gigantic sigh, sending up a little cloud of dust around his cushions. "I was promised new imprints. I liked the look of that one. Where'd she go?"

I didn't have an answer for Carl, so I headed into the bedroom and found Willa there, face down on the bed and snoring as if her life depended on it. She had one hand grasped around the covers as if she'd been turning down the bed for me, and her bare feet stuck off the side, dangling over the floor.

With a soft grunt, I gave Willa a light roll onto the bed and tucked the covers around her. When it no longer looked like she was smothering herself, I stepped back, glanced at her for a second, and wondered why I'd waited twenty-eight years of my life to find a friend. I liked having a friend.

I closed the door behind me and crept to the couch. As I sat down, Carl let out a disgruntled huff. "How much pizza did you have tonight?"

"Shut up," I told him. "I'm a healthy weight. I have to fight were-wolves, you know."

"She's a stick," Marla called from the corner. "I like women better the way they were in my day. Curly, curvaceous, simply marvelous like that Willa darling."

"I'm trying to sleep," I told the group. "Can y'all pipe down?"

Curling up, I snagged a blanket from the back of the couch and pulled it over me. I snuggled into Carl who, despite all his grumps and groans, was a true old friend. My eyes closed in minutes.

"Hector!" Marla shouted. "That means you, too. Silence!"

Hector reluctantly quieted the tick to his tock.

Then I slept, and I didn't hear a thing more until the unwelcome click of the lock woke me in the wee hours of the morning.

This would go down in history as the night that refused to end.

Chapter 26

My eyes flicked open, but I didn't move.

The doorknob twisted, glinting in the moonlight, moving when it should have been still. The turning of the lock had woken me, though I hadn't moved fast enough to get to my feet and hide.

The door opened partially, and I quickly scrolled through my options: my Stunner had been confiscated as evidence earlier in the evening, and I didn't have a backup. The kitchen was full of knives, which I couldn't reach. My other defensive spells and potions were in the bedroom where I normally slept. Right where I'd have access to them—if I'd been sleeping there.

A foot entered the room—I glimpsed a male shoe, unfamiliar to me. Not Jack, who I'd hoped had snuck upstairs in search of a comfier bed. Not Matthew, who had a tendency to make locks vanish when he wanted access to a place. My heart raced, and I wondered for a fleeting second if it was Trenton coming back from the dead.

I had hoped I'd gotten rid of these sorts of late night visitors when I'd retired. Making pizzas wasn't supposed to be dangerous. Unfortunately, I hadn't made many pizzas in the last few days.

Another footstep. The man moved slowly, cautiously. He was going for the element of surprise and not force, which benefitted me. I kept my breathing steady, most of my body obscured by the blanket. The longer he figured me to be sleeping, the better a jump I'd have on him.

I scanned the room once more for a weapon. There was a vase on the coffee table, but it was too far away to grab and not powerful enough to fight off a fully-grown man. The kitchen was across the room, and the heavy bookend on the living room shelf was right in the spotlight.

I was running low on options when I heard the slightest cough. As if my couch had a hairball. I almost growled at Carl for exposing me before I felt something poke me from between his cushions. *A knife*, I realized, as my fingers closed around the handle. A small, dainty knife, but a utensil all the same. Before I could wonder where it came from, I thought back to the past weekend when I'd brought my dinner to the couch, propped my feet on the coffee table, and read a book while I lounged and ate. A quick think back told me I'd cleaned up everything but had somehow missed the knife. Had Carl eaten it?

If I had more time, I probably would have realized that a lot of things had disappeared into the couch. I generally chalked the missing items—Chapstick, keys, a few bucks here and there—to my scatterbrained housekeeping, but now I wondered if there wasn't a more nefarious party responsible named Carl.

I clutched the knife, grateful. I'd thank him later. It wasn't a huge weapon, but it would be something—better than my fingers, at the very least. I could conjure simple spells, but that required words and usually brought light to my fingertips, and I was wary of risking my own element of surprise.

Even more, I didn't know who—or what—I was dealing with. I didn't want to curse one of my brothers, though it'd serve him right. If it was a sorcerer, I didn't want my spells bouncing off an invisible shield and setting fire and wreaking havoc around my apartment. So, the way I saw it, my only option was to wait.

The man completely entered my apartment and closed the door behind him. He stood masked in shadows. From what I could see around Carl's arm, I didn't recognize the build or the face. It was far too dark to get a proper hair color.

The intruder stepped further into the room and edged toward the kitchen. I wondered if he'd missed seeing the sleeping lump on the couch. Carl sat perpendicular to the door, so it was possible my body was hidden and lumped about in the shadows behind the arms and back of the couch. At first, that brought a wave of relief washing through me, but the relief didn't last long.

With the realization that the attacker *hadn't* noticed me, came another—he was heading straight toward Willa.

I couldn't let anything else happen to Willa—especially not on my account. I'd already cost the poor thing her job, though that might have been a blessing in disguise. This time around, however, there wouldn't be any blessing or any disguise. I had no doubt the man who'd entered my apartment wanted something from me, and I had a bad feeling that his goal was to end my life.

"Steady..." a voice whispered.

I shifted ever so slightly at the noise, until I realized it was all but a breath from Carl. It was so soft, so wide and thorough in its surround sound, that the man didn't even pause in his footsteps.

"Hold..." Carl murmured. "Wait."

I felt a rush of gratitude for Carl. I'd lost sight of the man as he'd disappeared behind the backrest. My timing would be crucial as I prepared to make my move. Jump over the couch too soon, and he'd have enough time to recover and attack. Jump too late, and he'd be well on his way to taking down Willa. Jump right on time, and my chances at defeating a murderer with a tiny knife were still small, but better than the alternatives.

"Ready..." Carl murmured in that elusive sound of his that was nothing more than a tremor in the air. "Go!"

I wasn't ready, and I didn't want to go, but I leapt on Carl's command and landed on the other side of the couch in one lightning quick motion. Years of hanging out with Matthew had taught me tiny ways to perfect the gracefulness of my movements, and while I would never have the skills of a vampire, I landed with a smooth quiet that startled the intruder.

"Cha—Harry!" I said, raising the knife. "Why are you in my apartment?"

"Got the HoloHex, have you?" he murmured. "I knew it would only be a matter of time before someone put my name with the picture."

"Why'd you kill Mayor Lapel?"

He laughed. "Put down the popsicle stick, Detective. Or, maybe you'd recognize me if I said *Can I get you more coffee?*"

The sick, twisted look in his eyes hit me hard. It was familiar, something I'd seen before in Trenton. An aversion to all humanity and reason. Harry had a plan, a mission—I just hadn't figured out what.

"Listen to me," I said. "I can help you, Harry. I promise. Let me help you."

"Just like you helped Willa by getting her fired?" Harry's light red hair glinted under the moonlight, and the whites of his teeth glinted maliciously bright in the dimness of my apartment. "I figured Willa would recognize me if she saw the HoloHex. Yes, I know about the HoloDisc. Stupid Willa. Blott never did like her."

"Did Blott plan the murder of the mayor?" I asked. We'd frozen in some sort of unmoving statue-like dance. "If Blott had anything to do with this, you have to tell me. I can help you."

Harry laughed. He shook his head, as if I just didn't understand, and then reached into his pocket. I raised the knife in response, but he gave me a calm down gesture. I watched as he pulled a tiny little pillbox out of his jeans and popped it open. His reddish hair gleamed as he dipped his head, studied the contents there.

I barely breathed, inching forward, the knife raised. "Don't move," he said, his head flicking up at me. He pulled a gun similar in style to my Stunner out from his pocket and pointed it at me. "I wasn't done talking to you."

My palms had begun to perspire, but I stopped in my tracks. "Good. Let's talk then. What do you have there?"

"You know what this is." He held up a tiny little pill no bigger than a half carat diamond. It sparkled, glistened like captured moonlight in an iridescent sort of glow. "PowerPax."

"Just turn it over to me, and we can work out a deal, Harry," I coaxed. "Please—"

Harry gave me a terse, wicked little smile, and in one smooth motion, he dropped the pill on his tongue.

"No!" I yelled, lunging for him.

I hit him hard on the chest and tackled him to the ground, but he fought me off with a swift blow to the face. My nose spurted blood while I rounded up for a second attack. I drove my knife toward his shoulder, but he rolled at the last second and sent me flying.

My head clocked hard against the wall, dazing me for a second too long. Harry got on his feet, returned to my side, and held the Stunner over me. He favored his shoulder, wincing as he adjusted his position over me, and I distinctly remembered the injured werewolf limping into the forest. But that made no sense—Harry wasn't a shifter.

"PowerPax will kick in after ten minutes," Harry said, nodding toward himself. "You'd be *lucky* if I killed you before that happens."

"Why'd you come here tonight?" I asked, struggling to a seated position against the wall. My head killed me. "What could you have possibly hoped to achieve?"

He laughed. "Well, you dead for starters. Grey will take the fall for it, as with Lorraine."

"What does Lorraine have to do with anything?" I asked. "A shifter killed her. You're not a shifter. It's the full moon, and you're standing here as a human."

"I'm not, but I am a sorcerer," he said, reaching into his front pocket and pulling out a vial the size of my pinky finger. "And I made a Cloning Spell with the hair of a fully transformed werewolf. In fact, here we have it. I'll just take that in a few minutes and it should do the trick."

"But the PowerPax—"

"The drug of the future," he boasted. "Ah, yes. It amplifies one's powers by tenfold. You're a witch? Imagine powers ten times stronger. A vampire? The strength, speed, and agility would be out of this world."

"Right," I said. "But you're a sorcerer."

"Exactly. We create spells, and I've created a Cloning Spell that will copy all the attributes of a fully formed werewolf. I can *become* something else. Sure, it's only for a short time. But my goal is to kill you—and I don't plan on that taking long."

"And the PowerPax strengthens your transformation into a werewolf?" I asked, suddenly seeing things click into place before my eyes. The psychedelic Residuals around the werewolf that had injured Matthew were the same as the ones sparkling around Harry now. The unlisted werewolf who had killed Lorraine wasn't documented because he *didn't really exist.*

"Even if you kill me, they'll find you." Nerves tingled down my spine. If I didn't move soon, he'd transform, and I'd be a lost cause. If I did move, he'd Stun me, and I'd be out for ten minutes. An absolute sitting duck for a werewolf. "They know it's not an average werewolf. Plus, the Residuals match those at Lorraine's crime scene."

"With you gone, the Residuals won't be an issue." Harry's eyes flicked up then, drawn to a sound behind me. His gaze pulled back to me. "You're not here alone. Who's in the bedroom?"

"Leave her alone," I said. "Willa didn't do anything to you."

"If you cooperate, I won't have to hurt her," Harry said with a dull smile. "Or your brother."

I didn't believe him for a second. In werewolf form, he would attack anything that breathed—especially with his powers amplified tenfold.

"If you touched Jack..." I growled, thinking of my brother on the bench. "What did you do to him?"

"He's alive—remember, I'm framing Grey? He's just in a deep sleep."

"Where is Grey?"

"How should I know? All I know is that it's the full moon, so he won't have an alibi tonight. In fact, his alibi will be that he had transformed—but that's not much of an alibi when claw marks are the cause of death."

"Why have you not rolled on Blott?" I threw every last bit of ammunition on the table that I had. He was intent on killing me anyway—that much was clear. "You know one of us isn't walking out of here alive, so what does it hurt to spill if Blott was involved with any of this mess?"

"Blott had nothing to do with it!" A flash of fury streaked through his eyes. "Blott was eating out of my hand."

"Then why murder the mayor? What did Lorraine have to do with anything?"

"This isn't about the mayor position! Who gives a rat's ass about that job, anyway? It's pointless! This is about PowerPax, plain and simple." He shook his head. "Lorraine was...shall we say, an unfortunate casualty. She thought she saw Grey slip something into Joey's drink, but it wasn't him. I stopped Grey next to Joey's table and we talked for a minute. Bumped into each other—on purpose. I dropped something into Joey's drink."

"Why?"

"We needed to test it on a powerless creature," he said. "Everyone who'd tried it noted magnified powers, but we needed to test it on someone who we knew had little to no natural powers. Joey was a prime candidate: There wasn't much special about him, and better yet, he was a well-known recreational drug user. But it's not like we could walk up and ask him to be our guinea pig, you know? He wasn't into the real hard stuff."

"So, you drugged him."

"It didn't do much, as you saw. Just sent him into a bit of a daze. I guess it was too much energy and not enough outlet for it. Not like when I take it."

"Lorraine must have seen Grey talking to Joey at the Howler," I said. "And she was trying to protect him."

He nodded. "I used to think it sucked that I wasn't memorable. All Lorraine remembered was seeing Grey—it didn't even dawn on her it might've been me. But I had to take care of her before she remembered seeing me there. I left her a note, said I could fix her problems and tell her the truth about Grey—and she agreed to meet me in The Depth. Well, you saw how that ended."

A wave of nausea washed over me. Poor Lorraine. Poor Grey. They hadn't asked for any of this mess.

"The mayor, well—he was looking too much into my business," Harry continued. "See, I'd worked my way up the ranks over the last few years. The office job was a cover." He laughed. "I made my real cash running drugs. Started low level, gained some experience. You know, I have ten people working under me now."

"Gee, congrats."

"The mayor stumbled over PowerPax. He took it to be his passion project and was intent on exposing us as a way to secure his win for office." Harry gave a disappointed cluck. "Bad decision. His little government position wasn't going to ruin my life's work. He had to go."

"Just like that. You killed him. And the Goblin Girl?"

"She was his informant. Smart little hooker, that one. She hadn't even had a client, you know that? On her first night out, she caught wind of PowerPax and skedaddled. Went squealing straight to the mayor, hoping he could take care of the problem. They decided to work on it together and thought they could do it all themselves."

"Why wouldn't they call the police?"

"Oh, they were ready to, but they wanted the credit. The votes. They'd done all the work, after all." He gave a salacious smile. "So, they earned the reward. The dump site at the Motel Sixth? That was nothing more than a distraction—I figured it'd kick off a wild goose chase. Finding the mayor in a hotel room with a hooker? The media would be in a *frenzy*. The real problem would..." He made his fingers wriggle into the distance. "Disappear."

"But what about—"

I lost track of my next question as Harry held up a finger, then raised the uncorked vial to his lips while holding the Stunner straight at my chest. "I've had enough of our chat and now I'm bored," he said, and then let a small drop of solution land on his tongue. "Adios, Detective."

Harry closed his eyes and swallowed the potion that had been created to turn him into a werewolf—or something. I knew in my mind that I wasn't facing off against a true werewolf—just the illusion of one—but even that would be enough to kill me. I'd seen what he'd done to Matthew, and that man was nearly indestructible. If I let PowerPax combine with the Cloning Spell, I'd be a dead woman—and he wouldn't stop with me.

I lunged, taking advantage of the momentary shudder in his body as the potion slithered through him. My knife plunged into his existing shoulder wound, and by the time Harry realized what had happened, he was blindsided by pain.

The cry that came from him was half human, half animal, and it was enough to raise the dead. There was a squeak of surprise from behind my shoulder, so I spared a glance back and found a ruffled-looking Willa standing in the doorway to my bedroom. Her hair extended from her head in all directions and a bedsheet was hanging from one hand. If she stuck her thumb in her mouth, she'd look like an oversized toddler.

"Dani?" she asked, her mouth parted in horror. "What's going on?"

"Willa, close the door!" I shouted at her. "Get inside!"

Willa took a step forward and slammed the bedroom door shut behind her.

"No," I said. "Get inside the bedroom. Lock the door! He's going to come after you!"

"No way, I'm here to help." She dropped the blanket and rushed toward the couch, her eye on the figure crumpled beneath my knife. "That's horrific. What is he?"

I pulled my knife from Harry's shoulder and backed away as he started to transform. He was bleeding badly on my floor, a pool of gleaming red. I dared not leap for him again as his body shivered, shuddered, and then sprouted fur from head to foot.

"Come on," I yelled to her, "there's a fire escape, but we'll have to bust the window. We've got to get out of here—he's transforming!"

"Into what? Is that Harry? He's not a freaking werewolf—he *can't* transform!"

"He will be for—oh, I'm guessing the next five minutes!" I grabbed Willa's arm and dragged her toward the window. "If we don't get out of here, we're dead."

I let the knife clatter to the floor since the tiny blade wouldn't do us any good against the wolf. Our only hope was to escape. I pounded against the stuck window, struggling for the words of a magical spell that I'd lost in the fury of the moment.

"I know this, I know this," Willa said, putting a finger to her lip as if she had time to think. "One second—my idiot cousin taught me some stupid charm that was supposed to fix a window, but instead it shattered it. I got in trouble; he got off scot free."

"No time," I said, glancing over my shoulder. "He's almost changed."

Harry had pulled onto all fours, his nose elongating, his teeth lengthening. He let out a test snarl that was an odd mix between a human whine and a doglike bark.

"*Bippity boppity boom*," Willa said, pointing at the window. "*You shouldn't have gone kaboom. Mother sent us to our room, so fix yourself real soon!*"

"That's not a real spell," I said. "Here, let me—"

I reached for the paperweight on my bookshelf, but even as I turned away, the tinkling sound of glass cracking filtered through the room. Then, with one giant *crack*, the window shattered into millions of tiny pieces. Half the glass landed inside my apartment, while the other half skidded down the exterior of my building.

"Wow," I said. "I can't believe that worked."

She giggled. "He's an idiot, but I love him."

I ushered Willa out first, flinching as the first real sound of a growl began. "I don't think he took enough potion to last longer than five minutes or so. Just long enough to get the job done."

"The job done?" Willa asked, one leg out the window.

"Killing me," I said. "Now, *go*!"

Willa began scrambling down as fast as she could move.

"Wake Jack," I yelled after her, realizing I wouldn't have time to climb out the window behind her. "He's downstairs—he can help. Get Matthew."

"But—"

"Go! I need help!"

She turned, her face pale. "Don't die! I already know that you're my best friend, Dani DeMarco," she shouted as she began clattering down the flimsy fire escape. "Hang on, Detective!"

I turned away from the jagged, partial panes of glass, and circled the now full-sized wolf. He didn't give me a moment to pause. As he leaped, I sidestepped him, hearing the sickening crunch of his body as it crashed into the wall below the window. He stood, shook himself off as the remaining shards of glass rained down on him in glittering spikes.

"Harry," I said, crouching. "Stop it. This is insane—you're going to get caught."

As I suspected, there was no recognition in his eyes. This was equal parts terrifying and thrilling—terrifying because absolutely no logic would get through to him. Thrilling because any clever scheming was gone, and all that remained of Harry was brute force. He'd inherited the strength of a werewolf ten-fold, but it had dampened his strategic movements.

"Fine," I said. "Have it your way."

I retreated to the kitchen as the wolf's claws clattered against the floor. I snatched the largest knife on the block; it was big, as long as my arm, and I hated having it in the house. It terrified me, but it'd come as part of a set my mother had given me for my birthday, and I hadn't wanted to throw it away. *Thanks, mother*, I thought dryly. She'd be properly appalled.

I held it in front of my body as Harry crept closer. He continued to approach me, but less aggressively. The knife held the glint of universal danger.

His teeth bared, and a low growl came from his throat. As he lithely crept forward, I saw the couch—enchanted old Carl—inch back slightly, as if an attempt to block the wolf's path. *Good old Carl*, I thought. I'd miss him.

I'd miss him dearly after the wolf's claws ripped through my skin.

Hurry, Willa, I pleaded silently. I needed to stall for five minutes until Harry's Cloning Spell wore off and he transformed back to human. That's when I would be able to make my move. Until then, I needed to keep him occupied.

"Come on, Harry," I coaxed. "Jump, you asshole."

If he leapt, I could possibly aim the knife toward the softer part of his stomach. I hadn't wanted to kill him, but I would. In a choice between my life or his, I'd always choose mine. Especially after seeing what he'd done to Lorraine.

We moved at the same time. I ducked around the kitchen table and went for Harry's legs as he snapped at me. We both missed, recoiled, recovered, and launched again. This round, I hit fur.

The wound wasn't deep, but it hit his injured shoulder and stopped his attack. He licked at himself as I moved through the living room, keeping the couch between us as I inched backward toward the door to my apartment. If I could just make it to the door...

I turned as the wolf limped toward me and sprinted. I lunged for the doorknob, but the wolf sniffed out my escape route and leapt past me, skidding to a stop in front of the door. He snarled at me, teeth gnashing as his body covered the frame. My only option was to head for the window, and now was my opportunity. Harry was off-balanced and injured, if I could just make it to the fire escape, I might survive.

If I missed, I would die...

I had a split second to make my decision. As Harry pulled himself back to launch at me from the doorway, I tossed my knife onto Carl's cushions. It was too big and unwieldy to move with, and once I fell from the window, I didn't want to be landing anywhere near the blade.

I sprinted, my legs burning, lungs gasping as I propelled my body toward the fresh air. My fingers dug into the ragged glass around the edges as I pulled myself up and over the sill.

Behind me, Harry let out a howl. A bloodcurdling sound that drew the howl of wolves around the borough toward him.

I had a single leg inside the window when my pajamas caught on the ledge. Stupid flannel shorts. I was bleeding from my hands, from scrapes on my legs. My awful shorts held me back as a feverish wolf launched straight for me.

His teeth gnashed at my clothes, dragging me back from the window. I managed to dodge his bite, but the weight of him curled around and dragged me under. I collapsed on the floor, bleeding and injured, as the wolf hovered over me. Drool dripped from his lips. His bared teeth were ugly white, stuck into ugly pink and black gums.

I closed my eyes.

"Dani!" The sound was a *woof* of air. "Roll!"

I didn't think, I just did. I rolled, opening my eyes as I ducked and fumbled toward the voice. Only as I moved did I realize it was Carl who had spoken. I looked up just in time to see my coat rack rock back and forth, tipping herself over toward the werewolf.

"Marla to the rescue," she cried as she landed with a *thunk* on the werewolf's bad shoulder. "Take that, you scoundrel!"

As he howled, Carl propped himself forward. I reached for the knife from his cushions then stood and gave the big old piece of furniture a push. My couch toppled forward, landing with a *thud* over the howling wolf and trapping the animal beneath its weight.

Suddenly, the howls stopped. They turned into desperate human pants. While Harry was still wedged under my couch, I realized that as he turned human, he'd no longer have the rapid healing abilities of a werewolf. He'd bleed, and he'd bleed quickly. I'd gotten a few pricks in with the knife, and though they'd healed somewhat, he hadn't been transformed long enough for them to heal completely.

At that moment, a figure flew through my window, and I whirled around at the distraction. It was another wolf, but one so completely different than Harry's version it might have been another species entirely. The newly arrived animal had a coat of pure white and eyes of the darkest sapphire blue. He howled, a short sound, more of a yip to get Harry's attention.

There was a *thump* from behind me, and I whirled back to find Harry on his feet again. He looked terrifying, standing there, bleeding from his lip, his nose, his abdomen, but he stared down the wolf and flexed his fingers. Then, he turned his sights to me. "You're dead, witch," he said, and leapt for me with his bare hands outstretched.

I ducked off his attack, but I needn't have moved. One leap from the huge, regal wolf knocked Harry flat to the ground.

The white wolf barked toward me, and I snapped to action. I rushed to the bedroom and grabbed the Immobilizer Incantation—an absolute blackout of poison—and returned, pouring it down Harry's throat while the newest wolf stood guard.

Within seconds, Harry fell into a coma-like state. He'd be revived later, but not until he received the antidote in a holding cell.

"Thank you," I whispered to the snowy wolf. I collapsed to my knees, leaned on him. It was only then that I realized I was bleeding from a plethora of wounds, and my bright red blood smeared on his coat.

The wolf nuzzled me, licked my cheek, and then ran his tongue along the worst of the wounds. I curled into the floor, dizziness pulling me from consciousness.

As I started to drift away, I pulled him closer. "Don't leave me."

The wolf whined. I wanted to ask his name, but I couldn't summon the breath—and he couldn't respond. My voice had gone, along with my energy. My vision went next, and just before my hearing faded, I heard the opening of the door and a collective gasp.

Chapter 27

"Jell-O?" Nurse Anita asked. "I have purple, blue, red, or this new multi-colored flavor."

"Since when is multicolor a flavor?" I grinned at Anita. "That has me concerned."

"Since when is Jell-O a food?" She shrugged. "How are you feeling, darling?"

"Better," I said. "Still a little off, but much better."

"That'll be the Diagnostic Deep Dive," she said. "The charm is working its way through your system now, so I expect you'll be a little out of it. Checking for infection and whatnot. Let me see your scrapes."

I offered my right arm first. It killed, burning from the goopy purple potion she'd slathered over the open wounds. Nurse Anita clucked over me, fussing and examining every inch of my skin before nodding and giving me a pat on the head.

"You're lucky to have made it out alive, you know," she said. "And thank goodness for that bubbly little thing running to get help. Did she put some salve on you? Your wounds are healing far quicker than they should be, frankly. I haven't even applied the healing spells yet, and already, you're sealing up quick."

I thought of Willa, and of the mysterious white wolf. I remembered the feel of his rough tongue against my arm, and I had to wonder if there was something in him—some wolf magic that'd gone to work on my wounds from his care.

It was well known that werewolves, vampires, and many other paranormal species healed faster than normal humans—much quicker than witches and sorcerers and other spell-based supernaturals.

I shivered, thinking of how close everything had come in the end—if some old witch hadn't enchanted my furniture; if I hadn't gotten Willa fired from her job; if the white wolf hadn't heard the howl from a wounded Harry...I likely wouldn't have made it through the night.

As it was, Matthew, Willa, Nash—and a slew of other officers—had arrived at the scene of the crime shortly after I'd blacked out. Jack had been found downstairs, unconscious but healthy save for a deep sleeping potion. The officers had then climbed to my apartment and found me nearly dead. They'd brought me to the hospital where the nurses had put me into a deeper unconsciousness—a medical one—and set to work on sealing my wounds.

I'd awoken just a few minutes ago to see the sun well on its way to noon. A bit of grogginess lingered from the combination of pain medicine, aches, and pure exhaustion, but otherwise, I felt fine. Great, actually—seeing as I was alive, relieved, and curious to learn the details I'd missed in my sleep.

"Is there anyone else here?" I asked lightly. "I mean, I guess I have a few questions, and—"

Nurse Anita rested a hand on my forehead. "Matthew stayed through the night. I kicked him out when I started doing your bloodwork."

"Matthew is controlled around the sight of blood, and he has been for a long time—"

"I know he's controlled, but this was *you*, darling."

I suspected I knew what she was getting at, but I equally suspected she was wrong. "We're just friends."

"Sure, honey. I'll let him know you're awake. Your friend has been dying to see you, too. She tried to climb into your bed and sleep next to you. Claimed she didn't want you to feel lonely."

"Oh, Willa." I grinned. "Send her in too, please."

Nurse Anita left, and seconds later, a blond head whizzed into the room and shot straight toward me as if from a cannon. Willa collided hard against my chest, slowing just enough to exaggerate gentleness as she hugged me.

"You're okay!" She gasped for air. "God, when I saw that huge wolf! You fought him?! How? You're just a... I mean, no offense, but you have human skin. He was a huge old werewolf! I hated to leave you, I swear it. I would never have run if you didn't tell me to go, and—"

"Willa." She was still hugging me, and I pressed a hand to the back of her head and gave her one big squeeze before letting go. "Breathe. Relax. You saved my life. It's me who should be thanking you."

"Don't be ridiculous! I was in there snoring up a storm, and out in the living room you're dueling for your life!" She held a hand to her forehead and mock fainted onto the bed. "What a disaster. Do you see how I'm horrible at my job? Completely oblivious. What a mess. I'm a hot mess, Dani, and I'm sorry."

I laughed, unable to help myself even as her eyes teared up with remorse. Even in utter despair, there was a bounciness to Willa's voice, the very spirit of her. I wondered again why she'd chosen me to be her friend, and then pushed past the thought. I already loved her so easily I had no desire to question the magic of it.

A shadow in the doorway made me glance up, over her shoulder, where I found the captain leaning against the door. "Matthew," I breathed, an involuntary sound.

His face was worn, drawn with worry and frustration, but as I murmured his name, he looked up, his eyes lighting as they landed on my face. "Detective. How are you feeling?"

"Is he always so formal?" Willa thumbed over her shoulder. "I really should call you detective too. I think it suits you."

"Dani," I said, resting a hand on her arm. "Willa, do you mind if we have a minute?"

"Fine, but I'll be waiting outside..." Her voice trailed off as another woman stomped through the door. Willa's eyes immediately shot up to study the woman's hair, pants, and shoes—all dark, and the utter opposite of Willa's brightness. "I take that back. If *she's* staying, I'm staying."

I snorted. Willa huffed herself into a corner chair and picked up a magazine, which she pretended to read.

"Uh, Detective, Captain?" Sienna raised her eyebrows. "May I have a word?"

"Sure." I watched the necromancer's eyes flick over to Willa. "It's fine—she's in this with us. Close the door behind you, please."

Sienna kicked the door shut with her combat boots. Today her hair was fire engine red and her shirt of choice had a large expletive printed on the front. I halfway wondered how she'd gotten past security at the hospital, and then I figured she must be a frequent flier around these parts what with her skills and connection to the NYPD.

"I've got some updates for you," she said, looking down at her clipboard. "The body I got in last night? Cause of death was—" she paused as Willa squeaked in the corner with concern—"well, I won't go into it, but Lorraine was slashed with claws and bled out. However, there's a catch."

Matthew shifted his weight from one foot to the next. "A catch?"

"I initially thought werewolf, what with it being the full moon, but that wasn't right," she said. "Most wolves have a bit of healing magic in them, ironically. It helps them heal quickly from wounds—that's one of the reasons they might lick a scrape while it's still bleeding. The magic is healing, and it will help bind the injured area and seal it off to infection."

I had suspected as much after having heard Anita's summary of my own scrapes. Once again, I wondered who the wolf had been and why he or she had chosen to save me against all odds.

If I had to guess, I would wager the identity of the wolf to be Grey. After all, who had more of a desire to slaughter Harry than the man who'd lost his love to the sorcerer?

Either way, the wolf hadn't succeeded in killing Harry. Harry had been taken into custody when Matthew, Nash, Willa, and a slew of others had arrived at my door. The wolf, it seemed, had chosen to save my life instead of taking his revenge on Harry.

"Except..." Sienna blew out a frustrated breath. "The healing magic wasn't there. Lorraine—poor thing—had absolutely no signs of healing on her body. It's as if the creature wasn't actually a werewolf."

"He wasn't."

Her eyes flicked up from the clipboard. "Excuse me?"

"It wasn't a werewolf," I said. "We caught the man responsible for her murder, and he is a sorcerer. He used some sort of complex Cloning Spell to transform temporarily into a werewolf and steal the attributes of their powers—not the real thing of course, but an imitation."

"Hence the lack of healing magic. It's not a perfect clone." Sienna caught on quickly. She bit her lip, then frowned. "Why does nobody ever tell me these things? They just give me the dead body and then expect a report. I swear. It's the most thankless job in the business."

"I'm sorry! I was unconscious," I said. "I didn't even know you had the body."

Sienna rolled her eyes. "What's your excuse, Captain?"

Matthew didn't comment, but his eyes slid toward me.

"Right. Fine," Sienna said. "Well, I'll get back to my friends then—corpses don't talk, which helps us to get along just fine. Plus, hospitals make me itchy—I get too many people asking me to bring their grandpaps back to life, and it creeps me out."

"Sienna," I said with a smile. "Thank you."

She harrumphed and stomped out.

"Interesting lady," Willa said from the corner. "A real necromancer? *Yowza.*"

We didn't have long to marvel about the magic of the dead because two more visitors arrived before the door had even slammed shut.

"Felix!" I grinned, then saw the second figure and straightened in bed. I glanced down, made sure all my skin was covered, and pulled the sheet up higher. "Chief, *uh*, hello! To what do I owe the visit?"

The chief of the Sixth Precinct—an orc who challenged Matthew in size but not in beauty—nodded toward me. "I came to thank you for your help, Detective."

"It's Dani, please," I said. "I'm retired."

"Once a detective, always one," Chief Newton said. "I owe you an update and wanted you to hear it straight from me. Well, from both of us. Felix?"

Felix coughed, then handed over a second pink balloon that said GET WELL SOON. I debated sending a pen through it like Matthew had, but Willa was too entranced by the glittering letters, so I refrained. I nodded for them to hand it to her, and she beamed with delight as she grasped the string.

"Who is she?" Felix asked as he watched her with interest. "And why's she here?"

"A friend. Trusted—if it weren't for her, we wouldn't have found Harry, and I wouldn't be alive."

"Understood. Pleasure to meet you," Felix said with a hopeful grin. "Felix. I'm the tech guy for the Sixth Precinct, and if you ever fancy a tour of the place—"

"Felix," the chief snapped. "Your report."

"Right, right," he said, flustered. Felix toyed with the buttons on his jelly-stained shirt. "Let's see here. Good work and all that, Detective. We have Harry in holding, and he's starting to talk. He's rolling over on a bunch of other midlist drug runners. In fact, that's the sole reason Nash isn't here."

"But," I interrupted. "Nash is Homicide."

"He's helping Narcotics on a huge bust that's spread throughout the borough—they needed extra guys. We've nailed seven upper level dealers already this morning. We have yet to get the head honcho, but that's a different case entirely. The narcotics team will handle that one."

"Wow, that's great," I said. "I forgive Nash so long as he didn't tell my mother I landed in the hospital. And what about Jack?"

"I have no comment on the location of your mother," Felix said just a little too smoothly, too practiced. "As for Jack—he is fine. They took him in, did a full scan, and after flashing his puppy dog eyes, he got the Comm address of his nurse. I think he's fine."

Willa inhaled a gasp. "That ass! He asked for my number just last night. Pig!"

I winced. "Did you give it to him?"

"Of course not." She crossed her arms and pouted. "But it's still rude."

"That's Jack." Felix laughed, grinning to himself with a bit of admiration for my brother before the chief cleared his throat. Felix's grin faded, and the tech shot straight back to business. "Right-o, let's see. I'm combing through Blott's office, Comms, etc. We got a warrant for everything thanks to Harry's confession. So far, we've found nothing linking him to the drugs or the crimes. Seems Harry just wanted to buddy up to the new mayor so he was in a better position to run his business. I'm sorry, Dani, but we don't have anything that can be used to hang Blott."

I caught myself frowning, thinking I'd wanted Blott to be guilty. I'd wanted him in jail for the murder of Mayor Lapel, but it looked like that might not be happening. I wondered, not for the first time, if I'd let my emotions get the better of me. I hated how he'd treated Willa more than the way he'd treated me, but being a jerk wasn't cause for a murder one charge.

"I know," Willa said softly, as if reading my mind. "It's okay, Detective. It's for the best that he wasn't involved."

Willa was right. Without looking at her, I nodded for Felix to continue.

"As for Mayor Lapel and Crystal—we're still searching for the Goblin Girl's real name—it's as Harry said," Felix said with a sigh. "He killed them with runes in his house at Sorcerer's Square. Lured them there by saying he had information on the drug issues and wanted to help their campaign. When they arrived, he had the runes set up and murdered them—I assume you can derive the rest from there."

My confirmation was interrupted by an outburst from Willa.

"It's just so unfair!" she burst. "That sucks! For both of them. Poor Crystal. Poor Mayor. Poor Mrs. Lapel. That really bloody sucks balls!"

The whole room fell into silence.

"Yes," Felix wandered eventually. "I guess one could say that."

Then Willa laughed, giggling hysterically as she realized her misstep. Her face was red as holly berries, and she slid lower into her chair and pulled the magazine up higher. "Sorry for interrupting. Continue."

"Yep, I'm not sure how to follow that up," Felix said. "Chief?"

Orcs probably didn't blush, but the chief had come close. He gave a hearty, manly sort of phlegm-busting cough that made me wrinkle my nose and set down the Jell-O that Anita had left on the table.

"We just wanted to say thank you. We know you retired, and this was a special consultant job," the chief said. "We owe you, Detective. If ever you decide the pizza industry isn't where you belong, we'd welcome you back as our resident Reserve."

I gave him a genuine smile. "Thank you, Chief. That means a lot."

"And in the meantime!" Felix raised a finger and grinned. "We've ordered DeMarco's pizzas for the entire office today."

"Poor Jack," I said. "I should probably hire extra help."

"That's what I'm for." Willa stood. "Out, gentlemen. This girl needs to rest and I need to go make some pizzas. Matthew?"

"I'm staying," he said.

"Fine." Willa kissed me on the cheek, then with the confidence of a Brazilian supermodel, she clucked at the chief of paranormal police and the tech guru. "Let's go, gentlemen. She needs her rest."

I'd never seen the chief look befuddled, but that would be the word to describe his expression as he was herded out by an annoyed blonde. Felix grinned and gave me the thumbs up, mouthed *keep her*, and then followed his boss.

"Alone," I said a moment later, after the door closed and left me and Matthew in silence. "Finally. I've been wanting to ask you—"

A tentative knock sounded before I could finish. Matthew strode to the door and cracked it open, sending a poor aide scrambling away with a growl.

"What exactly did you want to ask?" he murmured as he swiveled back. "Sorry about that."

"Never mind," I said. "Now's not the time. How are you feeling? Your leg can't be healed."

"It's fine," he said, rubbing a hand self-consciously over his knee as he watched me cautiously. "I hold together a little better than you. Heal quicker, too."

"Yeah, rub it in."

"Dani," he said, pausing as his gaze leveled to meet mine. "I haven't thanked you. I probably shouldn't have come to you for help on this case in the first place, but we were at a loss. Thank you."

"I'm glad you asked for my help, Matthew," I said, feeling a new heaviness come to rest on my shoulders. "Also, I know you heard the chief's offer today. I don't think I'm ready to come back. I don't know if I ever will be."

"Nobody expects you to return to the precinct. That doesn't mean the door closes on you. Ever."

"But Lucia..."

Matthew's eyes flickered. "We received her resignation letter this morning. It's postmarked from The Isle. She—well, read it yourself."

He handed over the letter. It was handwritten in simple language:

Dear Chief Newton,

Unfortunately, I have opted for early retirement from the Sixth Precinct. Please consider this my formal resignation.

Lucia Livingston

"This doesn't make sense," I said. "She was so excited about her career—excited to take over for me. To help bring justice to those who deserve it. I don't buy this."

"*You* retired, Dani." Matthew's words were soft and gentle, but they were packed with meaning. "Things happen."

"I know that better than anyone." I blew out a breath of frustration. "That's why I'm skeptical. I know what it's like—how *things* happen, and it's not like this."

"We're looking for her replacement," Matthew said. "The chief wanted me to ask if you'd be available to help train a new recruit. Paid, obviously. Part time."

"I enjoy the training," I said. "I'd love to help. As long as it's not a full-time thing. I can't keep abandoning Jack at the pizzeria."

"We won't be ready for your services for some time. You know how hard it is to find a Reserve, let alone one as talented as you." He trailed off in thought. "Enough about work. Are you okay, Danielle?"

"I'm sore, but I'll get over it."

"That's not what I meant, and you know it."

"What do you want me to say, Matthew? Everything has happened so fast. I feel like I don't know what's up and what's down right now." I sighed, gestured for him to come closer. "I'm sorry. It's all a lot to deal with right now."

"I know it is, and I wasn't asking for any answers. I can't seem to give any myself."

"Aren't we just a pair." I gave him a wry smile. Then I opened my arms and pulled him to my chest. "I do love you, Matthew—I hope you know that. I always will."

"I know," he breathed against my neck. "I love you too, Danielle."

We parted, and both knew those words didn't mean the sort of love we craved. It was the sort of love that had nothing to do with physical attraction or romance and everything to do with the knowledge that we'd dug through hell together and made it back again. The sort of love that can't be wiped away by distance, by time, or even by a broken heart. The sort of love that permeates the heart.

Before we could better voice our true sentiments, we needed to heal from the past. To each become whole. Because two halves don't make a whole in a relationship: Two wholes make one. One stronger, more powerful union. Only then can it last a lifetime.

"The white wolf," I said, my voice sounding froggy and worn. "Do you know who it is? Or, *what*, I should say?"

"White wolf?"

"The one who saved me," I said, gesturing toward my arms. "Licked my wounds."

Matthew still looked mystified. "Danielle, I'm worried about you hitting your head—"

"He leapt through the window and took down Harry just before Harry killed *me*," I said. "I thought maybe it was...why are you staring at me like that?"

"You lost a lot of blood. Are you sure it wasn't..." He cleared his throat, struggling. "The blood loss might have affected your vision."

"I'm not imagining this wolf, Matthew. I didn't dream up a savior or hallucinate him. My eyes weren't playing tricks on me." I thrust my arm forward, again revealing the wounds there. The roughness, the warmth of the wolf's tongue against my flesh was as real as anything in this room. "I felt his tongue. He helped stem the bleeding. You heard Sienna—wolves can do that."

"Werewolves, sure. But they're not—ah, sensitive enough in their transformed state to help a human," Matthew said. "And I've never seen a white wolf before. I'm sorry, Dani—when we found you in your apartment, you were alone except for Harry."

I swallowed my bitter recourse when I could see it wouldn't get me anywhere.

"Danielle—"

"It's fine. Maybe you're right," I said, even though I knew that was a lie. I just couldn't fight him anymore on it because I would never win. If I wanted the answers, I'd have to follow them myself. "Say, do you know when I can get out of here? I'm feeling much better and I have things to do."

Matthew laughed, and we returned to our usual, friendly selves. "Yeah, you're fine. Anita said to stay one more night."

"I'm not—"

Matthew raised a hand. "I'm going to let Anita fight with you." He called for the nurse, then turned back to face me. "I hope you know I believe you. But I also know what I saw, and you were alone when I broke through that door except for Harry. I remember the sight vividly."

He swallowed, and I imagined him picturing me bleeding out onto Harry's limp body, and I understood. I'd felt the same way watching him fight the crazed werewolf over Lorraine's corpse.

"I know," I whispered. "It's okay, Matthew. I promise."

He nodded, but before he could respond Anita arrived and shooed him out with a wave.

"Sorry, Captain," she said, "I'm helping this pretty lady with a shower. She smells like death warmed over."

Matthew got an interested gleam in his eye for all of one second. However, his professionalism won out. Mostly.

Before he left, Matthew leaned forward and circled his hand behind my head, dragging my lips to his and crushing them with a scorching, tender kiss. My hands found the back of his head as we lingered together, oblivious to the outside world.

"Matthew—" I gasped as he pulled away. "What was that all about?"

"I told you," he said with a dry smile. "The deal is off."

Then he turned without a backward glance at Anita, his hulking figure striding silently out the door. My gaze flickered toward the grinning nurse.

"Friends," Anita said, resting her clipboard on a hip. "*Right.*"

Epilogue

The week after my release from the hospital flew by. I returned to the pizza shop and so did my mother. Permanently. She flounced about for hours on end, worrying over me and wondering why I hadn't called her from the hospital.

Willa, Jack, and I settled into a nice routine at the pizzeria. Our door never seemed to close fully with all the guests coming and going. I suspected the flow of activity might slow to a more relaxed pace after the hype from the recent murders died down.

Most of the details had been withheld from the public, which made the gossip mills only churn quicker. It'd been impossible to keep my involvement a secret. Between the shattered glass on the ground outside the pizzeria and the late-night procession in and out of my apartment—complete with handcuffs and stretchers—word had zipped through Wicked like a forest fire.

The only disappointment in my week was that I hadn't been able to find Grey. I'd asked around the second I got out of the hospital (much to Matthew's dismay), but nobody had seen him since Lorraine had gone missing.

Therefore, on the first Friday evening after returning to the pizzeria, I was surprised when a knock sounded on the door at one thirty in the morning.

"We're closed," I called cheerily. We kept the place open technically until midnight, but our last customers (my mother and father) hadn't left until a few minutes after one. "We open tomorrow at eleven a.m.!"

"Detective, may I have a word?" The voice came through the door, husky and deep, and familiar in a distant way.

A tingle skittered down my spine as Willa glanced my way and mouthed, "Who is *that*?"

I shrugged, went up to my tiptoes, and peeked through the peep-hole. I almost had a heart attack at the handsome face staring directly back at me. I put a hand over my racing heart, wondering if, like Matthew, Grey could hear the surprise in my visceral response.

"Do you guys mind if I have a few minutes outside?" I looked back to where Willa was smacking Jack with a dish towel. "Okay, you two are obviously occupied. Jack—*Jack*!—walk Willa home, will you? And close up when you leave, please. I might be a bit."

"Who—"

I left before I gave them an answer, grabbing a jacket from the rack next to the wall. This hat rack was completely unenchanted. I'd always had a fond spot for this delightfully boring piece of furni-ture, though Marla's recent display of loyalty upstairs had changed my tune a bit.

"Hi," I murmured softly to Grey as I stepped outside and closed the door behind me. "I looked for you all week, but I couldn't find you."

"I didn't want to be found."

He waited for me to shrug into my jacket. I'd worn only a tank top and jeans, my hair pulled back into a high ponytail since working in the kitchen got hot. My leather jacket battled back some of the cool air from the night breeze.

Tonight, the moon was hidden behind clouds, and the only light was a faint glow from the flickering lamp-like torches along the path-ways.

We walked in silence for a long while. I supposed Grey led the way, though it was difficult to tell since he held back his supernatural pace, walking easily and relaxed in time with me.

I didn't bother to ask him how he was doing, how he was feeling, or where he'd been. All of that was inane small talk. I could feel the hurt radiating from Grey—the heartbreak, the distress, the hopeless pieces he was supposed to pick up alone. Even if we didn't speak a word all evening, this would be enough for me.

He took me to the place where Lorraine had been killed. The sandy white banks of the stream gleamed bright—reflecting the squiggling motion of water in the fractured beams of starlight with one difference: Where she'd fallen, someone—probably Grey—had scattered an armful of flowers.

There was no particular rhyme or reason to where they'd fallen. Some petals were broken and other leaves were wilted. Roses, daisies, ferns, baby's breath—and many, many more still bloomed beautifully. They released a soft floral scent as Grey held up a hand and gently helped me to rest atop the cave.

Beneath it all, however, was the damp odor of death from the flowers that had dried and crumbled, now left to wilt into the sand. The sweet smell mixed with the odor of decomposition in a frighteningly irresistible melody.

"She wasn't *mine*."

Grey spoke in a voice that sounded hoarse and unused. Thanks to Matthew's explanation of the way vampires and werewolves viewed love and soulmates, I understood immediately what he meant. It didn't seem like Grey wanted a response, so I didn't offer one.

"But I loved her," he said, and his voice cracked. "An incredible amount."

"I know," I said, and I reached for his hand. I squeezed. "She loved you, too. She died thinking she was protecting you."

"That makes it worse."

"It's not your fault," I said. "It's the fault of the horrible man who killed three people. He's the murderer, Grey—you couldn't have foreseen this."

"I should have known—"

"That's not going to get you anywhere." I spoke sharply. "I'm sorry that's harsh, but it's the truth. I don't think you came to me tonight because you wanted coddling and sympathy."

He gave a wry smile. "They told me you were tough, Detective."

I gave a hoarse laugh. "I don't know if that's a compliment."

Grey looked at me, his stunning face worn, wilted—just like the dying flowers. Though I barely knew him, I couldn't help but want to see it alight with life again. To see joy in his smile, even if it wasn't aimed at me.

"I have been through the *what if's* and the *why me's*. Why didn't I look closer? If only I'd done something—anything differently," I murmured to him. "And it doesn't work. There's no peace in those questions."

"When I said you were tough, I meant it as a compliment." He blinked, his pure eyes gleaming at me as if one with the moon. I supposed in a way, he was linked exquisitely to it. "I came to you for a reason, Detective."

"Dani," I said. "It's Dani. I'm retired."

"You've been through loss?"

"I don't know if you'd call it a loss, but..." I shrugged. "I grieved in my own way. For other things. My last relationship—well, the man I dated is dead."

"I just needed a companion tonight," he said. "I thought you might be the only person in my life who would understand."

"Our situations are different, Grey. You were in love with Lorraine, and she was a good woman. That's not how things ended for me and...*him*."

"Things haven't ended for you, Detective."

"Maybe." Sitting next to him was like having a space heater pointed straight at me. He ran warm, like most shifters. "I haven't gotten the chance to thank you, yet."

"You don't owe me any thanks," he said. "I came to your apartment selfishly that night. I came to kill him—I didn't come to save you."

"I know," I whispered. "But you changed your mind, and that saved my life. I don't know how to repay you."

"You already have." Grey stood. "Can I walk you back?"

"But—"

"I just needed some company." He hesitated, knelt before the flowers and picked up a halfway wilted rose. He tossed it into the stream and we both watched as it sailed away. "I needed help to say goodbye to her."

We began the trek through The Depth back toward my house. Our walk hadn't lasted more than an hour, but it had felt like a lifetime. When we arrived at the pizzeria, he reached toward my chin and tilted it upward. He looked directly into my eyes, and gave a sad, heartbreaking smile. "See you around, Detective."

Then he was gone, into the night.

MATTHEW STOPPED IN his tracks outside of the pizzeria, his eyes adjusting as he watched the wolf and Dani standing together on the front stoop. When Grey reached for Dani's chin and looked into her eyes, fury burned through Matthew. The vampire's fists clenched with enough power to crush rocks to dust.

Matthew forced himself to take a deep breath and duck into the shadows as rage boiled through him. He forced himself to be calm, to remember that he was neither dating Dani, nor did he have a claim to her. *He'd* broken things off. She'd had another relationship after him.

And, more importantly, the werewolf truly cared about her. Grey had gone into Dani's apartment to tear the head off the man who'd murdered his girlfriend, and instead he'd let the killer go in order to save Dani's life. Matthew knew Dani hadn't been hallucinating.

After Dani's recollection of the night, Matthew had been forced to remember the events differently. The soft thump of a pawprint on the fire escape, the light fur that he'd found on her body. Matthew hadn't gotten there in time to save Danielle's life, but the wolf had—and for that, he was both bitter and grateful.

Matthew thanked his lucky stars that Grey didn't kiss Dani on the stoop. She didn't seem inclined romantically toward the wolf at all, though Matthew wondered if he'd read the scene all wrong. If anything, there was a melancholy tone to their touches, the look of loss that Matthew knew too well.

After all, when one lived for centuries, one said goodbye to many dear friends and family. Until one learned that being alone was the only way to stay sane. If the wolf hadn't learned that yet, he would soon enough. The realization hurt, Matthew knew.

He almost felt sympathy for Grey. At least, until Danielle closed the door behind her and Grey turned directly to face Matthew. If Matthew would've had a pulse, it'd have stopped cold. *Of course the wolf had sensed him.* Matthew wondered if Grey had been toying with him, putting on a show. Or if it was quite the contrary, and he'd backed away in a grudging form of respect?

Grey marched directly toward the vampire. He only stopped when they were a few feet apart. The torchlight gleamed above them, burning, licking into the night. King and Grey faced off underneath it, shadows dancing across their faces.

"Is she yours?" Grey asked, and Matthew understood.

He didn't owe the wolf an answer, so he stood perfectly still and simply waited.

Grey ran a hand through his hair. He looked tired, but Matthew knew he was no better—probably ragged with despair.

"I'm not going after her," Grey said, his voice low and even. "I loved Lorraine, and I'm not ready to move on."

"But?" Matthew raised an eyebrow.

"But if she's yours, you'd better claim her."

"And if I don't?"

"Then under different circumstances, *that*—" he tilted his head back toward the scene at the door—"would've ended differently."

Grey moved away from the vampire, neither threatening nor friendly. Matter of fact, as if there were some mutual respect they had for one another—a line they wouldn't cross because of Dani.

Matthew was fueled by frustration as he moved toward the pizzeria and left the wolf behind. Grey wasn't a typical shifter werewolf. The scent was all wrong, something Matthew hadn't noticed in a shifter bar where the smell of werewolf permeated everything. *What is he, then?* Matthew wondered. *And what does he want?*

As Matthew reached the front door to the pizza parlor, his mind was churning. He knew he had one thing working on his side. Dani wasn't over him. He knew that from their kiss at the hospital, from the way she looked at him. From the way they simply existed around one another.

Still, Matthew was upset enough that he fumed right past the front door lock, picking it quickly with the nails that descended into claws. He normally kept them retracted at all times unless he was alone. It creeped people out otherwise, and he couldn't blame them.

Matthew climbed the stairs and raised a hand to knock on the door to Dani's apartment, pausing to listen. It sounded like she had company.

"Carl, give me the damn pen!" she barked. "You have my complete collection now. That's ridiculous! You're a couch."

There was a loud belching sound, and Matthew realized she was having a chat with her annoying furniture. Matthew raised a hand and knocked.

"Matthew!" Dani looked surprised to see him as she opened the door. "What are you doing here?"

She hadn't changed out of the jeans or the red tank top—blood red, he noticed—but she'd thrown the leather jacket over Marla.

"Well hello, hunk," the coatrack purred to the vampire. "Can I take your coat, sexy?"

Matthew ignored her and stepped inside. "I have to tell you—"

"Listen!" Dani's eyes beamed bright. "I was out walking tonight with Grey, and my mind was wandering. I thought of something, and sure enough...I think I have a clue."

"A clue?"

"Yes, look!" She beckoned Matthew over to the coffee table where she knelt on the floor before it. "Stupid pen. Carl, I need another. You gave me a dud."

Carl coughed this time, and a pen flew from his cushions and landed on the table.

"Hey, Carl," Matthew said. The vampire and Carl had an awkward relationship. "Good to see you again."

"This isn't a letter of resignation." Excitedly, Dani pulled the crumpled letter from Lucia closer. Matthew had forgotten to take it back. "It's a cry for help."

"A cry for help? I don't know, Dani—Lucia just left. She's not interested in..." He trailed off and watched as Dani waved a hand over the sheet of paper.

Her hand glowed, illuminating the words there. "It's vague, but I think it's on purpose. She's smart—really smart, and I trained her myself. I know she's resourceful. I thought about what I might do, and if I were held against my will, I'd be trying everything I could to get out. Look here. She double traced some of the letters. They're just slightly off, but there's a pattern."

Dear Matt**h**ew,

Unfortunate*l*y, I have o*p*ted for early retire*m*ent from the NYPD. Please consider this my formal resignation.

Lucia Livingston

"Help me?" he murmured, sounding out the bolded letters. "But this would mean..."

"She's been kidnapped!"

Matthew blew out a sigh. "I'm sorry, I have to get going. I'm calling in the chief on this one—too much time has passed already."

"But she's still alive." Dani stood. "This is recent. Her captor must want something. I have no clue what, but we need to find her."

"We?"

"I know, I'm retired." She gave a tremendous sigh. "I'll stay out of your hair, but don't hesitate to ask for help if you need it. Okay, King?"

Matthew reached into his coat and removed a long, thin, enchanted metal box that had been weighing him down for hours now. As he tossed it on the table, he watched Dani's eyes grow to the size of saucers as she read the name stamped on the exterior.

"Twenty-four hours," he said, "and then they're gone for good."

Matthew left, his mind spinning with the outcome from the night. A fellow officer was missing. He'd handed over The Hex Files to Dani—a collection of information that might get her killed. He'd been warned by a werewolf to sort things out with her, or else.

As Matthew moved with lightning speed back to the station, he realized with relief that he had one huge advantage over Grey. Matthew *knew* her. He understood Dani. They'd been together enough to know the other inside and out.

Matthew couldn't help but smile as he thought of the detective's independent streak. If he knew one thing for certain, it was that Danielle DeMarco wasn't a woman *for the taking*, as Grey had insinuated. Dani was an equal partner who made her own decisions.

By the time Matthew reached the station, his focus had shifted back to the files waiting inside the metal box staring up at his mate on the coffee table. The ones she'd so desperately desired; the ones that could get her killed.

Blood had been spilled before over The Hex Files, and if they were reopened, it would happen again. He closed his eyes, hoped Dani would do the right thing, and stepped into his boss's office.

"Chief," he said. "We have a problem."

THE END

Author's Note

Thank you for reading! I hope you enjoyed spending some time in Wicked! If this is your first foray into the Wicked universe, I'm excited to let you know there's another series already available on Amazon set on The Isle. It features a different set of characters, but it is based in the same world. Feel free to give it a try! The title of book one is *Hex on the Beach* by Gina LaManna.

If you'd like to read more about Matthew King and Dani DeMarco, good news! Book two, **THE HEX FILES: *Wicked Long Nights*** is available for order on Amazon now.

To be notified of new releases, please sign up for my newsletter at www.ginalamanna.com.

Thank you for reading!

Gina

Gina LaManna is the USA TODAY bestselling author of the Magic & Mixology series, the Lacey Luzzi Mafia Mysteries, The Little Things romantic suspense series, and the Misty Newman books.
List of Gina LaManna's other books:
The Hex Files:
Wicked Never Sleeps
Wicked Long Nights
Lola Pink Mystery Series:
Shades of Pink
Shades of Stars
Shades of Sunshine

Magic & Mixology Mysteries:
Hex on the Beach
Witchy Sour
Jinx & Tonic
Long Isle Iced Tea
Amuletto Kiss
MAGIC, Inc. Mysteries:
The Undercover Witch
Spellbooks & Spies (short story)
Reading Order for Lacey Luzzi:
Lacey Luzzi: Scooped
Lacey Luzzi: Sprinkled
Lacey Luzzi: Sparkled
Lacey Luzzi: Salted
Lacey Luzzi: Sauced
Lacey Luzzi: S'mored
Lacey Luzzi: Spooked
Lacey Luzzi: Seasoned
Lacey Luzzi: Spiced
Lacey Luzzi: Suckered
Lacey Luzzi: Sprouted
The Little Things Mystery Series:
One Little Wish
Two Little Lies
Misty Newman:
Teased to Death
Short Story in Killer Beach Reads
Chick Lit:
Girl Tripping
Gina also writes books for kids under the Pen Name Libby LaManna:
Mini Pie the Spy!

32139428R00180

Made in the USA
Lexington, KY
28 February 2019